Speculation

Speculation

Edmund Jorgensen

Inkwell & Often

ISBN: 0984749292
ISBN-13: 978-0984749294

For Jim Devlin, in Memory

CHAPTER ONE
The Law Offices of X, Y, and Z

By the time Buddy Johnston vanished, his humiliation had become so abject, and so public, that I don't suppose many people would have been shocked if he had washed up one morning on the banks of the East River with rocks in his pockets and stones in his shoes. But after more than ten years of acquaintance—or friendship, as he and I both charitably called it—I knew Buddy too well to imagine that he could have committed suicide without leaving a note. A note at the very least, and more likely a tract, a manifesto, a complaint in the classical sense and quite possibly in classical meter. He was just the sort of man who could have begun composing a suicide note and so lost himself in admiration of his own prose style and depth of feeling, become so overwhelmed by the pathos of his own situation, that he forgot entirely he had intended to do away with himself. Then he would have published the note in *The New Yorker* with an introductory remark explaining how writing had "literally saved my life."

During most of those years of friendship I would have laughed at the suggestion that I would someday feel sorry for Buddy, not only because he had so much that anyone would have envied—the moneyed family, two bestsellers, those famous affairs—but more importantly because I knew deep down that he was a closer friend to Sothum than I was, and someone whom Sothum considered almost an intellectual equal. But Buddy believed that merely by virtue of his being Buddy Johnston he deserved everything he had and more, and the strength of this belief made him unusually vulnerable to the vicissitudes of real life. This belief was the keystone of his model for all order in the world, for justice and rationality, and when fortune gave that stone a few good raps—the mean-spirited coverage of his breakup with Alyssa, the terrible reviews of his second book, the mocking movie adaptation of his first—the structures of Buddy's ego threatened to come tumbling after.

Although I might have disputed the justice of Buddy's success, I had no immediate doubts that he would be restored to it quickly. I was sure that he had only gone to ground for a while to lick his wounds and repair the esteem in which he held himself. He lacked neither the funds to support himself meanwhile nor the network of fellow celebrities to shelter him. One of these days he would emerge from another writer's cabin in the woods clutching a new manuscript; or from some Eastern monastery, decked out in novitiate's robes and claiming to have seen right through the false fame and fortune to which he would so eagerly return. His big bald head would glare again in the flashbulbs, and his next book—no doubt inspired by his brief experience as a pariah—would be trumpeted as a return to form. He would resume his trips to Boston to visit Sothum one or two weekends each month, and the three of us would again have early Sunday dinners at Huanchen America's on Beacon Street before Buddy caught the shuttle back to New York. In short, all would return to normal.

But as the months went by Buddy didn't emerge from a cabin or return from any meditative sojourn. He didn't wash up on the banks of the Hudson either, or the Charles, or the Ganges. He didn't turn up anywhere, though eventually there were quite a few people looking for him. There were publishers looking to give him money and tax men looking to take it away. There were journalists looking to scoop his story and women looking to tell him off or to console him. After a while there were detectives hot for evidence of foul play. And eventually I joined the search party myself, hoping against hope to disprove my growing suspicion that Sothum had somehow been involved in Buddy's disappearance.

Sothum had seemed as concerned as anyone when Buddy first went missing, but I found it strangely difficult to engage my normally voluble friend in conversation on the subject. He relished analyzing characters and their motives and could happily theorize for hours about whether Bush had given Saddam Hussein tacit permission to invade Kuwait, or why a professor from our college days had really resigned, but he was unwilling to venture even a single guess as to the whereabouts of his oldest friend. Initially I thought that perhaps Sothum did not disbelieve the more unpleasant possibilities as categorically as I did, and was just too frightened to give voice to his fears, but as time went on his apparent disinterest began to get under my skin, and I took it as a personal mission to provoke some reaction from him. I finally succeeded, but it was not a reaction I could have expected.

We were dining as usual at Huanchen America's House of Authentic China Food, in one of the dusky rose-curtained booths toward the back, and I was telling Sothum about the recent rash of Buddy sightings that had been reported in the press. It seemed our old friend was popping up all over the place, like Elvis or Whitey Bulger. One man swore he had seen Buddy on top of the Eiffel Tower, snapping photos and speaking French without an accent. A honeymooning couple had spotted him slurping noodles in a small Thai village. A waitress in Atlanta's Little Five Points neighborhood claimed that she had served

Buddy and Salman Rushdie Sunday brunch—they had both ordered eggs Benedict.

At first Sothum had not shown any interest. I could feel his refusal to turn that vast intelligence to the topic I was proposing. It was the same feeling I had whenever I asked him about the possibility of his leaving finance and returning to philosophy: the odd disappointment of a powerful rifle trained ten feet above your head, as if you did not even warrant assassination. Or perhaps the feeling an actor might get if during his monologue the spotlight swung away from him to focus on some vase or bowl on a card table—props that apparently commanded more attention than he did. I was just about to give up and move on to other topics—but when I mentioned the brunch in Little Five Points Sothum's attitude changed completely. He turned a color I had never seen him before—whiter than the unopened menu on the table in front of him—and then his face flooded with blood.

"I'll be damned," he said.

And then as quickly as the change had come, it was gone. He manufactured a chuckle.

"Maybe I would have believed it," he said, "if he had been breakfasting with Stephen King. Buddy would never share a table with anyone whose novels were better regarded than his own."

I was not fooled by this recovery, swift as it was, but I sensed something in Sothum's reaction that made it socially impossible for me to acknowledge, just as one must pretend not to have noticed when another guest burps at a cocktail party. There was something in Sothum's "I'll be damned" that went beyond mere surprise or recognition—something that struck me as almost shameful. After a moment it dawned on me that what I had sensed seemed very much like guilt—as if my friend had been speaking of literal, not idiomatic, damnation.

Conversation over the rest of dinner covered the usual topics—books, movies, philosophy, politics—but the immediate change in our relationship was both subtle and profound. Sothum almost allowed that my critique of Reagan as both actor and politician had some merit, for instance, and he let me pay for dinner—the first time, excepting birthdays, that I could remember that happening.

After that dinner Sothum and I fell out of touch. We exchanged one or two emails and I called him on Christmas, but our communications were strained and perfunctory. I felt a strange relief at this new distance. Not seeing him made it easier to pretend that I had noticed nothing odd in his reaction to the Buddy sightings, and I wanted so little to acknowledge that moment that I did not even tell my wife Cheryl about it, though she commented directly on the cooling between Sothum and me.

"Has some kind of rift formed?" she asked, managing not to sound hopeful at the prospect. "As long as I've known you he's been such a huge part of your life. You talked so much about how you were going to have the chance to see him regularly when he moved back to Boston, and now that he's a few miles away you see him less than you did in Texas. You don't even email like before. Don't you miss him?"

I assured her that everything was fine—that we were both just unusually busy. And of course I did miss my friend, but I assumed that eventually the awkwardness between us would be explained away or forgotten, that we would reconnect and things between us would be as they had always been. As is the way of the young and healthy, I thought that we had plenty of time to work everything out.

I did not see Sothum again until the April wedding of a mutual friend. He had arrived without female company for once, and near the end of the reception I cornered him at the bar. I paid for his scotch and tried to strike up a conversation, but it remained clear that there was something I didn't have the courage to ask him and he had no inclination to offer up, and when—at a loss for anything else to say—I inquired whether he had been working on anything philosophical lately he excused himself to pay his compliments to the bride.

I ended up getting most of his basic news from Cheryl, who chatted with him while I walked a few blocks in an early spring rainstorm to retrieve our car. He was still not seriously involved with anyone, business was booming at Babel Investments, and of course we must get together sometime soon. Cheryl said he had seemed "almost entirely absent" from the conversation. Or as she put it the next day after some more thought: "inhumanly free of nostalgia." She remarked on how thin he looked. I worked out later that he had already been diagnosed by then, and would have known that we were unlikely to see each other again.

Five weeks later my cell phone rang in the middle of my office hours. As I was coaching a student through Plato's "Apology" and did not recognize the number, I let the call go through to voicemail, and when I listened to the message later I was both alarmed and suspicious. I could think of no good reason why anyone from the improbably named Law Offices of X, Y, and Z would need urgently to speak with me, and suspected a prank or a scam. Nevertheless after confirming on the Internet that the firm existed I did call back, and a lugubrious lawyer whose name I heard and promptly forgot informed me that I had been named in the will of Stanley Riordan.

It took me a few seconds to realize who the lawyer was talking about—it had been so long since I had heard Sothum called by his real name. The lawyer dodged all the questions I asked about the circumstances of Sothum's death. I could not fathom his calm and even manner in the face of this impossible news. It angered me. He must have been mistaken. The very idea of Sothum's death was absurd: he was a giant of a man, larger than life, too big to die, and this lawyer, whoever he was, should have understood that.

But once the lawyer had managed to convey the salient facts over my protests and questions—where and when to present myself to move the process forward—he did allow himself to express that he was sorry to have been the one to break the news to me. I suppose that was true in its most literal sense.

Even though Cheryl was in her own office just across campus I did not immediately tell her about Sothum's death. I didn't even tell her at dinner that night, though she asked me several times if everything was all right. Nor did I bring it up while we watched the History Channel's evening special on "Battles of the Bible." I didn't tell her until we were in bed that night, breathing quietly in the unseasonably chilly apartment, having just made a strange, silent kind of love.

For a moment she said nothing, just continued to breathe in the same regular manner, until I began to wonder if she had heard me.

"When?"

"Three days ago."

"How?"

"I don't know. The lawyer couldn't tell me anything."

"Or wouldn't."

"Yes, or wouldn't."

"I'm sorry," she said after a long pause, and her hand found mine under the blankets.

Cheryl was always better than I was at navigating such practical matters. When I awoke late the next morning she had already been working the phones and had managed to connect with Sothum's Aunt Rosemary and to extract the facts from her.

"It was a brain tumor—a very rare type, very fast. When they diagnosed him they gave him six months, but it only took three. Per his wishes there was no funeral, which Aunt Rosemary thought very peculiar. She also didn't hide her irritation not to have inherited a single cent from her wealthy nephew."

Up to this point I had not considered the nature of Sothum's bequest, but all of a sudden there it was, hanging between us: the disorienting thought that perhaps we had been rich for three days without knowing it. Within a few hours we might have hobbies instead of careers. Neither of us wanted to discuss the possibility openly. It felt cheap and vulgar to think about money, and impossible not to. I went to take a shower.

Some years back Sothum's doctor had ordered an MRI after a fainting scare. Sothum had mentioned it to me offhand, explaining that he had to hang up in order to make his appointment, and I had demanded so many details and become so upset that he finally agreed to call me as soon as he had the results.

That same night I answered the phone to hear him greet me with such energy and amusement that I was instantly sure the test had been negative. In fact he was only delighted to report that he had not even undergone the scan, since just as it had started—"the moment the waves hit the brain," according to the technician—the MRI machine had crashed spectacularly. Something had gone wrong with the magnet, the manufacturer would have to be called in for repairs, and the test postponed for another time (when it would prove negative).

To Sothum, who knew all about the anatomy and chemistry of the brain, the incident was an amusing coincidence, but while I laughed right along with him I was not convinced it had been anything of the sort. I found it eminently possible that his brain had *done* something to the MRI machine—emitted some radiation or dazzled it with neural incandescence. If anyone's brain could have done it, it was his.

So naturally it was his brain that had killed him. With that brain Sothum had subdued philosophy, computing, finance—everything he had turned it to. What else could have undone him but that brain itself? Only diamond scratches diamond.

Cheryl offered to accompany me to meet the lawyer the next morning, but I went alone. The experience was sure to prove surreal and unpleasant, and without my wife present I hoped I might be able to treat the ordeal as a play in which all of us were only actors speaking our lines.

Parking was scarce near Post Office Square, and finally I gave up, parked in a garage near the aquarium, and found my way on foot to India Street. Given the size of Sothum's estate I had assumed he would have hired an exclusive firm to manage it, and as I wandered past long stretches of concrete and brick unbroken by doorways and indifferently maintained, I wondered whether I had mistaken the address. But then after a block or two there were also a few pubs that appeared simultaneously depressed and upscale, and clusters of converted brownstones that housed private tax preparers and vaguely named companies offering all manner of "solution." It was on one of these brownstones that I found the simple black and white plaque marking the Law Offices of X, Y, and Z.

The outer door of the building was locked. I rang suite #3 and stated my name and business to an anonymous and unimpressed woman. She kept me waiting for an unreasonably long time before instructing me to take the elevator, not the stairs, to the third floor, and requiring me to acknowledge these instructions before she would buzz me in.

That ancient elevator gave me some misgivings. It was cramped and unashamed to complain at even the modest burden that I presented, and I began to wonder whether I was really going to leave these premises a wealthy man. When the car stopped abruptly and I had pushed back the scissored metal door, my first view of the offices themselves did little to rekindle any hopes of fortune.

It was a high, badly lit space, becoming downright dark along the two hallways that split to the left and the right. The reception desk was unattended and empty except for a potted pincushion cactus in desperate need of water and a black rotary phone that was not obviously connected anywhere. High up along the walls of both hallways stretched balconies lined with mostly empty bookshelves, and standing on one of these balconies, engaged in browsing one of the more populous sections of shelf, was a portly, whiskered gentleman with flowing white hair and a tan vest and pants. When he heard me come in he took off his glasses and looked down in my general direction.

"Mr. Wrangles?" he said, as if he had just come upon me in the jungle after much searching.

"Yes."

"Half a minute, please." Now his tone suggested that I had been pressuring him in some way.

After thirty seconds or so, good to his word, he replaced the volume he had been consulting to the shelf, reclaimed his suit jacket from where he had draped it over the railing, and with a good deal of puffing climbed down the ladder to join me.

"How do you do?" he asked. His accent was slightly Midwestern and at odds with this formal greeting. His recent exercise had produced beads of sweat on his forehead, but the hand he offered me was dry and a little cool.

"Why don't we conclude this matter in my office," he said, apparently skipping right past the continuation to the conclusion, and without any inflection that might suggest that he was asking a question.

He led me down the left hallway, his walk blending a southern gentleman's decorous pace below the shoulders with the head-bounce of a strutting pigeon, and I began to understand what might have drawn Sothum to employ this eccentric instead of a more conventional lawyer. He was just the kind of character my old friend had always appreciated, absurd and idiosyncratic to such a degree that you could never be sure whether he was being entirely earnest or completely ironic.

When we entered his office I formed a theory on where all the books missing from those high bookshelves might have gotten to. Books covered every available surface in the room— even the surfaces that had been created by stacking other books. Many of the volumes had bundles of paper sticking out at wild angles. The radiator was surrounded by a few decades' worth of legal magazines, which did nothing to prevent the room from being stiflingly hot.

My host transferred a stack of books from the chair in front of his desk to the floor and then swatted at the seat cushion a few times, producing an impressive cloud of dust. Wheezing a little from the dust and the exertion that had raised it, he plopped down into the desk chair and indicated the other to me. When we were both seated he made a pyramid with his fingers around his red nose, reclined deeply, and proceeded to wait. He seemed to be waiting for me to say something.

"Mr...I'm sorry, I never got your name."

"Mr. X," he said, without a trace of irony. I wondered whether he weren't also Misters Y and Z.

"Mr. X, I received a call from...someone in your office about an inheritance that was left to me. By Stanley Riordan?"

"Yes, of course, why else would you be here? Here's the file. I was looking at it again just this morning." The amount of dust he brushed from the manila folder contradicted him, but as he handed the folder to me and kept speaking he did appear to be familiar with the facts of the case. "An interesting testament. We don't get many conditionals here."

I had started flipping through the twenty or so pages in the folder, but they were black with legalese, and I stopped as soon as it became clear that Mr. X was going to summarize the contents for me.

"Firstly, Mr. Riordan has willed you three boxes of assorted papers. These are on the premises and you may remove them today if you can transport them. I hope you will, since as you can see we are not equipped for long term storage here.

"Secondly, Mr. Riordan has left two articles, between which you may choose one. These are, in the first case: a fraction of the liquidated value of Babel Investments, arriving at the sum of ten million US dollars; and in the second case: a standard business-size envelope, sealed."

"I'm sorry?" I said.

"Not at all," answered Mr. X.

"No, I mean I don't understand. I have to choose between ten million dollars or an envelope?"

"You have understood perfectly."

"What's *in* the envelope?"

"I have no information regarding the contents of the envelope."

"Can you at least tell me what it looks like?"

"It is a standard business-size envelope addressed to you in, I believe, blue ink."

"And I have to choose right now?"

"The will in your hand clearly states that this offer expires only with your own death. Allow me to express the wish that this day is a long way off."

"And what happens to the money if I choose the envelope?"

"The money will be disbursed among various charities as specified in the will. If you choose the money, the envelope is to be destroyed. Have you decided which you prefer to receive or will you require some time?"

"No, I'm...I'm going to require some time."

"Then I hope you arrived by car today rather than the subway, and will be able to take immediate possession of the three boxes?"

I said I would, provided that the boxes were not too large, and by way of answer he pointed them out to me amid the chaos of the office: three identical cardboard boxes, each about two feet cubed, sealed with packing tape, and numbered on the side in permanent red marker.

Mr. X agreed to transfer the boxes to street level while I fetched my car.

"Thank you, Mr. Wrangles," he said as I signed to confirm receipt. "Please inform me directly when you arrive at a decision on the matter of the envelope and the monetary inheritance."

The drive back to Cleveland Circle was uncomfortable. I had packed the boxes into the rear passenger side, one in the well and two stacked on the seat, and more than once as I looked in the rear-view mirror they gave me the impression of a mute human passenger.

Back at our apartment I lugged the boxes in three trips up to the second bedroom, which Cheryl and I shared as a study. I was both eager to see what they contained and reluctant to cut the first strip of tape, as if that act would be a final acknowledgement that there had been no misunderstanding, that I would not wake up from any dream—that Sothum was really dead. I paced back and forth for a few minutes, slapping the flat of a serrated kitchen knife against my palm until I had worked myself up sufficiently to slice the packing tape sealing the first box and throw open the flaps.

I had been hoping to find order. A note, perhaps. A listing of contents. But there was no note or catalogue. There was not even a semblance of order or intention. Papers were folded and stuffed and jammed everywhere, crammed in at the sides when there was no room left to stack them higher, and without any sorting or grouping in evidence. The box could very well have been filled by sweeping everything off Sothum's desk, or by pulling out one of his desk drawers, turning it upside down, and shaking it empty. I held out some faint hopes for the other two boxes, but they held two similar explosions of paper. Feeling almost desperate I began to rip through the sheets: some jots about the performance of the Eastern markets on a particular Tuesday; a stack of receipts for books, mostly philosophy and math; the sheet music to Chopin's Nocturne in E-flat major—Op. 55, not Op. 9—the love of which had been behind Sothum's sporadic attempts to learn the piano; Venn diagrams with single-letter labels, entirely opaque to me; unopened junk mail; a short prose poem.

When I had finished my frenzied and useless tour through the boxes I was disappointed and a little angry, but after some calmer reflection I realized that I had been unreasonable to expect an immediate resolution to the riddle Sothum had left me. He had loved puzzles and riddles—both solving them and inflicting them—and moreover in our friendship he had always played the part of teacher and guide, the enigmatic mentor, beckoning and challenging his disciple with conundrums of increasing complexity. If I wanted to know what was in that envelope, I was going to have to figure it out—he was not going to tell me. So I stopped, took a step back, and tried to approach the problem as Sothum might have led me through it.

"First principles, Andy. You're so focused on what I *have* left you. What haven't I left?"

Any explanation of your intentions or my next steps, really. A note, a message.

"More generally?"

A clue.

"Conspicuous by its absence, no? But without a clue this entire exercise is only a joke, not a riddle. So the lack of a clue..."

Must *be* the clue. All right Sothum, I thought. I see it. I don't get it yet, but maybe I see it. The disorder and apparent irrelevance of this blizzard of paper was random, but it was not an accident. Sothum had left me a meticulously constructed chaos, and I was supposed to understand and do something with this fact.

I began to look through the papers again more carefully, categorizing and cataloguing them until the afternoon sun slanting into the study made me squint and think to check the clock. It was already four o'clock, and Cheryl would be home soon.

My wife would not care to dissect the nice difference between a joke and a riddle, I was sure, or speculate about what might be in that envelope with my name on it, or dig through three boxes of papers for supposed clues. Once I told her about the ten million dollars she would have heard all she needed to hear. Who could blame her? But I was not ready to make that decision, and after a frustrating day pawing through the detritus of Sothum's desk with nothing to show for it, I was not prepared to argue my side either. So I chose the coward's way out.

After a few quick phone calls I stuck a note on the refrigerator reporting that I'd gone to have a drink of consolation with some of my colleagues in the philosophy department, which was true—though I worded it to imply that they had invited me rather than the other way around—and that I would tell her everything when I got home.

Usually I am only good for a round or two, but on this occasion I did my level best to drown the unpleasant memories of my day and my anxieties around tomorrow in single malt scotch. A few of the younger members of the department, who had never even met Sothum but who rarely turned down any opportunity to drink, closed the bar with me. When I finally staggered back to the apartment I saw with relief that Cheryl had already gone to bed, and with some difficulty I read her note on the kitchen table: "Hope you had fun, see you in the morning." I slept on the sofa to avoid waking her.

CHAPTER TWO

Cherry Lips and Missed Connections

"Hello stranger," said Cheryl as I shuffled into the kitchen. It was seven o'clock, and I considered the scrambled eggs my wife had left on the stove for me with nauseous interest. The morning light was a fine silver, and large clouds must have been on the move, because every few minutes the entire kitchen would go dim for a moment—a moment that my eyes and head appreciated dearly.

"Hello yourself," I said. "How was your day yesterday?"

"Oh—fine."

"Nothing memorable or newsworthy?" I asked.

For a moment my wife looked at me with arched eyebrows, perhaps undecided whether I was delaying my news in order to toy with her or on account of brain damage brought on by alcohol poisoning. Then she shrugged, as if to say that if I wanted to play the situation casually, she was game.

"Remember the Middle Eastern student I told you about?" she said.

"The one who said that he didn't understand why people bothered to put quarters in the meter, since the fine is only 25 dollars anyway?"

"That's the very one—his father's in oil, rich as God. I saw his car the other day, it would make you sick. Promise me we'll never get a car like that, even if we can afford it."

She paused, in case I wanted to inform her whether we could now afford it or not, but then continued with her casual act.

"Anyway, yesterday he doesn't show up for the exam, and not only doesn't he show up, but there's some other Middle Eastern young man whom I've never seen before sitting at his usual desk and waiting for a copy of the exam. When I ask this young man who he is, he stands up, bows, and tells me very courteously that he's here to take the test for our young petroleum prince. Apparently this is a normal and accepted practice in his country."

"Anything requiring exertion is below a gentleman—even mental exertion? What did you do?"

"I dumped it on Shelley. If she wants to be Dean of Students so much then she can handle it from here. I have no desire to deal with the parents on this one."

"Never a dull moment around that place."

"No, try as we might."

We sunk into uneasy silence as I poured some coffee and ventured a few bites of egg.

"So," Cheryl said finally, "that was *my* day. How was yours?"

"Interesting."

"Damn it, Andrew," said Cheryl, breaking the act with a nervous laugh, "just tell me. Was there anything besides those papers in the study? Do I have to go to work today, or can I call Shelley and finally give her a piece of my mind? Are we..."

"Rich?" I said. "It's not a simple answer. On the one hand we have the option of receiving ten million dollars."

I saw right away that for all her jokes my wife had not allowed herself to hope so big. Her brown eyes widened as she attempted to process this number. She really could park illegally with impunity now, just like her student. She really could call Shelley and tell her a thing or two. These and a hundred other fantasies were no longer fantasies when backed by a number like ten million, and on Cheryl's face a struggle played out: did that mean that these fantasies were now reality, or that reality had become a fantasy? She seemed to be swaying between the two conclusions, so that she had to reach out and steady herself with the table. Then she remembered a particular word I had used.

"Option? What's not simple about the option of ten million dollars? Unless you have to cut off an arm or kill someone or something like that to get it? What's the alternative?"

"I could also choose an envelope that Sothum left me."

"With what in it?"

"I don't know, that's the thing."

"What do you mean you don't know?"

"It's sealed, addressed to me. Even the lawyer doesn't know what's in it."

"You're joking."

"No, I'm serious."

"Then *he's* joking. Sothum is joking."

"Maybe," I said. "Maybe not."

"Am I missing something here? Unless there's a check for eleven million in that envelope, I think your choice is pretty clear."

"You're probably right," I said. "But what's the rush? There's no time limit on the choice."

"Andrew, really—'what's the rush?' What's the point in waiting? It's ten million dollars or an envelope."

"It's a riddle. Don't look at me like that. Just think about it for a moment—and remember, this is Sothum we're talking about. I see two ways to look at the choice he left. One is definitely to say that there can't possibly be anything in that envelope worth giving up ten million dollars for. But the other is to conclude that just by setting up the choice as he has, Sothum is implying that there *is* something in the envelope that's worth it—or that there might be."

Cheryl continued to stare at me until I tried a different tack.

"My best friend just died—I hadn't talked to him in over a month, and things hadn't been right between us for a while—and now he's left me a sealed envelope and a bunch of papers and no explanation. I'm not saying that I'm going to choose the envelope. I just want a day or two to catch my breath and look through the papers and get my head on straight. Seriously, is that too much to ask? One or two days is all."

"I knew there was something going on between the two of you," she said, and the confirmation that she had been right appeared to please her just enough that I wondered whether she might grant me the days as a reward for this concession.

But the question of whether or not my request was reasonable was not one that Cheryl seemed to be able to answer for herself right away. Still staring at me she put her hand over her mouth and rested her elbow on the table while she thought about it. I was considering whether telling her about my suspicions of Sothum's involvement in Buddy's disappearance would help or hurt my case when she made up her mind.

"All right," she said, making every effort to sound tolerant of my argument. "A day or two is fine. A day or two is reasonable. Just promise me you won't make any decisions without talking to me."

"Come on," I said, "you know me better than that."

She did not answer with the strong affirmative I had been expecting, and the clinking of flatware against plate seemed very loud for the next few minutes.

"Then at least tell me what's in these mysterious boxes," said Cheryl finally.

"So far just a bunch of miscellaneous crap," I admitted.

"Like what kind of miscellaneous crap?"

"Like sheet music, and some photos, and a prose poem."

"A prose poem that Sothum wrote?"

"I think so."

"There's something I would never have thought to have seen. Can I read it?"

I paused my breakfast long enough to fetch the poem, and then continued to pick at my eggs while Cheryl read it out loud.

I am sitting inside a pentagram and a salmon, human-sized, is sitting with me. It is cramped, as the pentagram is small. We are eating eggs for breakfast. Benedict Arnold is our waiter. But even as we eat I know that I am not really having this experience— that I am being mistaken for someone else. Actually I cannot shake the feeling that I am dead.

"Creepy," said Cheryl, handing back the sharply creased piece of paper. "It sounds less like a prose poem to me and more like a dream he wrote down. Either way it doesn't seem as if he's been very helpful with these papers he left you."

Cheryl seemed to expect me to agree with her, and appeared a little miffed when I didn't. We sat for a few minutes in silence as I finished breakfast.

"Well," she said finally, "I have to get ready for class."

"Me too. I cancelled yesterday but I don't think that would fly again today after going out drinking with half the department."

We started to clear away the dishes.

"So..." she said in a falling tone, "a day, right?"

"A day," I answered. "Two at the outside."

She nodded and gave me a kiss.

"I'll finish these up," she said, taking the dishes from my hands. "You go get ready. Even a philosopher can't show up to work looking like that."

She did not push me further on the subject of the boxes or the envelope as we took the T to campus together. My wife has always had a light touch, and furthermore she didn't need anything heavier to convey the point. I needed no reminding of what she had given up on my account.

I met Cheryl not long after I met Sothum. It was just turning to spring in our sophomore year, and the entire campus was soggy and charged. Midterms were coming up and I was studying in the campus café.

That café was always noisy and crowded, probably because no matter how long you had occupied one of the precious chairs, none of the students or recent grads who worked there would dream of pressuring you into buying another cup—or even a first cup—of the strong home brew or the exotic "varietals" they featured occasionally. The employees were content to fraternize behind the counter and compare piercings or challenge each other with trivia about increasingly obscure bands. They refused to represent "The Man" and declined to protect his interests, happy enough to be demonstrably hipper and less conformist than thou, the Consumer—an unspoken title that was yours whether or not you were actually consuming anything.

On this rainy Thursday afternoon I was sitting in the café pretending to read Kant. I should not have been pretending, as I was well behind in my reading that semester—the result of too many late-night discussions with Sothum and Buddy. But *The Groundwork of the Metaphysic of Morals* is weighty stuff to be attempting in a buzzing café at the best of times, and on this particular Thursday one distraction proved insurmountable.

A group of four comparative literature majors had arrived at the café before me and snatched my usual table, around which they were now chattering away endlessly, having purchased among them for this privilege not so much as one cup of coffee or a single croissant. For fifteen minutes I had been eavesdropping on their conversation while sniffing righteously above my second shot in the dark, enjoying the hint of moral imperative in its aroma. After all, who cared whether the employees minded or not? There were higher principles at stake.

Their conversation was typical graduate student fare—departmental yarns and gripes, rumors of cutbacks, critiquing of professors by their first names.

"So I told Christopher I thought he was dead wrong in this case..."

"And Geoffrey said, in that way he has—you know the way..."

"...but Rosanna always thinks every poem is too long..."

If there had been nothing else remarkable about the group I might have been able to ignore their freeloading theft of my table and these loud pretensions, but I had not flipped a page of Kant in fifteen minutes because one of the two women had a mouth that it was impossible to look away from.

She was not quite beautiful. There was something, as with Scarlett O'Hara perhaps, inharmonious in her makeup, a slight error of proportion that prevented her claim to that adjective, as well as ten or so pounds. But it was precisely these imperfections of hers—the plump curves where her jeans creased at the thighs, the French snub nose set between the rosy English cheeks, and especially the shape and deep cherry-redness of her mouth—that saturated her with sexual energy. In the steamy spring air of the café with its fogged up windows it was almost too much to bear, an exquisite pain of not-having as I followed every smile and twist of those deep red lips. Their owner sat quietly listening to the others banter, and her silence only increased her appeal—or prevented her from ruining it.

At some point one of the literature majors introduced the term "dramatic monologue," prompting one of the men to jump in. He dressed and cut his hair like a skateboarder and clearly enjoyed the "tension" between his appearance and his scholarly pursuits.

"Dramatic monologue—that pretty much sums up my last relationship."

"Who did all the talking?" the other woman, a sharp blonde, asked.

"Guess," said the thrasher/scholar.

"Wait," said the other male—a clean-cut Joe College type, who had clearly set his eye on Cherry Lips—"there's an idea for a good contest—who can come up with the best lit-crit term to describe a relationship?"

"Extended footnote," said the blonde as quick as anything.

"All right," Joe College said, "give me a second to do one too. How about negative capability?"

"Works for you," said the blonde.

"Ouch," said Joe College, looking at Cherry Lips for comfort. She smiled at him a little too encouragingly for my tastes.

"Beast epic," offered the thrasher/scholar.

"What the hell is a beast epic?" said the blonde. "Did you just make that up?"

"Absolutely not. It's a medieval thing—stories of animals with human characteristics. Allegorical stuff. It goes all the way back to Aesop."

"I'll allow it," the blonde said.

"Who made you the judge?"

Before she could answer—if she was going to answer—Joe College broke in, with a significant glance at Cherry Lips.

"Occasional poem."

"Hovering stress." (The blonde again.)

They were all silent for a moment, aware that the contest was still up for grabs, combing their memory banks for some jargon with the perfectly barbed double-entendre that would bar the gate to new entries. And then the blonde smiled.

"Pathetic fallacy," she said with the smug air of a winner.

A howl of respect went up from the table—Joe College waved his hand as if he'd touched something hot.

"It's over," said the thrasher/scholar. "I'm calling it—time of death..."

As he looked at his watch to complete the joke, a female voice—definitely female but not the sharp blonde's—broke in.

"Artful enjambment," said the voice.

At this I was all but swooning—ready to throw Kant aside and, hell with her friends and everyone else in the café, jump over the table and kiss those cherry lips, which had finally broken their silence with such an erotic rejoinder—until I realized that the cherry lips had not moved—that no rejoinder had in fact passed through them. As the four grad students turned to see who had crashed their party I followed their collective gaze until it rested on a woman, two tables away from them and three from me, who had put her hefty book down on the table (I could not tell what book it was, though I tried to tell) and was—I saw to my shock—looking more in my direction than towards the competition she had just demolished.

This woman was neither exactly beautiful or even, like Cherry Lips, immediately sexual. She had lovely hair though— black and long and spring-loaded. And her dark eyes—stuck in the middle of a face that was a little too puffy and somehow cold like clay around the chin—were vital. What was more, they were glittering at me in particular, as if she and I were sharing a joke that the literature students couldn't quite get in on.

"Sorry," she said to the gang of four, "I didn't mean to interrupt. Not the kind of lit-crit term you meant? Maybe?"

Joe College mumbled something and the four of them turned—properly shocked and chastened, I trusted—to another topic. I don't know what topic, because I was no longer listening—I was watching in disbelief as the dark-haired woman rose from her chair, smoothed the wrinkles from her long green skirt, and with unexpected grace navigated the three tables and eleven chairs between us until she reached my table, where she sat down without being invited—which is not to say that I would not have invited her, had I been able to say anything. She extended her hand for me to shake. As I took it I noticed she had narrow wrists and—I thought at the time—stubby fingers, which were quite strong. She gripped my hand in introduction almost as a man would have. Her skin was a shade of olive, and an especially smooth expanse lay above the neck of her white blouse.

"Cheryl Walker. You weren't really reading your book, were you?"

She spoke quickly, but her voice was deep and smoky—as if she should properly have been speaking Spanish. I found that I could not even speak English at that moment, but she took my silence as admission that I had not been reading.

"Eavesdropping, right? So was I. Fascinating stuff, wasn't it? The human interest, I mean," she said, leaning in towards me and dropping her voice. As she did so the loose blouse fell somewhat away from her neck. "What have you got here? Oh, Immanuel Kant? Have to admit, I've never made it through. My father used to say 'Immanuel? I Kaaant stanhim.' You've seen *Singing in the Rain*, right?" She was genuinely concerned that I might not have gotten the reference, and genuinely pleased when I nodded to indicate that I had. "I'm supposed to be reading *How to Kill a Dragon* myself. Watkins. Do you know it? It's great but awfully dense—nice and erudite, if you know what I mean. I could use a break, actually. Maybe a walk in the rain?"

Finally I managed to find my voice long enough to say that I would join her, and even to add that I had an umbrella big enough to share.

"Great," she said. "You looked like the practical type. But before we share an umbrella there's a question I need you to answer."

"What's that?"

As soon as I'd spoken I realized it must be my name she wanted, which I had been too off-balance to offer yet. But the clay-like flesh around her cheeks and chin suddenly became animate, a golem bolting upright into life, as she made a wicked grin.

"Which term did you like the best?"

We walked all afternoon and then had dinner together at a Japanese restaurant Cheryl knew. She introduced me to sushi, which I have never learned to appreciate as she does. After dinner we saw a movie—a terribly stupid comedy about lesbians becoming straight and straight men gay, though I was hardly watching it. That was our first Thursday movie night.

I have been blessed with an excellent memory. My easy recall of things I have read has always given me an advantage on tests, though the work ethic my stepfather extolled and personified has driven me to put in at least as many hours studying as my peers regardless. A fine memory has also proven to be an advantage in my chosen profession. While I was teaching in Texas I achieved a certain level of notoriety for being able to identify plagiarized papers. Mystical powers were attributed to me, but it was nothing more than a simple feat of memory and attention to phrasing—and a bit of elbow grease in the stacks or on the Web. If a certain phrase, or even the rhythm of a paragraph, recurred among several papers—even if those papers were submitted in separate terms—bells would ring in my head, I would be off to the library or to the Internet, and posthaste the offenders would find themselves before the Academic Conduct Board. I generally advocated leniency for first-timers who confessed.

More important than the academic and professional advantages that a fine memory has bestowed, however, are the hours of comfort—the "sessions of sweet silent thought"—which my detailed recollections have provided during hard and lonely times. Foremost among these are the memories of meeting Cheryl and our courtship. Even now when I close my eyes and concentrate I can see it all in my head running like a movie, or frozen moments hanging like glossy stills on a museum wall. The raised hem with the floral pattern of white knots on the blouse she wore that first day (I had occasion to feel the knots rub against my neck when she leaned over during the abysmal movie to whisper some witticism in my ear). The low honey and smoke of her voice in my ear again, not too many nights after that, when she invited me to stay with her. Discovering the odd geometry of her body—the conical forearms, her almost triangular thighs, her squarish feet—the only feature of her body I have ever heard her complain about.

Cheryl chose me. There in a few words lies expressed one of the great mysteries of my life. She picked me out in that crowded café and claimed me for her own, and for years I could not bring myself to ask her why, afraid that even after so much time together she might have been unable to come up with a reason herself and begin to doubt the wisdom of her choice. Apart from the bald spot about which I was always so self-conscious I was an unremarkably handsome young man in my college days, standing out neither as one of the heartbreakers or the heartbroken. Why had she noticed me? When I finally asked her this question, on the night of our first anniversary, she made a few jesting dodges—it was my powerful bushy eyebrows, or my fashion sense, or my raw testosterone—until I forced the matter.

"It was just the way you reacted to that red-haired girl when you thought she'd been the one to speak. It was instantaneous, your face just froze in this mask of determination and you even started to put down your book, as if you were going to walk over there and plant one on her. And I thought to myself 'Maybe here's a guy who can keep up with me.'"

My feet did not touch the ground for days.

We were inseparable from that first night at the café, and though I think I assumed from that first evening that we would someday marry, Cheryl and I were not engaged when we received our undergraduate degrees. We made a point of waiting, and then waiting even longer, until both of us were well advanced into our respective graduate programs. We waited so long that when we made our announcement at Thanksgiving dinner back in Illinois my stepfather almost fell over himself in his eagerness to spring the gag he'd been hoarding (or the gags, really—apparently he couldn't pick between them, though they were incongruous): clutching at his chest in mock cardiac arrest and then, after a miraculous recovery, lifting his watch to his ear to check if it were, like his heart, still ticking.

But because we were not engaged I experienced some anxiety as the last semester of our senior year wound up and the responses from graduate programs started rolling in. Cheryl got into all the top linguistics programs—in London, in Chicago, in California. And I began to wonder: would she really follow me to Texas, as she had indicated—to their decent but less-respected program—if the philosophy department there accepted me?

It had to be Texas for me. I had no choice, because Sothum had once mentioned that if he'd decided to pursue a degree in philosophy instead of computer science, he would have gone to Texas to study with Featherstone, "the greatest philosopher still alive today."

In fact I was so worried that Cheryl would not come with me that on the day I received my acceptance to Texas I considered proposing before I showed it to her. But my worry proved ungenerous. When I arrived at her apartment, letter in hand, she took one look at it and fell on me with a flurry of kisses that turned into a blizzard. Things took their natural course, and I woke up the next morning and found her in the kitchen.

She was sitting at the small circular table, and as I entered the room she looked up at me and smiled, her face so aflame with love that I was stopped in my tracks, as if I had stormed into a burning building without thinking and been knocked back by a wall of pure heat. It was a love that shamed me in its simplicity and directness and selflessness. Where her worn white robe parted over the knee of her crossed leg, or fell loosely away from her neck down to where her breasts began their sharp curve, it revealed that every inch of her olive skin was flushed as vigorously pink as her cheeks with the pleasure of what she was doing—which was filling out her acceptance to the linguistics program in Texas. She had been just about to sign it when I walked in. On the table an envelope lay open and ready.

"Are you sure?" I asked her.

Her face fell ever so slightly, and I began to think the flush had gone from pleasure to anger. But then she sighed affectionately, shook her head, and signed without making a flourish. She folded the paper, stuffed it in the envelope, and stood as she was licking and sealing it up. Then, tapping the envelope rhythmically across her left palm, she walked over to me, taking her time, and when she got close enough she touched my nose with one of the envelope's sharp corners.

"Mail this for me while I take a shower, would you?" She was speaking more slowly than usual, and her voice was even deeper, almost thick, and I think that was the first time in my life that I realized how much more women understand about sacrifice than men. I nodded and kissed her.

I'd found my coat and was nearly out the door when I heard Cheryl call my name. I turned around to see her head and one bare shoulder peeking out around the edge of the bathroom door. She had tied her hair up with a quick abandon that was irresistible—her neck was entirely exposed and a few stray curls of hair bobbed in the warm breath of the shower.

"Pick up some oranges and bacon too, and we'll have fresh juice with brunch."

"But it's Wednesday," I said lamely.

"Baby, this is not going to be our usual Wednesday."

And she disappeared back into the shower.

In the end it was Featherstone who prompted me to marry, whether he meant to or not. He was getting very old by the time we arrived in Texas, feeling his mortality, without fear but with immediacy, and he was interested in using the time he had left listening to his much younger wife, a brilliant concert pianist, give him private performances of Mozart—or in wandering through his rose garden and touching the petals—or in meditating further on the nature of logic and its relationship to the divine.

He was not particularly interested in spending too many of his remaining hours bringing a graduate student like myself up to speed, or listening to my vague proposals for a course of study, and even I could not blame the man—especially since I had read his considerations of the afterlife and knew that he considered it highly improbable.

I now think he was also in the process of becoming a kind of saint—a process that I did not understand but sensed dimly, and had no desire to interrupt. On occasion when I managed to catch his eyes—which had sunk so far amid his wrinkles they looked like twin wells, deep and dark and cool—I felt them look through me, as if I were a cactus on the edge of a vast spiritual desert,

31

waving my arms in a doomed attempt at grabbing his attention while he was already wandering deep in the tan-blue distance, leaving no footprints. He seemed to be shrinking daily, becoming more wrinkled and more frail no matter how much whole milk his wife made him drink, as if everything impure in him were simply being breathed away in the night as he slept, everything that was gross and necessary for surviving in this compromised world, and his mind was picking up the slack—for a little while, at least. His hair, which had long been grey, turned white during the first months of my study there. He might stop and smile, sometimes to his immediate peril, when a breeze blew as he crossed the street, or if he heard music begin to play somewhere down the hall, looking up, and suddenly you could see his eyes under the wrinkles of his brow, and they were always joyful and filled with a wonder that was not naive. How do you bring yourself to interrupt such a man, even if he has posted office hours?

Usually I didn't. At most I followed him around silently, almost as a witness, or I sat at the table with him and his wife for a while, silently, while he drank his whole milk. I didn't seek a different advisor either, though all his other graduate students did. Several of the professors in the department took it upon themselves to pull me aside and to warn me in whispers that Featherstone didn't have long left. They assured me that no one would blame me for looking around. In fact Featherstone held out longer than any of them expected, long enough to sign off on my dissertation topic, though not to read the dissertation itself (not, I'm sure, one of the chief regrets he took with him when he went).

I was one of the last to see Featherstone alive. I may have been the last to speak to him except his wife. I had just helped him to move a few boxes of books from his home to his office— why he was moving them that way instead of from office to home, where he was spending more of his time, I don't know. As we were walking back to his house he stopped suddenly and touched my arm. This was unusual—besides our initial handshake it may have been the only time he touched me. His fingers were almost bone and nothing else. His touch was not much heavier than if a butterfly had landed on my forearm and kept flapping its wings. Then he began to speak to me—I managed to make out my name but little else—because just then a motorcycle gang came roaring down the street in the strong sunshine of Texas noon.

I had never seen a gang so large. There must have been fifty cycles, Harley Davidsons and massive Goldwings, all of the engines tweaked to run as noisily as possible. They came riding two or three abreast down the westbound lanes with a lazy determination. Perhaps there was a convention in town, I don't know. But as they revved by they inspired such vibrations that the ground shook and every car with an alarm began to protest. Most of the bikers were huge men and dangerously out of shape, as if mere mass could convey strength and viciousness. Some had women with half-shirts clinging on behind them, and there was a dizzying variety of leather chaps and boots and black glossy helmets and mirrored shades. I could not take my eyes off them, or stop myself either from hating the self-satisfied and aggressive way they inflicted themselves on the world or from wishing to some extent that I could do the same. So I was not listening very well to Featherstone. But as the last few motorcycles passed and he wrapped up I realized he did not want me to come with him any further—he wanted to walk home alone. So we parted.

The next day the department secretary called me at home. Cheryl and I were having lunch on our cramped concrete balcony, eating tacos off the crudely painted earthenware plates she had picked up for almost nothing and drinking cheap

Mexican beer from those bottles that seemed to remain dusty no matter how much cold water we rinsed them with. We almost didn't answer the phone, but I insisted—I have always had trouble letting a phone ring unless I am with a student.

Evidently he had died peacefully in his sleep, a "real blessing" as the secretary said. She offered me so many condolences that I began to feel as if I had been related to the man. She was apologetic and delicate about bringing up the fact that I would need a new advisor for my dissertation as soon as I could find one.

In fact I was not sad, except in the abstract sense. The way Featherstone had lived his last days it was impossible to be too sad. Death waits for all of us—as everyone who has not just had someone die is quick to remind us—and Featherstone's death seemed to be what death almost never is: not a decline or an interruption but a culmination. And of course I hardly knew the man except as a figure, a symbol, an ideal so advanced into mind and quiet and light that he was impossible to get to know "as a person." But I did regret, all of a sudden and quite sharply, that I had not asked him to repeat what he'd tried to say to me the day before. What wisdom—practically words from the other side— had I lost forever through my inattention?

I regretted it so much that when I asked Cheryl to marry me three weeks later I convinced myself that this was exactly what Featherstone had been saying. He had been advising me not to put it off any longer but to marry this woman I loved immediately, because life was short and she was splendid. He had met her once, and I think he had liked her. And after all who cared if she and I had agreed we would get our degrees first? That had been a young idea in all the wrong ways something could be young. It was time to put aside childish things. I stopped short of spinning the story thus for Cheryl. And in my heart I knew how improbable it was that Featherstone, who never spoke to me about my personal life, had said any such thing. But still I tried very hard to believe it myself, and sometimes I succeeded. I did, to my shame, tell Sothum the invented version of the story, and he was delighted by it. Given his feelings on marriage I'm not sure anything else could have made him agree to be my best man.

So Cheryl and I married the next May in a small ceremony in Austin, with Sothum as best man and Cheryl's girlhood friend Mary as matron of honor, and at the reception under a rented tent with yellow and white stripes everyone danced and drank too much, and Sothum's speech was a little ironic but also quite beautiful, quoting Woody Guthrie that for him to talk about marriage was like "a cowboy talking about the sky," and my stepfather pulled me aside for a drunken and incoherent talk about how proud he was, though he hoped I was taking concrete steps towards eventual financial solvency, and my mother could hardly say anything the whole time, she was so choked with tears, and Cheryl's parents managed to keep from fighting until almost everyone else had gone, and even then the fight was mild by their standards, probably because they were both so exhausted from dancing.

Buddy was at the wedding too, dressed impeccably and wowing all of Cheryl's friends with his look of undeniable success, and his presence is the only bad memory I have from that day. Not even his whole presence, because the brief conversation I had with him was pleasant enough. Just the moment, as Cheryl and I were dancing, when I looked over and saw Buddy standing by the bar with Sothum, making him laugh as he had always been able to do. Somehow I got the feeling that they were talking about me, or at least something that I wasn't privy to, and all of a sudden we could have been back in our undergraduate days at a meeting of The Three Wise Fools,

Buddy and Sothum sharing some look or chuckle at a remark I had just made.

As I recall, Buddy gave us a fondue pot.

I was distracted during the day's classes thinking of all these episodes from the past, but on the T ride back to the apartment I did not relish the prospect of returning to work on Sothum's papers. Although I hated even to consider the possibility, after another hour or two among the boxes I began to wonder whether Sothum's mind had been all there as he had been preparing these papers and drawing up the terms and conditions of his will. Or perhaps there had been a clerical error and I had received the wrong papers? It was all very well to speak of riddles and clues in chaos, but as I flipped through the papers again and again I could find nothing. Why on earth would Sothum will me sheet music? A receipt for oil delivery from two years ago? An unopened solicitation to join AARP? Really, what purpose or clue could these represent?

Cheryl did not ask for a progress report at dinner that evening, and I did not offer one, but when she went off to grade papers until bed I returned to the study. I could hardly find it within myself even to pretend to go through the papers again, and when Cheryl knocked at the door and came in to say good night I did not bother to make it look as though I had been busy.

By the time I followed Cheryl to bed a few hours later I had decided: at breakfast I would tell her that it was clear that I—we —should take the money, and we could begin making plans about whether we wanted to teach any more, where we would live, and so on. She had been more than patient with me—on more than one occasion—and I had found nothing in the boxes even to suggest that the contents of the envelope Sothum had addressed to me were worth anything, let alone ten million dollars. I was profoundly at peace with this decision as I began to drift off.

Then something startled me fully awake. Careful not to disturb Cheryl, I stole out to the study and began to dig through the pile of miscellaneous papers until I found it: the single page on which was written the prose poem or dream-record that I had shown to Cheryl. The page had been ripped from a bound journal, and now that I examined it more carefully it did not appear to be Sothum's handwriting. It appeared to be Buddy's.

I am sitting inside a pentagram and a salmon, human-sized, is sitting with me. It is cramped, as the pentagram is small. We are eating eggs for breakfast. Benedict Arnold is our waiter. But even as we eat I know that I am not really having this experience— that I am being mistaken for someone else. Actually I cannot shake the feeling that I am dead.

With trembling hands I tore into the filing cabinet. I was quite sure I had saved the clippings of every Buddy sighting I had found, and in less than a minute I was holding it: the crudely clipped gossip column I had summarized for Sothum during our last dinner together at Huanchen America's, shocking and alarming him so profoundly that he had ended our friendship as I knew it.

"Atlanta, GA: A waitress at a diner in the trendy neighborhood of Little Five Points says she spotted novelist-in-hiding Buddy Johnston breakfasting with Salman Rushdie, who is long officially out of hiding himself. According to our source, both ordered eggs Benedict. For the record Elvis was spotted at the same diner last year, eating banana and chocolate chip pancakes. Readers are left, as always, to draw their own conclusions."

CHAPTER THREE

Monica D. Feather and the Three Wise Fools

In the broad daylight of morning the coincidence did not seem quite as earth-shattering, even to me, as it had all alone in the small dark hours. Cheryl listened without interrupting as I finally told her what had happened during my last dinner with Sothum at Huanchen America's. She read carefully the newspaper clipping reporting the sighting of Buddy and compared it to the prose poem in Buddy's handwriting. She was at obvious pains not to jump to any conclusions before letting me finish—or at least not to give the appearance of having jumped to any conclusions.

"Andrew, this is pretty thin stuff," she said when I had no more evidence to present.

"I know, I know. Let's call it what it probably is: crazy. But it's also the only hint I've found that gives me any clue why Sothum would have left me those boxes."

Cheryl sighed.

"Honey," she said, and I knew right away that she had something to say that she expected me to find unpleasant, as we did not often call each other by the standard names that couples use, "that's exactly why you're seeing this connection. Because you're looking for it. If it weren't this, it would have been something else. You have an associative mind, and you spend half your life trying to make connections where others don't see them. It's how you make your living—it's part of why I love you.

But there probably aren't three boxes of papers anywhere in the world that don't have *something* you could have connected to Sothum and Buddy *if you were looking to make connections.* I think it's possible that Sothum was...what? Playing a joke on you? Or not quite sure himself what he was doing?"

"Now we're getting down to the crux, aren't we? Go on, you're not going to make me angry by asking it. I asked it myself yesterday: was Sothum in his right mind at the end? That's the real question we're asking here. Because if he was still in his right mind, then there is something in the boxes worth sending to me—and maybe something in that envelope that is worth giving up a fortune for. And if he wasn't, then every day we wait to claim the money is just another day observed in honor of madness."

"Well, yes. Now that you put it that way, that's exactly what I think is going on. You are doing observance to madness."

"And you're sure? He was crazy at the end?"

"Sure is a strong word, but Andrew, really—if he had wanted you to get something out of these boxes, why seal the message with seven seals? Why not just tell you what he wanted you to know, or at least leave a very clear path for you to follow?"

I shook my head.

"You may be right. You're probably right. But I have a really hard time imagining him as crazy."

Cheryl moved her chair closer to mine and put her hand on my shoulder. She intended the gesture to be comforting, but I did not find it entirely so.

"Of course you do. He was your brilliant friend. He was so young. I hate to think of it too. But he had a brain tumor. Cancer of the *brain.* Don't you think if we were talking about someone else—anyone else—that you would have found it a little strange if he hadn't gone a bit crazy near the end? Seriously, if you had to estimate the odds, where would you put them?"

"I don't really feel like putting odds on this, Cheryl."

"That was a bad way to put it, I'm sorry. But let's assume for a moment that Sothum was as sharp as ever near the end, or at least sharp enough, and that he really was trying to send you a message with the papers in those boxes. What would you do now? Where do you go from here?"

"Is that rhetorical, or are you asking that for real? Because it's exactly what I spent all last night thinking about."

Cheryl nodded—she was really asking.

"I would go to New York to see Buddy's mother and then see where that takes me. I think that Sothum intended me to figure out what happened to Buddy, and I don't really have any other place to start an investigation. But I don't want to do this without your agreement—I want you to be on board with this."

My wife did not answer right away, though I had the sense that she had already decided on her answer. I think that she wanted to convey to me just how much I was asking for at this point.

"This is that important to you?" she asked me.

"I don't know how important *that* important is, but it's important to me." I hoped "*that* important" did not translate to "important enough to put our marriage at risk."

"Use the MasterCard, not the Visa," said Cheryl as she stood up from the table, "and don't be away too long."

"I've only got the weekend and Monday before I have class again," I said, "so it can't be longer than that."

She didn't answer.

Once breakfasted and showered I packed light and quickly, afraid that Cheryl might still change her mind, and took the subway to Back Bay Station. Flying has always terrified me, and one of the attractions of a trip to New York from Boston is that the train is such a viable option. At Back Bay I booked a seat on the regular passenger train rather than the high-speed commuter. I was looking forward to the ride, and had no wish to shorten it.

Riding a train, feeling the slide and the clack of the rails, the occasional shudder of the iron horse, watching the world melt by through a window the size of a picture frame—who can deny that this is one of life's pleasures? A moving train is the perfect place for a certain kind of thinking, and as I settled into my window seat, pressing my cheek against the cool glass just for the sensation, and felt the train jerk into motion, I was not exactly happy, but I was happier than I had been at any moment since learning of Sothum's death. Soon I was half asleep, hovering equidistant between dream and reverie.

Back when I was still a sophomore wavering between an English and philosophy major, and with time running short to decide, I had picked up as much literature as I could find on both departments and headed for the campus café, where I planned to sift through all the available information and to make my decision in a single marathon session. With my customary shot in the dark beside me to ward off the eternal college fatigue and the December chill, I plowed through the course catalogues and the "What a Major in X Can Do for You" pamphlets with increasing desperation. There was nothing here but propaganda, nothing that would help settle the Platonic debate between poetry and philosophy, and certainly nothing that would help a bright young prospect like myself decide on the direction of his future. Without much hope I turned finally to the newsletters of each department: *The Unacknowledged Legislator* from English and from philosophy the more modestly entitled *Nous Notes*. With a fresh shot in the dark to give me strength I started with *Nous Notes* because it seemed a little thicker and more substantial. I never made it to *The Unacknowledged Legislator*.

The thickness of *Nous Notes* was occasioned by the inclusion of a philosophical dialogue by one "Monica D. Feather, Student of Philosophy." This caught my attention immediately, both because I could not think of a philosophical dialogue that had been written in the last 100 years, and—yes—because the author was female. The interlocutors were two businessmen, called only A and B, both of whom are up for the same promotion. They meet by chance in the corporate cafeteria and spend their lunch hour arguing about whether the term "identity" refers to that which is unique about something or someone ("my true identity"), or that which makes someone or something just like something else (e.g. "a trigonometric identity"). It seemed an interesting enough premise that I decided to give the dialogue a quick read.

Four hours later I was still in the same chair, re-reading the dialogue for at least the twentieth time.

Youth reacts more strongly to young, raw brilliance than to genius that has mellowed and developed. Today if one of my students had submitted the same dialogue to me I would have thought it promising—perhaps exceptionally so—but I doubt I would have been intoxicated. Back then it hit my sophomoric blood like kerosene or powdered glass. I read the dialogue over and over again that day in the café, and at least thirty more when I went home for winter break, each time increasingly convinced that I had discovered the work of a young genius.

Back home for Christmas I decided that when break was over I too would become, like Miss Feather (oh, it could not be Mrs.!), a student of philosophy—for I was truly in love for the first time in my young life, and the fact that I did not even know the face of my beloved only sharpened my righteous passion. At night I would imagine a parade of the ugliest women I could, some of them almost leprous, and then ask myself as each marched by:

"Could you love this woman?"

The answer was always the same.

"If that is the woman who wrote this dialogue, then I have no choice: I already do. Platonic love is the only real love. Sexual love is for the vulgar masses that she and I do not inhabit." And then, silently even in my thoughts, I would always add a footnote. "Unless, of course, she happens to be beautiful."

My first order of business returning from winter break was to look up Monica D. Feather in the campus directory. I was not surprised when the search proved fruitless: many female students kept their details unlisted as a protective measure against stalkers. But I was not discouraged, either—kismet was at stake here, and I would just have to get creative.

Taking advantage of the trip to the philosophy department where I would declare my new major, I sought out the coordinator and asked if she could put me in touch with Miss Feather. I presented my dog-eared copy of *Nous Notes* as evidence that my intentions were honorable, and delivered my well-rehearsed invention: I was forming a philosophical discussion society, and Miss Feather was just the kind of student I was looking to recruit.

The coordinator—a thin, icy blonde—took great pleasure in explaining why she must deny my request. Laws forbade it—and even had they not, university policy forbade it—and even had it not, she personally did not feel that it was appropriate. I suspected that even if she had somehow managed to overcome law, policy, and her own scruples, some other power would have contravened. With reluctance she did agree to accept a note to pass on to Miss Feather. In these days of letter bombs and anthrax I wonder if she could not have found a way to deny even this favor. But in those simpler days my message in a bottle was on its way, and now I could only wait.

Two days later the phone rang, and my roommate Ryan answered.

"Dude," he said, "it's for you."

"Thanks," I replied. I did not know whether to add an answering "dude" or not—both approaches felt transparently uncool—and my indecision blossomed into the negative choice as I took the receiver.

"Hello?"

"Is this Andy?" No one called me Andy. Normally I would have corrected anyone who tried, but this voice already had me off balance. It was deep and powerful and unmistakably male, and something about this last fact disturbed me.

"Yes?"

"You left a note for me in the philosophy department."

You could have knocked me down, as they say, with a feather. Suddenly I was not feeling so well, or even so Platonic. This was a twist that my fantasies had never taken. New questions were being raised.

"What?"

"You left a note for me in the philosophy department."

"A note?"

"Can you hear me all right?" the voice asked.

"You're a man," I answered.

I could sense Ryan's sudden interest in the background.

"Last time I checked. You're interested in a philosophical discussion society?"

"But your name..."

"Monica D. Feather, Moniker D. Feather, Nom de Plume. It was a joke. Look, are you in the market for a society or a date?"

"A society?" I might have been asking for a definition.

"Then you're in luck. I've already started one. We meet at Huanchen America's on Beacon Street every Wednesday at eight. You know the place? You in?"

"Yes, but..."

"Okay, then we'll see you tomorrow night."

"Wait, what's your real name?"

"You might as well call me Sothum," he said, and hung up.

I attended my European history class that afternoon, but to this day I know less about Charlemagne than I should. My mind was consumed with a single, burning question: was I gay? More properly: *could* I be gay? Decide to be gay? *Will* myself gay? Even to love the genius behind the dialogue? What if he were attractive, beautiful, an Adonis even?

He was not beautiful—not in the usual sense. His eyes were beautiful. It was his icy blue eyes that women always commented on. At times his eyes could appear so blue and detached that they seemed floating, holographic, a projection from the dream-logic apparatus humming away in his skull. It was his eyes that gave him away that Wednesday outside of Huanchen America's. He was standing on the sidewalk and looking up and down for me, but I could have picked him out of a lineup of twenty. The moment that I saw him I knew both that I could not love him as I might love a woman, and that I did love him.

I stand a hair under 5'11" in stocking feet, but Sothum had a good six inches of perspective from which to observe the beginnings of my early male-pattern baldness. He was rail thin, and his joints protruded so that he looked cheaply welded or glued together. The odd angles of his body made clothes fall awkwardly on him. One hip was thrust out slightly and the corresponding arm pressed at an uncomfortable angle against the restaurant's facade, so it almost seemed that his sleeves, one of which flapped free while the other was pulled tight to his forearm, had been harvested from two different black raincoats. He had light brown, unruly hair, which refused to surrender to the freezing drizzle trying to slick it down, and an incongruous face, babyish and a bit chubby, that gave the impression of an orange stuck on the end of a shish-kebab. Although it was quite chilly that night he was wearing only a raincoat, which would prove to be his usual outerwear in all four seasons. He simply did not get cold or hot, or at least did not admit to it.

Buddy was waiting there with him, handsome and well-groomed and still with his hair. He had that air of boredom that communicates superiority to one's surroundings. I walked up to the two of them, unsure how to introduce myself.

"You must be Andy," said Sothum, and once again I did not correct his use of the nickname. "I'm Sothum, this is Buddy. Let's get a table."

Buddy managed to hold the door in a manner to suggest that he might have been only suffering a moment of doubt about patronizing this establishment, and if a couple non-entities managed to slip through meanwhile, well, he was great-souled enough not to make a fuss about it.

Since that first night Huanchen America's has remained my Platonic ideal of a Chinese restaurant. It was a dark place with dust floating in the glow of red hurricane lamps on each of the dozen tables. The statues of dogs and dragons at the edges of the floor and the trellis work in the corners of the doorways must have been gaudy once, but time had flaked away much of the gold leaf and dust had muted what remained, so that the patches of revealed plaster appeared natural and appropriate, like wrinkles on a human face that has the dignity to wear them well. The carpet was deep red and black, and worn noticeably along the waitstaff's alleys among the tables. But I did not notice all of these details immediately upon entering for the first time, as my attention was absorbed by the small Chinese man headed our way at perhaps ten miles an hour.

Huanchen America was small in every dimension but well-proportioned, as if he had been shrunk using sophisticated digital techniques or some expensive dry solvent. The print on his shirt that evening was of endless brilliant butterflies, and the shirt itself was open a few buttons past what common sense might have dictated, showing off a thick gold braid against his hairless, wrinkled chest. He looked delighted to see us, pushing his expensive cross-trainers along the carpet to intercept Sothum even before the hostess could greet him.

The two of them clasped hands and Huanchen America bowed over the handshake, Sothum not bowing but undergoing a visible expansion of mood that seemed to come from his chest and to build upon itself like an atomic pile, until you would have thought that he had never been so happy to see anyone or anything in his life as he was to see Huanchen America at just that moment. Experience would teach me that this was his standard greeting for anyone of reasonable fellowship.

"Give us the quietest table you have, Mr. America," Sothum said, and the proprietor took back his hands and stood for a moment holding his chin, eyes darting around the dining room as if he were tracing the path that different sound-waves would take through it, trying to identify the acoustical pocket they would all mostly miss. Then with an "ah-ha" gesture and a lot of nodding he led us to a round table right in the thick of things.

"Mr. America," said Sothum, feigning indignation, "don't you have anything quieter than this?"

"Ah!" answered the proprietor, adding in an accent so thick it was clearly theatrical: "Sorry, language barrier, language barrier!"

I suspected that this was a running joke between them, and would turn out to be correct.

Huanchen America then led us to the back of the restaurant, where the wide dining room narrowed into a passage that ended with the kitchen door. On either side of the passage were three booths with high wooden backs and dusty rose curtains that could be drawn for privacy.

"Thank you," said Sothum, "this is much better. Don't you agree, Andy?" he asked, as Huanchen America receded and the three of us scooted in, Buddy and Sothum both sitting across from me.

"It's quite a place. I've never seen booths like this."

"Did you notice the octopus chandelier?" said Buddy, letting me look before he drew the curtain. It was a huge, sprawling thing in brass, its eight spreading arms each lined with tiny bulbs that gave a dim, creamy light. "This used to be a seafood restaurant. The owner had these booths put in to facilitate his assignations with the more receptive waitresses. A nice idea until his wife caught him. In the ensuing divorce he was forced to sell the place for a sea shanty, so to speak, and Huanchen America happened to be looking at the time. This was a long time ago of course."

I nodded, I hoped with sufficient appreciation.

"So Andy," Sothum said, only to be interrupted by two wrinkled arms that parted the curtain long enough to deposit a pot of tea and three white cups. "Ah, the dragon tea. Which cup do you want? As this is your first time with us, I think you should choose first."

I took a closer look at the three cups: a scarlet dragon was painted on the inside of each one. Each dragon made unique coils with his body and the smoke from his nostrils, and displayed a different unclassifiable emotion with his smiling mouth and eyes.

"It's an edible paint made of spices," Buddy said, continuing his role as unofficial tour guide. "It will dissolve when you add the tea. A transitory piece of art."

"I don't like the flavor much myself," said Sothum. "Too much anise. And it costs an extra two dollars per. But where else can you see a dragon dissolve in your tea?"

48

"Huanchen America keeps the artist on staff." Buddy again. "He's from the old country, fled for political reasons I suspect, though Huanchen won't tell us. Huanchen calls him 'The Scholar,' and he doesn't cook or serve, he only paints the cups for dragon tea. I think he must have saved Huanchen America's life back in darker days."

"So," said Sothum, "which one do you want?"

"Well, it's hard to say...each is interesting in its own way..."

"Go ahead," urged Buddy. "You can't go wrong. They're not Rorschach tests or anything."

I chose the tightest, most regular design.

"Interesting," said Sothum, giving Buddy a significant look. I panicked.

"Interesting how? I really liked the others too. Did you want this one?"

"Relax," said Buddy. "There are no right or wrong answers. It's just a kind of Zodiac, and we had a bet running on which you'd choose."

"Who won?"

They just smiled at me, and while I silently cursed myself for choosing so poorly Sothum poured the tea and my shameful selection began to dissolve into the steaming amber. When I took the first sip I found I agreed with Sothum: too much anise.

"I'd never heard the name Sothum before," I said. "Is that your first name or your last?"

"You've read *Mount Analogue*?"

This would prove to be Sothum's grammatical formula for answering questions with questions. He did not tack "of course" on, as others with his knowledge would tend to do. But his tone, more hopeful than arrogant, and the inversion at the beginning—not "have you" but "you have"—these inspired a desperate desire to answer with a strong affirmative, or to be able to answer so.

"No," I said, "not yet." As if it were on my bed stand beneath a few other books that I just had to get through first—when in fact I could not have named the author or his century (René Daumal, I now know indelibly, 1908 to 1944).

"There's a character in it named Father Sogol," said Sothum, "which is *logos* backwards."

"The Greek word for 'word,'" I said. It is terrible how much there is in one's past to make one's cheeks burn.

"One of them—*muthos* being another. Buddy here is pretty keen on nicknames—it has something to do with the class he was born into. After reading *Mount Analogue* he took to calling me Father Sothum."

"After reading it *at your suggestion*," said Buddy.

"At last, after much begging, I at least convinced him to drop the 'Father.'"

Buddy pantomimed a tip of his hat.

"But *muthos* backwards would be Sohtum," I said, "not Sothum." Did I really believe that the author of that dialogue had missed this? Then I added my *coup de grâce*. "You must have changed it for reasons of euphony."

"No," said Buddy, "'tee aitch' in Greek is one letter. Theta. So *muthos* backwards would be, and is, Sothum."

"I haven't taken Greek yet," I said.

"Or written a symphony yet," said Buddy without missing a beat.

"No."

"Or climbed Mount Everest yet."

"No." This was beginning to get uncomfortable.

"Can you believe it?" asked Buddy, turning to Sothum. "The elusive Yeti, pursued in vain by so many, and we find him right here at our own table."

And just like that I had earned my own nickname from Buddy, though he never managed to convince Sothum to use it.

"So what *have* you done, Andy?" asked Sothum.

Even in retrospect I am not sure how I should have answered this question. Perhaps I could have said something oblique: "I'm still young." Or: "Less than Mozart, but less than Hitler too."

"Nothing," was what I managed. At least I did not attempt a curriculum vitae.

"Good," said Sothum, leading the double ohs up a tonic hill and down again, "you'll fit in just fine. So Andy, what is it you're looking for in a discussion society?"

"This," I answered without thinking.

"And what's this?" said Buddy. "Local restaurant history, potable art, and mild hazing?"

"No, I..." I could not express what I felt so clearly: that in these two men—and especially in Sothum—I already felt the stirrings of a wild intellectual power that I had been vainly seeking since my first days at college. "Well, what kind of society do you have?"

"That's an interesting question," said Sothum, "and in fact that happens to be on the slate of topics for tonight's discussion. But first I think we need a name. What should we call ourselves?"

"You already know I'm partial to the Zeitgeists," said Buddy.

"Yes, but it's so optimistic."

"Then the Hot Air Society?"

"Excessive honesty, like any form of excess, is not a virtue."

"Are you both sophomores?" I asked.

"Yes, why?"

"Then how about the Three Wise Fools?" I think even then I was trying to keep the membership down—fewer members meant less competition for Sothum's attention. And I still thank God I did not make explicit my knowledge that the word "sophomore" meant "wise fool" in Greek.

"Perfect!" said Sothum, to my delight and Buddy's tight-lipped smile. He picked up his tea and raised it in toast. "To the Three Wise Fools!" And we began to hash out the bylaws of our new society.

"The ancients understood destiny. The medievals explored free will. We moderns are obsessed with origins. An indication of this is the time we spend arguing 'Nature vs. Nurture,' so hypnotized by the chiming similarity of the two words that we do not notice we have surrendered without blows to being determined by our origins, and are now reduced merely to arguing which form of origin it is—genetic or behavioral—that determines us."

I remember being very excited by these words when I wrote them, imagining how they would be received at the first official meeting of the Three Wise Fools. I thought they would serve as quite an opening to an argument that I intended to make both persuasive and inflammatory at once, threading that perfect line between convincing the listener that resistance was futile and calling his blood to resist anyway. I had only one small problem: I had no idea what that argument was.

Over the next two pages I felt my optimism flag as I tried and failed to answer the question that Sothum had assigned me: "Origin, destiny, or will—which is the primary force in man's life?" Here and there I thought I had turned a decent phrase. I was particularly proud of accusing modern science of a perverted fascination with the "four-letter words of DNA." Moreover I hoped that the splendor of my final image would so dazzle my listeners that they would not even notice I had never really answered the question:

"In short, man is a missile launched powerfully by his origins, which have programmed and flung him in a direction he can barely recognize. His destiny, a magnetic target, tugs at him always like a moon, pulling him towards a different but equally alien destination. To counter these man has only his will, a booster of variable, unreliable, and sometimes dubious strength. Consider then with some pity the state of poor man, the tortured missile—for it is the state of us all."

The next Wednesday night I let this powerful conclusion hang in the air for a few seconds. The Three Wise Fools had congregated in a private conference room on the library's fourth floor—I had signed it out because I did not relish the prospect of reading my first philosophical essay out loud in Huanchen America's or any other public space. As the dramatic pause after my final sentence stretched into awkward silence, I looked directly at Sothum in the hopes that he would be moved to comment. But Buddy responded first.

"What splendid crap you've regaled us with, Andrew. All those words and the images they paint are really intended not to reveal, but to hide the secret message of your essay: that you personally have nothing interesting to say about origin, destiny, or will."

I began to squirm.

"I had some hopes there for a moment," he continued, "that maybe you were going to posit the three as distinct expressions of a single force, like physicists positing that the four fundamental forces of nature are all the same at sufficiently high energies. Take Macbeth, for instance. After the witches deliver that poisoned prophecy to him, is there any difference between his will and his destiny? Or in that heightened, dramatic state, are the two the same? One can imagine an even more fundamental state in which all three—will, destiny, and origin— are shown manifestly to be one and the same. One can even imagine a name for the hero—perhaps something like Oedipus would do. But unfortunately you went this other way."

I began to clear my throat as if I were going to respond, but it was pure bluff. As angry and humiliated as I was, I found myself agreeing with Buddy.

"Now come on," said Sothum, "let's go easy on the new guy. I think there's a seed of merit in Andy's idea that history has progressed through an obsession with each force. I wonder if you could correlate the fundamental views of God these same epochs had. Is it the case that polytheists tend to think in terms of fate, monotheists in terms of will, and atheists in terms of origins?"

"Do we have to drag God into this?" said Buddy.

"We don't have to *drag* Him into anything," Sothum said. "I think, quite the contrary, that you'll find He's already there long ahead of you, and pretty hard to get rid of."

"I was hoping we could have one discussion that didn't involve a being who shared so much with the Easter Bunny and Santa Claus."

I remained silent, horrified by the clash of the Titans that was brewing, but also relieved that my essay was being left behind in the process.

"Ah yes," said Sothum, "of course, I forgot that God doesn't exist. You're sure of that, right?"

"As sure as I am of anything."

"You know what I'm unsure of is whether or not *you* exist. It occurs to me that you can't prove it. I guess you're a fairly divine character yourself, in that you also share a lot with Santa Claus and the Easter Bunny."

"The difference being, I know that I exist."

"But *I* don't, and isn't the point of these discussions to convince others? Let's officially change tonight's topic. We are now arguing the following: 'Resolved, that Buddy Johnston exists.' You'll take the positive, naturally. So come on, why don't you convince me? Come on, prove to me that you exist and you win, no questions asked. I'll never bring up God again. Let's go,

I'm waiting, hop to it, quick like a bunny. Ho-ho-ho! Let's go, Santa, all I want for Christmas is you to prove it to me. Prove it! I dare you."

So saying Sothum scrunched himself up in that way that he had, hunching and making himself as small as he could (which was alarmingly small), bringing his chin down on his chest and drawing his elbows in until they dug into his stomach and almost touched each other. Below the table his feet were treading the floor in a mock-walking motion. This was Sothum's characteristic physical illustration of futility, whether it was the futility of his own efforts he wished to underscore, or yours—and when they were yours, it was infuriating.

What came next would have seemed inevitable to anyone present, whether they knew Johnson's refutation of Berkeley or not. Buddy thrust himself across the table, an improperly made fist at the end of an arm improperly stretched out and locked at the elbow (neither of them knew the first thing about real fighting). But he did not launch himself with enough force— maybe he underestimated the friction involved, or thought that his fury rather than his muscles would propel him—and he skidded to a stop halfway across the conference table with its phony granite finish. For what seemed like a long time Buddy lay there frozen, his fist still extended and his eyes wide, while Sothum regarded with apparent amusement the taut skin across his knuckles. For a moment I thought Sothum was going to laugh—and then, snarling, he thrust himself on the table and engaged his opponent in a different kind of debate.

They took each other in a hard embrace and began to roll around the table, kneeing at each other's thighs and swearing, their foreheads bumping at every revolution. Somehow I found the presence of mind to lift my coffee cup as the scuffle went rolling by me.

Then I gasped, unable to sound a warning at realizing they were reaching the edge of the table. I remember reaching out my hand as if that would somehow have helped. I still couldn't speak, but they wouldn't have heard me anyway, or have listened if they could have heard. And so with another roll over they went, Sothum on top at the apex but already rotating lower as the table disappeared beneath them. A dull thud followed, most of it absorbed by the baffles and curtains and panels of the conference room, so that the landing sounded neither painful or even particularly real. Then there was a long silence, as if they had both been knocked unconscious.

I sat there, stunned, until I heard Sothum's voice from over the ledge.

"I'm still only 85 percent sure you exist. But now I'm 100 percent sure you're an asshole."

And at that we all broke up laughing—even Buddy, who laughed so hard that he had to use his sleeve to wipe his eyes.

There was nothing for it—the meeting could not be brought back to order, and we disbanded. When Sothum asked me if I would be back the next week, I could only nod in awe. I had never met one person, let alone two, for whom ideas were worth fisticuffs, and though I hoped to avoid any actual wrestling myself, I was well and truly hooked.

Soon I was adjusting my class schedule to match Sothum's, reading whatever he read, and talking about whatever he had on his mind at the moment. Every few weeks he would mention some new book that was consuming his thoughts, and he would begin to find ways to bend any and every topic back to its central concerns. It was rare that Buddy or I had already read these books, and on occasion we had not even heard of them, and the two of us would race against each other to acquaint ourselves with the new material sufficiently to understand Sothum's latest theories. Generally we would succeed just before Sothum tired of the book in question and discovered some new and unrelated work that he found even more staggering, and which must be added posthaste to our canon.

I had never been happier in my life.

These days I believe that back in that undoubtedly ridiculous essay I happened onto an important truth. As intelligent and charming as Buddy's physical analogy was, origin, will, and destiny are three separate and antagonistic forces in human life. They cannot really be reconciled, and in general are violently at odds. I have seen this most clearly not in the case of fictional and dramatic figures like Macbeth and Oedipus but in the case of Sothum himself. If he did not transcend his origins then there was something in them that I have never been able to discover, because I have never seen much in that bland New Jersey stew to hint at the ferment that was to come.

His parents were decent, solid, unremarkable people. Their home was modest but warm and welcoming—although the unfortunate wall-to-wall carpeting always seemed to me the exact color of ill health. Over the next two years the Three Wise Fools would take frequent advantage of that welcome during long weekends and short breaks.

Sothum's mother Marjorie, stout and blonde and energetic, kept the table overflowing with homemade lasagna, chicken parmesan, cannoli. She always cooked Italian, but she was not Italian herself—she was a mutt of Northern European breeds.

Stan, or Big Stan as we called him—though Sothum had surpassed him in size while still quite young—might have been Sicilian. Then again he might have been Eastern European, or Black Irish, or even Arabic. It was impossible to tell, or to puzzle out how he had ended up with the surname Riordan. All one could say about him was that he sure looked ethnic. He could have put together a decent bit player career in Hollywood as mob or terrorist muscle—at least in non-speaking roles.

Big Stan almost never spoke, and this silence—along with his forehead, which jutted out like an ancient cliff, scrubby eyebrows just clinging on—could give people the impression that he was stupid. But I don't believe he was stupid at all. He was a plumber who had decided that life was not meant to reach far past what the profession of plumbing provided. Good work at plumbing meant good food, a warm house, a television to kick when the Jets lost. Other things—things like books for example, which purported to take you to other worlds—were a veiled insult to this home that good plumbing had built, and were not especially welcome in his house. I got the impression that Sothum had hidden volumes of philosophy under his mattress the way that most of us were hiding purloined copies of *Our Bodies, Our Selves.*

In short, there were almost no indications besides the physical even to hint that Sothum was the child of these two people, and I often imagined his parents eyeing each other suspiciously, each wondering whether the other had kept hidden some secret spark of divine madness and contributed it to the mixture of their genes. I have gone almost so far as to question whether Sothum had been the result of an affair on Marjorie's part—perhaps even some stolen beach weekend with Featherstone himself, which would have explained a lot. But no—Big Stan was neither foolish enough to be cuckolded without realizing it or flexible enough to forgive, and moreover in Marjorie's breast—good, simple Marjorie—could not have beat a cheating heart.

The train was emptying out as I came back from my daydreaming. We had arrived at Penn Station.

I was glad to see that the relatively cheap hotel right on the edge of Harlem, in which Cheryl and I had stayed on our last visit to New York, was still in business, and once settled in my room I called Buddy's mother. For some reason I had decided that it was important to call her from New York rather than Boston—as if she would find it more difficult to put me off once I had already made the trip—and it was not until the third ring went unanswered that it occurred to me she might have been out of town. But on the fifth she picked up, and after telling her my cover story (that I was in town for a conference) I asked if I might stop by.

She went on for a few sentences about how delightful that would be, delivering all sorts of superlatives in the weariest tone of voice that a charitable listener could still potentially classify as hospitable. We set an hour for the following morning, too late for breakfast and too early for lunch, and she made sure I still had the address. Then I set the alarm, raided the mini bar, and fell asleep to a muted television and the sound of sirens.

CHAPTER FOUR
How the Other Half Lives

Right after our undergraduate commencement in Boston Buddy had invited Sothum and me to visit his parents' brownstone in New York—probably because he wanted to make sure, in case we all went our separate ways, that we had seen at least once how rich he really was. Buddy had been born rich, as had his mother, who came from old tobacco. His father was at first merely privileged, but had made enough in the market to silence any whispers concerning a financial disparity in the match. The family had other homes scattered throughout the world, including a villa on the Italian Riviera and an apartment in Paris, but according to Buddy they rarely left New York, as it was only in that city, "the greatest in the world," that Buddy's father felt truly at home.

Being my stepfather's stepson I felt well prepared to be suitably unimpressed with Buddy's real parents' considerable wealth. And I felt fine when we stepped from the cab onto the wide avenue and looked up at three floors of brown brick drenched in summer light—above which peeked out a few slender branches from the roof garden. The look of Buddy's parents when they greeted us at the worked oaken door—the self-congratulatory look of people who are healthy and beautiful because they have enjoyed sufficient nutritional and educational advantages to unlock their decent genetic potential—neither angered me or made me feel inferior, nor did their expensive casual clothes, or the two grand pianos, or the calendar covered with names I had seen in the papers. None of it got under my skin until they showed me the library.

Then my knees went weak. I mean that literally—I had to sit down on the love seat uninvited, which was too plush and threatened to swallow me. I pled low blood pressure and an overly exciting New York cab ride. There were folios of Shakespeare in those glass-cased shelves, and first editions signed by Frost and Yeats, and, with a prominent glass case all to itself, an original Latin edition of Descartes' *Meditations on First Philosophy*. A number of those volumes could have purchased a small library in which to house the others. Then I was envious. Of course I was envious.

All eight meals I ate in that house—each one prepared by the family's personal chef, who had trained in Paris—were so rich that they upset my digestion. I hated myself for enjoying them so much. I hated that despite the supposedly good-natured mocking I incurred from Buddy's father I could not keep from reaching for seconds and thirds—and that I would wake in the night craving leftovers, seriously considering a raid on the kitchen with its marble floor of checkered black and white.

Buddy spent the weekend smiling at me as though I were a tourist too embarrassed to ask for directions, trying to pass this off as my destination but fooling no one. His mother—his slim beautiful mother, whose normal uniform seemed to be a tennis skirt, and who apologized for putting sugar on her rice—asked me questions about myself in her warm Southern accent and would nod or exclaim periodically while I answered as briefly as I was able, her chin bobbing like the hull of a bored, hospitable boat as she cut through my reply without absorbing anything.

During the initial tour of the house (which had been, as Sothum remarked later, "a three hour tour, a three hour tour") Buddy's father showed us what he called the smoking room.

"A room we use only for special occasions," he said, "though if you think about what paid for this house, every other room in here could be called the smoking room."

Buddy's shoulders had stiffened as he felt this joke coming.

Later that first night, after Buddy's mother had turned in, his father led us three boys—the Three Musketeers, as he referred to us—back into the smoking room. All the furniture was the color of wine with the exception of the white Baldwin grand piano. There was so much crystal—objects d'art and immaculate ashtrays and a low chandelier, all cut at hard prismatic angles—that specks of colored light jumped on the white walls as overloaded shelves rattled at our entrance, casting rainbow confetti over the family's inferior Picasso sketch.

Buddy's father removed two crystal snifters from a glass cabinet, the shelves and back of which were mirrored. Sothum and I had positioned ourselves as instructed on the burgundy sofa, which was also too plush, as all their sofas were, and we looked at each other with the same unspoken question—why two glasses? Were we the only ones who were going to drink? Meanwhile Buddy's father opened up the bar and, shielding the bottle from our view with his narrow back, filled both snifters up to where they bulged their widest.

When he turned around he was smiling at me, as was Buddy, who had perched on the white bench of the white piano like a hawk. In that moment Buddy seemed to me a deflated version of his old man—a little scrawnier, a little whiter—just as vicious but perhaps without the same energy to put his nasty intentions into action. But of course we were friends, so I pushed these thoughts away as quickly as I could.

Buddy's father handed me one of the glasses. I could see the blond hairs shine on his slightly orange arm, the tan-line his pink polo shirt exposed halfway up his modest bicep as he stretched forward. Instead of offering the other glass to Sothum, as I had expected, he took it with him to a matching chair on the sofa's left, where he sat and sighed and looked around the room once at the three of us, as if we were his three boys. Or as if, I thought on account of the drinks that only he and I were holding, we—Buddy's father and I—were the proud parents, and Sothum and Buddy were our recently graduated children.

"Cheers," he said, lifting his glass. He smiled in a way that made the nascent wrinkles on his face seem easy, no big deal, a graceful sign of age and experience that he would acknowledge in the same spirit in which he did not dye his salt-and-pepper hair.

"Cheers," said I, lifting mine and taking a small sip—but even that small sip left a line like a burning fuse as it trickled down. I was only used to drinking beer at the time, and have never been used to drinking while my friends do not. When I had taken my sip I switched the drink to my other hand, where I could pass it to Sothum more easily if the moment came to do so. I was thinking that perhaps the three youngsters were supposed to share this one drink. I remember I looked to Buddy for clues—and he smiled at me.

"Well?" said his father.

"It's good," I said.

"And?"

"Very good?"

"What's good about it?" he asked. "What can you taste?"

He watched closely as I took another sip, a bigger one this time, and I could see him suppress a smile as I suppressed my cough.

"What did you taste?"

What I had tasted was fire, pure and simple, but I doubted that was an answer that would please my host.

"Smoke?" I said. Where there was fire there should be smoke, I thought—and I remembered hearing once that scotch could be smoky.

"I'm impressed," he said. He swirled his own snifter, inhaled deeply, and took a meditative sip, half closing his eyes. "It's the rare gourmand whose palette can pick out smoke through the honey and heather of a floral highland scotch. I salute you, Andrew!" And he drank again, first thrusting the arm with his glass out as far as it would go, as if we were two gladiators taking a last drink together before a hopeless battle.

They tormented me like that all weekend, silent smiling Buddy and his father, but they left Sothum alone. Buddy's father in particular barely said a word to him, except to answer in a surprisingly polite and deferential manner Sothum's involved questions about the market. I suppose that Buddy's father was scared of him. Sothum was taller than he was, after all. And around that time Sothum was surrounded by the fire of brilliance that is only just discovering its limits. He was still measuring himself against the world, and he was ready for any and every fight that anyone might start with him. Everything in his manner attested to that readiness.

Sothum was especially ferocious that weekend, swiping and snarling like a cornered animal, because I think during those few days in New York so much of what he saw challenged one of his deepest held beliefs, his most dear: that money followed talent. More than that: he believed that money *was* the worldly, external manifestation of talent—and that therefore successful people deserved their success. Or he wanted very badly to believe so. Even years later, after he had seen enough to realize otherwise, Sothum could cling to this belief when he was tired or disheartened, pointing out that the rich Germans who were ruined in World War II were rich again ten years after the war was over. He might even make excuses for Buddy's father, who was rumored to have gotten his start with questionably legal trading tips obtained while performing favors of questionable legality in his capacity as a senator's aide.

The terror and humiliation of that weekend came flooding back to me all these years later as I paid my cab driver the next morning and walked up the stairs to the front door. The slabs of light hitting the walls were so similar to the ones in my memory, and the snaky branches above looked just the same as I recalled them. I knew that Buddy's father was long dead, but I could not entirely erase the irrational fear that he would answer when I rang, and all of a sudden I was tempted to turn around and forget the entire errand. But I had called ahead, and was expected, and the thought of having to call Buddy's mother again with some excuse was slightly more mortifying than going through with my visit.

I could hear Buddy's mother calling to one or more members of the household staff that she was expecting someone and would get the door herself, and she did. The years and their griefs had not been kind to her. The blonde hair that had once been her crown had grown thin and brittle, and she had refused either to take chemical measures or to cut it in a style more in line with its diminished capabilities. Her lips had always been thin, but now they also turned down at the ends, frozen into a permanent expression of displeasure. Her eyes were sad. It was unmistakable: she no longer knew what to do with her life, and I was suddenly quite sorry to be disturbing her, especially as I brought no offerings of cheer or peace.

"Andrew," she said, "how nice of you to come." And I had to give her credit: though her face had become eternally sour she still managed to pump hospitality and warmth into her voice, even if the edge of effort was apparent. I did notice the odd way in which she expressed her welcome—"nice of you to come," rather than "to visit" or "to stop by." It gave my visit the immediate air of a condolence call, especially since there had never been a decision to presume Buddy dead or an official occasion on which I could have offered her my sympathies.

She invited me in and offered me iced tea or water, both of which I refused, before leading me into the living room. She had been watching television when I arrived.

"The Home Shopping Network," she said as she found the remote and turned it off. "I can't for the life of me explain why I watch it—I've never bought a single thing from them. But I can spend a whole morning just watching the endless parade of trinkets and bric-a-brac. Sometimes I play a game with myself and see if I can guess how low they will drop the price. I don't often win: usually I guess far too low. It must be that I can't imagine anyone paying anything at all for most of that merchandise. Please, sit anywhere you are comfortable. It has been a terribly long time, hasn't it? How are you? What are you doing these days?"

I tried to give a very short account of myself and my current marital, professional, and medical situation, but she strung her questions into such an energetic chain, and asked them with such perfect rhythm, that I began to understand I was going to have to grab the reins of the conversation forcibly or she was not going to allow me to ask her the questions I had come to ask.

"Mrs. Johnston," I said, leaving her in ignorance of whether Cheryl and I were cat people or dog people, "I would like to ask you some questions about Buddy."

In response her thin lips showed me just how far they could go in the direction of displeasure, and her eyes narrowed as though I had said something in extremely poor taste.

"I have nothing to tell you. I don't know where my son is, or even whether he's alive or not, though I doubt it. If he is alive, I expect that he's run off with that friend of yours."

"You mean Soth—Stanley?" Parents generally knew Sothum by his given name.

"I never understood exactly what went on between him and my son, but I always suspected that I would not approve of it."

Something about the way she said it led me to think that she had suspected them of being lovers.

"Mrs. Johnston," I said, hesitating while I tried to find the right way to put it, "I can tell you with perfect confidence that Stanley and Buddy were not close in that way."

It took her a few seconds to understand what I was talking about, and then she started to laugh in an unpleasant fashion. I felt that I had managed to fall still further in her esteem.

"I never had doubts on that score. For small mercies God be praised. No, whatever that man had Buddy involved in, I don't believe it was homosexuality."

"I'm very sorry to have suggested it—I only wanted to put your mind at ease. But do you have any evidence to suggest that Stanley was responsible for...whatever caused Buddy to drop out of sight?"

"I have nothing concrete, and nothing I wish to share with either you or the public. I decided long ago that it is much better that my son remain a controversial suicide in the public's eye than whatever else he might really have been. I have thought once or twice about asking your friend straight out what happened to my son, but I am sure that I would not like the answer, even if he would give it to me. Which I doubt."

"Stanley died recently," I told her. "I didn't know if you had heard."

"I can't say that I am terribly sorry to hear that."

I was close to giving the visit up for lost, but having come this far I did at least want to play my last cards. From my pocket I took the notebook page—the one written in what I was fairly sure was Buddy's handwriting—and gave it to her.

"Does this mean anything to you?" I asked.

She unfolded and read the paper.

"Where did you get this?"

"Stanley left me some assorted papers when he died. This was among them. It is Buddy's handwriting, isn't it?"

"Yes."

"Do you have any idea what it means? What it's about?"

She did not answer right away, and she seemed to be thinking very carefully about what to say next. Finally she stood up and returned the paper to me.

"Please wait here," she said, and left the room.

She was gone long enough that I started to wonder if she had forgotten about me, or simply changed her mind about showing me whatever she had gone to fetch. But eventually she re-appeared carrying a small leather notebook, which she handed to me before she sat back down.

I began to flip through the pages. They were filled with the same crabbed hand and the same kind of surreal scenes as my single torn-out page. Near the middle of the notebook I even found the spot where my page had been ripped out—the torn edges fit each other perfectly. None of the pages were dated, and a brief examination found no explanatory notes or extra information besides the short, strange scenes themselves. After reading a few entries silently to myself I picked a page at random and read aloud.

"The tiger approaches, laughing and salivating at the same time, while the ground heaves and musical notes spring in pairs and triplets from the resultant chasms. Suddenly the sun is laughing instead of the tiger, and the tiger puts his paw over his own mouth, and in the same instant a cloud drifts across the sun."

I closed the notebook.

"Do you have any idea what these are about?" I asked.

"About? They aren't about anything. Buddy was a writer, and these are something he was writing. Absurdist prose poems, a dream journal."

"He told you that?"

"He didn't have to."

"Mrs. Johnston, where did you get this? Did Buddy give it to you? Did he give you an indication that it was special in any way?"

Buddy's mother looked around nervously as if for a cigarette. She seemed to be wavering in her resolve not to talk about Buddy, so I pressed the issue.

"Please look at this," I said, taking the clipped Buddy sighting from my pocket and handing it to her along with the page that had been ripped from the journal. "Compare the two. Doesn't it strike you as odd?"

"I don't see what you're driving at," she said when she had read the article.

"You don't think the two echo each other rather oddly?"

"There are some similarities. So what?"

"How about the timing? How long have you been in possession of this journal? Look at the date on the newspaper clipping. Is there any way Buddy could have read the clipping before he wrote the...absurdist poem?"

"Andrew, you seem like a nice enough young man, and you seem much more interested in Buddy's experimental writing than I am, so I'll make you a deal. If I tell you everything I know about that book, will you leave here and never come back? Furthermore, will you promise that you won't do anything, with that book or anything else, that might put Buddy's name in the press again? You'll agree that I've been through enough, and whatever happened to my son, it really isn't anyone else's business."

I promised her that I would hold to both of these conditions.

"The book was mailed to me anonymously, perhaps two months ago. I have no idea who sent it or why. As it was not accompanied by ransom demands or any information about my son's whereabouts or his condition, I can only imagine it was intended to twist the knife of my ignorance."

"Do you still have the packing it came in?"

"Of course not. Before you ask, there was no return address, and the postmark was from Eldred, New York. The police checked for fingerprints and didn't find any. They went to Eldred and found nothing. Now you know everything that I know about that book. Please honor your promise and leave."

I stood to leave and, thanking her, tried to hand the journal back, but she refused it.

"Just get all of this out of my house. You can see yourself to the door."

"Goodbye, Mrs. Johnston. And thank you."

I had already opened the door when I heard her call out to me. I started to walk back to the living room, but she met me halfway in the hall. All of her prickliness and armor had vanished, and she was on the verge of tears.

"If you find out what happened to him, do you promise you'll tell me?"

I promised, and for one awkward moment it seemed as though she would embrace me. Instead she took my hand, holding it for a few seconds in a feminine fashion, and walked back to the living room. As I opened the front door I could hear the Home Shopping Network start up again in the background.

While I waited for a cab to pass and take me back to the train station, I flashed back again to that weekend visit after graduation. I remembered how on the final morning, as Sothum and I climbed into a taxi, Buddy stood at the door looking pleased with himself but also a little jealous. At the time I assumed that he was jealous because I was about to have a cab and train ride with Sothum all to myself. But as I stood on the same curb all these years later I wondered whether he hadn't been jealous of both Sothum and me for a different reason. Perhaps he had been jealous that he was not, as we were, leaving that nest of wealth having been awed and impressed by it—that he was going to have to turn around and return to the breakfast table whose opulence had always been plain in his eyes, the house whose splendor he could only feel in the reactions of guests who were not accustomed to it. Perhaps he felt clearly that he would have to find some prick or itch against the comforts he knew he had not earned, and how difficult it might prove to find his way out of his father's large and not entirely honest shadow.

Now with the benefit of hindsight I could see what Buddy should have done. Right then he should have signaled us to wait, packed his bags—well, one or two of them—told his parents he'd probably see them in ten years or so, and come with us as far as the train station, where he could have picked his own destination. That's the kind of thing everyone thinks about and no one does. But it would have been better than taking the publishing job his father had secured for him and remaining within reach of that house's fair airs and poisoned spirit. If Sothum transcended—effortlessly it seemed—his origins, Buddy was never able either to accept his or to rebel sufficiently against them, so that he seemed locked in a psyche more resembling Sothum's boyhood home—with its claustrophobic spaces and bad carpets—than his own. In some crucial sense Buddy, for all his wealth and opportunity, had been far less free than Sothum and

I were as we started back for Boston, where Cheryl was waiting for me with her bags already packed for Texas.

CHAPTER FIVE

The Literary Crimes of Buddy Johnston

To pass the time on the train ride back to Boston I leafed through my old copies of Buddy's two novels. It had been a long time since I had opened either one, and I found it strangely affecting to see Buddy's signature on their front leaves. He used to autograph his books in an idiosyncratic fashion, crossing out the printed version of his name on the title page and signing below in green ink. That I know of, he never added a message of esteem or thanks or anything beyond his name—I suppose he thought his name should have been thanks enough for anyone. The signature in the first book was large and sweeping, an act of grand abandon—but by the second book his letters had become stingy and anemic, the loops pulled tight like nooses. In these two scrawls of ink I could discern everything that had happened to Buddy in the interval between their production. A different man had made that second signature.

When Buddy fell he fell so hard, and so fast, that only a heart of stone could not have felt a pang for him. Yes, he was arrogant and pompous and vain, and yes, his books were terrible, but it is a painful thing to see a man whose ego has become so large that only the adulation of the world can support it then be deprived so suddenly of his only prop.

I say his books were terrible. This opinion placed me squarely in the minority when it came to his first novel. Reviewer after reviewer praised Buddy's "postmodern fable" and the "fresh new voice" in which he had written it, and one distinguished critic, from whom I would have expected better, even entitled his review "At Last: Story Returns to the Novel." The best that any right-thinking critic should have said about the story of Buddy's novel was that at least it was quick and easy to summarize.

A Friend Indeed tells the story of Otto, a young and promising man whose career in public relations has nevertheless stalled somewhere in middle management. Even worse for poor Otto, Ramona—the gorgeous secretary on the second floor—remains ignorant of his existence, despite his many exertions to demonstrate it to her. But Otto's life changes one day with the arrival of a man named Jake.

Jake, a new hire in the mail room, latches on to Otto instantly, and despite the gap in rank the two become fast friends. Soon enough Jake (whom Otto affectionately dubs Jake-O) is providing Otto with all sorts of moral support and excellent advice. His position in the mail room allows him to give Otto advance warning of a memo sent to the powers that be from a rival who is attempting to destroy Otto's career. Instead the rival himself looks like a fool when Otto appears to have anticipated his every move. Jake-O also takes the liberty of forging a love note to Ramona that so unlocks the passions she was unaware of harboring that she marries Otto in a whirlwind of romance only a few weeks later—just in time, incidentally, to learn at the wedding that she is to be the wife of the newly named regional director. Otto is on cloud nine, his only regret being that Jake-O will not accept even a small promotion in the mail room in return for all the marvelous changes he has helped bring about in Otto's life.

Then one mild spring day a few weeks later Otto receives a call from Jake-O. He knows it's Saturday, but would Otto mind meeting him at the office? Jake-O has a surprise for him—"the biggest surprise you've ever gotten from me." Otto is only too happy to meet him, but when Jake-O has not arrived by the agreed upon hour Otto knows instantly that something is wrong. Only disaster could have waylaid this best and most punctual of men. With dread in his heart Otto takes to the streets in search, only to have his worst fears confirmed: he finds Jake-O in the street outside the office, struck down by a bus, dead.

Otto's life takes the predictable turns. He sees to it that the bus driver, who claims to have blacked out at the time of the accident, is prosecuted to the fullest extent of the law. He establishes a charity in his friend's name. He writes a book about Jake-O as well, which finds a publisher instantly. The book is called—of course—*A Friend Indeed*. An actor in Hollywood happens upon a copy and is so taken with the story that he adapts it into a vanity project, with himself in the starring role.

The final proper scene of the novel opens with Otto and Ramona at the L.A. theater where the film is to debut. Ramona is even holding their own little Jake-O on her lap, who is strangely quiet for a two year old, as if even an infant could sense the sacred nature of the moment. The lights go down, Otto's eyes start to fill with tears, the curtain is about to rise. Ramona takes his hand. The curtain rises...

And then, after this whole dreary affair of some 200 pages, comes the postlude in Heaven, which practically guaranteed, even more than the popular movie-within-a-movie motif, that this bad book would someday become a worse movie.

We see Jake-O on a cloud, surrounded by a splendorous light, picking his teeth with a feather and speaking, as it were, to the camera. In short order he fills us in on the real backstory. He is not now, nor has he ever been, a friend to Otto. He has intended him evil since before the day they met—he declines to reveal his motivations. But every kindness he has ever done Otto, every gift he ever bestowed upon him, was only to give the wretch more to lose when the malicious ax fell. It was supposed to fall, in fact, that very Saturday at the office, that very day that Jake-O was stricken down before he could bring his plan to its conclusion.

Nevertheless Jake-O can muster only mild regret at how things have turned out. His natural disappointment is soothed not only by the celestial delights he is experiencing (he has just come from a banquet he can only describe as "heavenly"), but most of all by the pride he feels in the performance he gave while he was still alive. His act as the perfect friend was so nuanced, so convincing, that, he says with a wink and an indicating thumb jerked over his shoulder, "I even had the Old Man snowed."

Sothum had a theory on the book, as he had a theory on every book. Although he agreed with me that the echoes, so very obvious, of Othello were not to the novel's advantage, that was just about his only complaint.

"It's a fantastic piece of work, although ninety-nine out of a hundred readers won't understand why—if there are a hundred readers left these days. The ending alone redeems any nits that might be picked in the earlier chapters. It's ironic to such an extent that I was disgusted myself until I realized what was really happening."

According to Sothum, what was really happening was that Jake-O had failed utterly, and not only in the sense that he himself thought. God's own hand had been driving the bus that lovely spring morning, and Jake-O, intending to do harm, had become an unwitting instrument for good, accomplishing nothing more with all his machinations than to bring a good man and woman together into an excellent life. Jake-O's final state, left for the reader to divine, was not Heaven at all but Hell—a Hell of his own making, where his ignorance and pride kept him in the loneliest state a human creature had ever found himself, believing that his true character was so secret, so unknowable, that even God could not penetrate it.

"And what about the bus driver?" I had asked him, indignant. "He goes to prison for longer than most child molesters while Jake-O goes to a Hell that anyone would confuse with Heaven?"

"Yes, that's the beauty part! The bus driver is a good and simple man. He has no doubt been praying for years to become an instrument of the divine, and he's wise enough to know when his prayers have been answered. That's why he's described as impassive at the trial—'almost cold,' remember? He knows why he blacked out that day. Rather, he knows enough to realize he doesn't need to know. His complete bodily deprivation in prison is a state of spiritual fulfillment, while Jake-O's myriad delights in Heaven—food, pride, comfort—are a state of utter spiritual emptiness. It's a thing of rare beauty that Buddy has pulled off. And even rarer is the restraint that he showed in not drawing the reader's attention to it. I didn't know he had that in him."

"Have you ever presented this theory of yours to him and asked him if that's what he really meant?"

"Andy," he said, "you know me better than to think that I would ever choose to be so vulgar!"

It was not that I could not see the charm of Sothum's theory. I much preferred it to what I knew the book really meant. Buddy would never have trusted a reader to figure anything out without a few hammer blows to the head, and he would certainly never have written anything to imply that man was finally incapable of outsmarting God. No, the ending of *A Friend Indeed* meant just what it purported to mean: a cunning man had fooled his fellow men and a buffoonish God, a man and woman had found a meaningless happiness based on a deep deception, and in short all was for the most arbitrary in this most arbitrary of all worlds. That is exactly, I am sure, what Buddy meant to say. But even so Buddy, like most who preach the fickleness of fate, was violently surprised and indignant when fate became a little more fickle with him.

The instant success of *A Friend Indeed* made Buddy rich and famous enough that even though he had been born into money and influence, he could start to pretend to be a self-made man. Reviewers hailed him as one of the best hopes for the American Novel, *A Friend Indeed* sold out its first three printings, and there were whispers of the inevitable cinematic adaptation. But Buddy got his first taste of *real* celebrity only when he began to be seen around town on the arm of Alyssa.

Yes, *the* Alyssa, heiress to the largest motel chain in North America, darling of the masses, "the working man's Paris Hilton" as she was always described in the press. They made quite a pair in the Paparazzi shots: the slim blonde with that permanent look of cheap seduction plastered on her face, and next to her Buddy, still a bit fleshy despite the personal trainers he had hired—that permanent glower on his face that he thought looked intellectual but I thought looked intestinal in origin, his big shaven dome of a head always shining in the flash of the camera like a fishbowl caught in the sun. I never saw a single photo where either of the two tried to block their faces or the camera with their hands. On the contrary, I imagine them as the first power couple that could have worn the Paparazzi out.

"All right, I think we've got enough here...why don't you two go into dinner?"

"Are you sure? Why don't we get a few more from three quarters?"

"We're out of film."

"Don't you use digital?"

"Out of memory, then."

I am not the only one who wondered what brought these two together, or kept them together through nine long months. In nastier moments I have theorized that perhaps they were each so self-absorbed as not to even notice the presence of the other, but with the benefit of time I suspect they were intensely aware of it, and must have disliked each other just as intensely from the moment they met. They were trophies to each other, nothing more: he gave her a stamp of intellectual respectability, and she gave him a pass into the limelight he had always sensed he would prefer to the flicker of the midnight desk lamp.

Once he discovered that limelight Buddy appeared to lose all interest in the literary world rather quickly. The establishment, after pronouncing him "one of the ten most promising novelists under 40," was kept wondering what the wonder boy had up his sleeve next. Every interviewer asked him what masterpiece he had in the works, and his answer was always the same: "Right now I'm focusing on some other things in my life." By which he meant: "When *A Friend Indeed* is re-issued with a Hollywood actor on the cover, and one of those silver explosions with embossed red letters informing you that it is now a major motion picture, then maybe I'll think about writing another novel for Hollywood to adapt into another film." He had caught the fever well and truly.

At first it seemed that Buddy's love for Hollywood would be requited. A major motion picture studio optioned his book, and some exciting names were floated around for the position of director. On the frequent trips that he and Alyssa began to make from New York to L.A. Buddy was lunching with everyone you read about in the gossip magazines and their handlers, and it must have seemed to him that he had finally found a crowd, a whole town, whose vision was worthy of his own. These were people who understood you were exactly as big as you made yourself, and that, if you knew you were better than everyone else, it made no sense not to say so. They even taught him some marvelous new dialects in which to say so: fashion, food, the after-party party.

You couldn't really accuse Buddy of selling out, though, despite what some—chiefly those in the literary establishment—have said to the contrary. Money for Buddy was always a secondary thing: nice to have, of course, but it had always been there and there was every reason to think it always would be. Selling a piece of art was a desirable and excellent achievement, but not so much for the cash the audience was forking over for your book or a ticket to your film. What was crucial was the audience itself, the hearts and minds you had a chance to reach and inform with your superior understanding. That they were willing to pay for your message just meant that they took it seriously. Words on the printed page were always, for Buddy, a medium like any other—a distribution channel for what he saw as the profound message he had to deliver. There was nothing mystical about the written word, nothing superior or close to the human core, and it had no special hold over him. If film—just another medium, another channel of distribution—had the power to reach more hearts and minds than the printed word, then it only made sense to cover the typewriter and spin up the camera, and any artist who told you otherwise deserved the inferior audience he got.

But Buddy's transition to film was not as effortless as his book's auspicious beginnings had led him to believe it would be. The options to *A Friend Indeed* fell into one of those bizarre Hollywood morasses from which it was not clear there would ever be an escape. The original director dropped the project for health reasons, then another dropped it to work on *Green Lantern vs. Green Arrow*, which had apparently been a dream of his since childhood. A third director walked when the studio refused to accept an unknown in the part of Jake-O, finally responding to the director's olive-branch proposal of Kenneth Branagh with a counter-offer of Keanu Reeves. After that the project sank into dormancy. Buddy meanwhile was becoming increasingly frantic.

He had other matters to be frantic about, too: he and Alyssa had finally called it quits, and the limelight was a little harsher for Buddy now that he had become "the man who broke Alyssa's heart." A tabloid photographer caught him holding a restaurant door for a strange brunette, sparking all kinds of speculation. In his black frustration he was on the verge of breaking down and hiring a second publicist when a superior strategy suddenly dawned on him, and he locked himself away in his Manhattan apartment and began breaking ground on a new novel. If the bastards were going to come at him, he would move the battle to ground where he still reigned supreme.

I can imagine Buddy well during those days, rising late as he had since college (you could not be Sothum's friend and keep early hours), hammering away furiously at the new book until early evening, and then, when late afternoon had arrived to the left coast, putting aside the new novel and taking up once again the cause of the old: making calls, sending faxes, leaving messages, attempting with his flood of communication to dislodge the boulder that was holding down his work of genius in Tinseltown. He flattered all the bosses he could reach and cursed all the assistants, and one day he must have used the wrong curse on the wrong assistant, because a short time later he received word that Smythe & Hammer had signed on to the project, were already in casting, and wanted to meet with him as soon as was humanly possible.

Smythe & Hammer were a—some would say *the*—avant-garde direction/production team out of England. Their first two feature-length films—*Guy in Effigy* and *The Sympathetic, Nervous System* had been well-received critically in their native land, but even there had not earned anything at the box office.

No one, not even the critics who reviewed them glowingly, could say what either film was really about, and Smythe & Hammer's line was always that if you had to ask, it meant you had already gotten it.

How these two ever ended up on a project like Buddy's would doubtless make a fascinating tale in itself if it could ever be uncovered. I imagine that some lackey, fed up with Buddy's abuse, either plucked them from a hat, or sicced them on Buddy with revenge in mind, or perhaps simply reckoned that men who made films without plots, characters, or soundtracks, could not be much stranger than someone who would actually take the time to write a whole novel based on something called *Othello* by some dead screenwriter named William Something, and gambled that they and Buddy would get along famously. Smythe & Hammer must have taken the project as a lark with money attached or vice-versa—or maybe through some snafu in communication thought it was actually *Othello* itself they were adapting, and only found out the truth too late.

For Buddy it must have seemed that Fortune's wheel had finally rolled back to its proper position, with him on top. Smythe & Hammer arrived from England with steamer trunks full of black notebooks, and Buddy spent the next three months refusing to make cuts to the new book with his editor in the mornings, and pontificating about the older one in the afternoons. Smythe & Hammer followed him everywhere, all the time, laughing at his jokes, flattering him at every turn, and appearing to fill those lovely black notebooks with copious notes as he held forth on the themes, conceits, and secrets of the tale told by a *A Friend Indeed*.

As fate would have it—or legend—Buddy delivered the proofs of the second novel on the same day that Smythe & Hammer started filming, which was also the same day that Buddy's father, Randolph Johnston, the well-known pundit and investor, stepped up to a podium to accept an award from an economic think tank and dropped dead of a blood infection he had probably picked up on vacation without his wife in South America.

During the period that followed, between the death of his father and the publication of his second book, I saw more of Buddy than I had since our college days. He would come up to Boston almost every week, sometimes twice a week, and when Sothum was busy or not to be found Buddy would stay with Cheryl and me in our Cleveland Circle apartment. I never liked Buddy more than I liked him during that time, either. He professed no doubt that both the new book and the movie would be smashing successes, that he would be back on top again in no time at all, but the obvious doubts that prompted him to insist so hard made him more human, easier to understand and empathize with.

Cheryl and Buddy became quite close as well—closer than he and I had ever been. Some nights I would go to bed early, leaving them to kill a bottle of the ouzo I could never learn to stand and talk the night away. Cheryl said that Buddy spoke a lot about his father—how angry he was that he had died while Buddy's life was at such a low point. Buddy did not like to think that was the last impression of him that his father had. Cheryl said that Buddy often mentioned how much his father had liked me, how he asked after me regularly and spoke again and again of the favorable impressions he had formed of me that one weekend we all spent in New York back during college. This hokum was such a bald-faced, absurd invention on Buddy's part that it was rather touching.

As the publication date of his second novel drew nearer, Buddy seemed to remember himself, to shake himself out from the rut he had fallen into. His visits to Boston became less frequent, and his visits to our apartment ceased entirely. His insufferable streaks reasserted themselves in anticipation of September 15th, the day that Buddy was to unleash his new vision on the hungry world. By the 16th of September, the world owed Buddy an apology.

Please don't misunderstand me—*The Four Seasons in Hell* did not deserve good reviews, but it did deserve differently bad ones. It deserved at the very least reviewers who bothered to read the whole tedious affair of 888 pages before confirming that this was quite a bad book indeed, transparently based on Buddy's nine month relationship with a motel heiress (though in the novel Buddy stretched their relationship to a whole year and, quite sportingly, transformed Alyssa into a proper hotel heiress on the order of Paris Hilton herself). It deserved reviewers who noted that in Buddy's case the tools of the writer's trade had apparently not been forged well enough to survive the vitriol that shot through every page, or reviewers who confirmed for Buddy that no one wanted to read a book about a man who, despite his intellectual as well as moral superiority to the lady, is somehow taken in completely by a shallow, no-good, nymphomaniacal, two-timing, three-timing, and eventually eight-timing shrew who never had more to offer him anyway than a bra stuffed with Daddy's dollars. Instead what Buddy's novel got, from the first reviewer in the Times to the last in the Podunk Literary Supplement, was treatment that never made it past the disclaimer on the novel's first page.

"This is a work of fiction," read the disclaimer. "Any similarity to any person, living or dead, is unintended and purely coincidental. Anyone who thinks to have found in these pages such a similarity to oneself should take a long, hard look in the mirror, and get a better grip on her raging ego."

You don't attack America's darlings. Buddy might as well have called Jackie O a prostitute. Article after article, website after website, critic after critic applied the magic formula: quote the disclaimer, level charges of misogyny and mean-spiritedness, and express sadness that such a talent had come to this. Never mind that the disclaimer was the only mildly funny or biting part of a book that was supposed to be a satire! Never mind that the Alyssa character "pouts" instead of "says" exactly 256 times in only 888 pages (as in, "Do we really have to see a movie with subtitles?" she pouted). Never mind the ultimate lunacy of pages 887 and 888, where our mightily wronged hero, by way of revenge, decides to make a randomly chosen man as miserable as he himself has been made, takes a job in a mail room in a distant city, and changes his name to Jacob—Jake-O for short—an idiotic twist that would not only have Balzac spinning in his grave, but which does retroactive injury to *A Friend Indeed*—an insult that the earlier work could ill afford.

If only Buddy had cared a little more about money and infamy than a more respectable fame, he might have come through everything just fine. Thanks to its "controversial" disclaimer the book was selling like mad. There seemed to be a law enacted that Alyssa could not be mentioned in the press without an immediate mention of Buddy, and Alyssa was mentioned a lot. But for Buddy's stinging pride all this was salt, not balm, and the world only had worse in store for him.

Buddy came out of the advance screening of the movie, *his* movie, the vehicle he had been counting on to bring his genius back to the people, threatening law suits, injunctions, even, according to legend, assassins. But there was nothing he could do, and two weeks later *A. Friend Indeed: An American Film with English Subtitles* opened on a few hundred screens throughout the country.

The story of the movie had nothing to do with the book— which, one could argue, was one point in the movie's favor. There was no Otto, no Jake-O, and no Ramona, no bus, no scenes in heaven. Instead the movie told the story of Smythe & Hammer, a—some would say *the*—avant-garde production/direction team from England, trying to adapt for the screen a novel by an American novelist, one A. Friend by name. The novelist's first name is never mentioned in the film—he is always addressed as Mr. Friend or simply Amigo, depending on who is addressing him.

The movie was actually quite good. The unknown actor who played Mr. Friend bore only a passing physical resemblance to Buddy—except around his eyes, which managed to be as glittering and greedy as the original's—but his performance was right on the money. His dismissive and self-important patterns of speech and movement could not have been closer to Buddy's own. Smythe & Hammer were interpreted by Hugh Laurie and a mute Stephen Fry, two masters of the raised eyebrow who played their parts as the ironic, disapproving Englishmen to the hilt. Alyssa even had a cameo as herself and, to be sure, nailed the part (which was far from the only thing on the set she nailed, if the rumors are to be believed). But the best part of the movie— the part that made me see it twice, even though Cheryl pronounced the second time to be sadism—and probably the part that launched this long shot of a film onto screens from coast to coast within a month—were the subtitles.

They were yellow, bright yellow like a hot English pub mustard, and they served various purposes throughout the film. Sometimes they interpreted what Laurie's or Fry's eyebrows were saying, though in the case of Fry this is done with typographical symbols only, such as "???!!!!!!?!" for extreme disbelief and "(~~~~~)" to indicate ambivalence. Sometimes they answered Mr. Friend's rhetorical questions for him, such as when he asked Smythe & Hammer if they knew how many women he'd bedded in his life who made Alyssa look like a dog. And sometimes they merely "corrected" Mr. Friend's American

English, for example when he admonished Hammer to "get that damn [read bloody] teacup off of [sic] my Mercedes before you scratch the paint job."

As my train back to Boston clacked and shuddered its way along the tracks, I put aside Buddy's novels and recalled these subtitles, chuckling at the memory of some of them and the accompanying scenes that played in my head. At one point I imagined involuntarily what it must have been like for Buddy to have read them for the first time, and I stopped chuckling and was almost ashamed of myself. Each new line must have felt to him like the next probe of a subtle, relentless scalpel, neatly cutting his vanity away from the ego that supported it. The thought made me remember how plausible it had seemed back then that he might have done away with himself—except for the matter of the missing note.

CHAPTER SIX
Envelope B

The evening of my return from visiting Buddy's mother, as if by tacit agreement, Cheryl and I ate dinner without discussing anything of my trip. She had prepared roast chicken in my favorite fashion, deglazing the pan with dry white wine at high heat, pouring the intense sauce over the carved bird, and accompanying it with sautéed spinach flavored by garlic and lemon. It was a simple and familiar meal for us, and it felt cozy and domestic to dine at the kitchen table and chat about our normal topics: the antics of students, the insanities of the administration, and the bumps and minor triumphs of Cheryl's research.

After finishing dinner we left the dishes in the sink and retired to the living room, again by unspoken agreement, where we arranged ourselves as if we were going to watch a movie— with me sitting at one end of the couch and Cheryl at the other with her feet in my lap. She was wearing white gym socks which were a little dirty on the bottom and left her ankles bare and irresistible. When I told her so she smiled, but not encouragingly. She was now prepared and determined to hear my story, and I was not going to escape with compliments and love games.

I removed myself gingerly from the sofa and retrieved the leather journal, which I figured was the closest thing to a prize my trip had yielded. I was not optimistic about my wife's reaction. I had arrived home more convinced than ever that I needed to find out what had happened to Buddy in order to understand what might be in the envelope, but I also knew that I had precious little evidence compelling enough to sway Cheryl to the same view.

I showed her the journal and told her the story of how I had obtained it, demonstrating how convincingly the origins of the torn sheet lay within those leather covers, but I could tell that I had done little to move the needle of her skepticism. When it was clear that I had finished presenting the fruits of my journey, she reached behind her to the side table and produced an exhibit of her own.

It did not surprise me that my wife had not been idle in my absence. A demon researcher lurks below that olive skin, spoiling for an opportunity to emerge and bury itself in the stacks.

"Take a look at that," she said, passing me a bundle of ten or so photocopied pages. I recognized them right away.

"It's Sothum's article on Newcomb's paradox," I said.

"Yes. Do you still think it's entirely impossible that he is playing a joke on you?"

Although I hated to admit it, my wife had a point.

Newcomb's paradox, as formulated by its creator William Newcomb: suppose a genie presents you with two envelopes, A and B. He opens A to show you that there is a certain sum of money inside—say 100 dollars. He then offers you a choice: you may take only envelope B with its mystery contents if you wish, or you may take envelope A and envelope B together. But, the genie cautions you as you prepare to make the boneheadedly obvious choice, there is a catch. The genie is a formidable but not infallible predictor of the future, and has attempted to predict which option you will choose. If he predicts that you will choose both envelopes, the genie will leave envelope B empty. But if he predicts that you will forego the sure 100 dollars in envelope A and choose only envelope B, he will prepare envelope B with a substantially larger sum of money—say 1000 dollars. Having explained these rules to you, the genie puts both envelopes on the hypothetical table and invites you to choose: will you take both envelopes, or envelope B alone? Debate about which is the correct choice has raged in mathematical and philosophical circles since Newcomb first presented the dilemma, and shows no signs of cooling down.

One school of thought insists that you would be an idiot not to take both envelopes. After all, the genie has already made his prediction. Envelope B either contains 1000 dollars or it does not, and your choice in the future cannot possibly change the past— so why deny yourself the sure 100?

Another school of thought counters: if the genie is really any good at predicting the future, then he is likely to have foreseen that you would make the above argument to yourself and take both envelopes, and has probably left envelope B empty. But if you think this through and take only envelope B then he is just as likely to have predicted accordingly, and you are about to be 1000 dollars richer.

Says another school: the problem is contradictory on its face. Either you can have free will, or a genie who predicts the future. You can't have both. Opinion splits on which of the two—the genie or free will—is real, and which a fantasy.

Finally there were those who looked at the whole mess and declared the paradox to be nothing more than an intellectual amusement. Whether it was *only* an amusement or not, it was an amusing thought experiment, and always good for generating a little debate among the Three Wise Fools.

Sothum was especially interested in the problem—so much so that in his junior year he wrote a term paper on the paradox for one of his philosophy classes. He argued that, as the genie only predicted probabilistically, free will was not vioalated, and that therefore the solution was actually quite simple, depending on only three variables: the amount of money in envelope A, the amount of money in envelope B, and the probability that the genie predicts correctly. He showed that with these variables in hand it is a simple matter to treat the problem as a wager, as straightforward as a bet in blackjack or craps. Take both envelopes and you are betting the amount in B that the genie is wrong; take B only and you are betting the amount in A that the genie is right.

Sothum's professor returned the paper with a B+ and a long note explaining that, while he enjoyed the "vigorous" prose and the clean solution, "I feel strongly that the simple mathematical model you sketch out is an illusion, since such a genie cannot exist, and therefore it is impossible to assign any realistic odds to its ability to predict the future." To his credit, the professor changed the grade to an A after Sothum built his working genie.

The insight that allowed Sothum to create his genie appeared almost ridiculously simple in retrospect, but that is one of the hallmarks of brilliance. He pointed out that most people had approached the problem as if the genie had to be able to predict the future. But in fact the genie did not have to predict stock prices, or the courses of wars, or the propitiousness of starting a love affair on a Thursday with Mercury in retrograde. In other words, the genie did not have to predict the general future—or even, in a larger sense, *predict* at all. It had only to *determine* which of two types of person it thought you were: the type who would choose both envelopes, or the type who would choose only envelope B. The genie was not a crystal ball but a personality test.

The experiment that Sothum designed over the next few weeks was imperfect in that any of his volunteer subjects might have chosen differently if presented with real envelopes holding real cash rather than the theoretical envelopes and hypothetical dollars that were all he could afford at the time. The results were still impressive.

After a few rounds of fine tuning Sothum produced a computer program that needed to ask only thirteen questions in order to predict with over 95% accuracy whether the respondent would choose both envelopes or envelope B alone. Several of the questions, like sex and age, were probably matters of public record. A few were derived from the Myers-Briggs personality test. But none of them concerned genies, envelopes, money, or anything else that could easily be construed to relate to Newcomb's paradox.

Buddy and I were among the first subjects tested by the finished genie, and it correctly predicted in both our cases that we would choose only envelope B. The genie did make a rare error with Cheryl, however, predicting that she would do the same, when in fact she took both envelopes on the grounds that one way or the other the contents of the envelopes had already been decided. She remained stalwart in her choice even after I had explained Sothum's argument and the nature of his genie to her.

"So? It's not like my choosing one way or the other now would change what type of person I am, or change what the genie thought back when he was deciding. Besides, why would I want to do anything any different? I'm the luckiest type of all—so complicated and difficult for the genie to understand that I end up with the money in both envelopes."

I laughed and agreed with her, adding that I hoped I could count on her continued assistance in my own quest to crack the tough nut of her character, and inquiring whether her windfall at the expense of the hapless genie meant that she would be inviting me to sushi that evening, rather than our going Dutch as usual. She responded in the affirmative and the negative respectively.

The mood was not quite so light all these years later, as we found ourselves discussing this same paradox again.

"No," I said to Cheryl, "I still don't think this is just some elaborate joke that Sothum is playing on me, even if the situation bears a passing resemblance to Newcomb's paradox. And it is a passing resemblance only—I have no option to choose both the money and the envelope, remember."

"The 'situation?'"

"Yes, the situation. The situation I'm in—or we're in."

"The 'situation' that we're in isn't an accident. It's the situation that Sothum *constructed*. It's a puzzle. He set it up, it's entirely contrived—as contrived as the paradox."

"Fine, this is a situation that he constructed. It is a contrived and unusual situation, on that we agree. The difference is that the more we see just how contrived and unusual it is, the more you think that there is nothing but a joke in that envelope, and the more I become convinced that what is in there might be deadly serious."

"You're right, completely right. I am now almost positive that what's in that envelope, if there's anything at all, is a note that says something like 'Andy, I always knew you were the type who would never learn the real value of money.'"

"Or maybe, in keeping with the Newcomb theme you've become attached to, there's a check for 100 million dollars in there."

"Maybe so, but as you yourself point out, you don't get to choose both envelopes in this experiment, do you? So are you willing to risk it? Would 100 million dollars really make that much more of a difference to our lives than a mere ten million anyway? Would a billion?"

I shook my head, took a few breaths to cool down, and patted her feet, which were still in my lap.

"It's a clever parallel you've found, I'm not denying that, but I think it's just a coincidence."

At that last word Cheryl smiled, and her eyes lit up with girlish mischief. For a moment the tension of the previous conversation was gone. Suddenly she seemed more concerned with the game than with the stakes, and I had just blundered into her carefully laid trap. She nudged my hand playfully with a stockinged foot, reached behind her once again, and from the same side table at the end of the sofa picked up a slip of paper, which she leaned over to deposit in my lap. She made quite a show of it, as if to demonstrate how perfectly she must have predicted my tactics.

"I found *that*," she said as she slapped the exhibit down hard on my thigh, "in Sothum's papers."

I looked at the piece of paper: it was a receipt from a department store. I failed to see any connection to our conversation, and I told my wife so.

"Look carefully," she said. "What did he buy?"

There were two items only on the receipt, so I read them out dutifully.

"Men's comb, black. Doc Martens Oxfords, black."

Cheryl looked at me with raised eyebrows, dropping her hands in front of her as if to express her wonderment at my density.

"Oh," I said, catching on and starting to smile. "Oh, come on. You cannot possibly be serious."

"Of course I'm serious! It's a clue, a message, a secret hint left just for you! A new comb—a pair of Doc Martens—a pair of Docs—Newcomb's paradox! What could be clearer?"

Now I was actually laughing.

"Did you even find this receipt in there, or did you run out while I was in New York and buy these items yourself in an attempt to show me I was being silly for finding clues hidden in the papers? I mean if so, brava! This is some clever work."

"Look at the date," she said, unamused. "He bought them about five weeks before he died. He already knew what was happening to him—he knew he didn't have much time left. Why buy a comb and a new pair of shoes when you have weeks to live? Simple, he didn't care about either—he just wanted the receipt. Another little clue to throw in the box to let you know, when you were ready to see it, that he was just having a little harmless fun with you, sending you on a wild goose chase before he made you rich."

"I don't know, it just seems so far-fetched—a pair of Doc Martens..."

"Oh, I'm sorry," said Cheryl, "I'm a little unclear on what you mean. Do you mean that this word game is a little far-fetched for someone whose pen name was Monica D. Feather, or for a man whose nickname was *muthos* backwards? Could you just clarify that for me?"

In a flash Cheryl had lost all innocent delight in the game. She was angry now, as angry as I had seen her in quite some time. She removed her feet from my lap and herself from the sofa.

"Jesus, Andrew. There's nothing in that envelope. And even if there is, it can't possibly do for us what ten million dollars could. I'm going for a walk."

CHAPTER SEVEN
Chilly Days in Boston and Austin

Cheryl was not around much during the next two weeks, and she offered neither notice or explanation of her absence. When I did see her—nearly always in the evening, when she would arrive hassled and taciturn from her unspecified activities—she would only say that she had already eaten, was exhausted, and was going to bed. She did always add that she loved me, but I began to wonder whether I should be hearing an implied "still" modifying that sentiment.

I was unhappy with this state of affairs, but I was equally unable to make the decision that I knew would rectify it. Instead I played dumb, fruitlessly looking for clues in Sothum's papers during the day and greeting my wife cheerfully as she arrived late each night, asking about her day without asking where she had been, taking it calmly when she brushed my questions off.

Beneath my calm exterior I was all nerves and fears. Cheryl and I had only experienced one such period of cold companionship before, and I did not like to be reminded of it. I was sure Cheryl liked to think of it even less.

The earlier rough spot had come after an almost preternaturally easy stretch in our marriage, when the tree of life seemed to be bending over itself to deposit fruit and fortune in our laps.

During our first few years as graduate students in Texas I became recognized as something of a Boswell to Featherstone's

Johnson. In the aging philosopher I thought I had found an ideal professional niche: a body of work that was reputed to be important and equally difficult and unpleasant to master. So I learned every one of Featherstone's arguments, rehearsing them in written form over and over until I had filled up stacks of notebooks and could give a simple, concise summary of any of them in any situation. And I do mean any situation—while driving, drinking, swimming the crawl, or listening to a blues band in a local roadhouse, I could still have explained those arguments.

At departmental parties I would perform a novelty act with this knowledge: one of my fellow students would call out the title of a Featherstone book and a chapter number, and I would attempt to diagram the perspectival logic found within before my challenger could pound a beer. I rarely lost, and when I did it was because of the inhuman drinking prowess of some of those graduate students rather than my stumbling over any detail of the argument. The most frequent request was for chapter 14 of *The Divine Logic*—the most famous and least read chapter of Featherstone's most famous and least read book, in which he claims to prove the existence of God.

Many of Featherstone's contemporaries would have despised him even if he had attempted no such thing. Something about the combination of that towering intellect with the bird-like physique and well-bred manner stirred up contempt in precisely those over whom he towered. But to claim to have proven the existence of God on top of that was simply too much for the philosophical establishment to bear. They would have liked nothing better than to have laughed him out of academia, but Featherstone's logical and historical work figured so crucially in their own systems that they could not mock him without risking collateral damage. So they contented themselves with a deep and silent antipathy, and for the most part Featherstone was simply ignored—ignored like the rich uncle at a family party who sings and dances around the room in a tutu while every potential heir steps out of his way without comment, lifts a martini to keep it safe from whirling arms, and, biting his tongue, smiles or gives a little grunt of encouragement when Uncle Crazy asks how everyone is enjoying his latest.

But restrained contempt, reluctant tolerance, and willful ignorance were not the only ingredients of the philosophical cocktail that went to the heads of Featherstone's contemporaries when they considered *The Divine Logic*. There was a dash of mortal terror in there as well. Late, late into those same graduate student get-togethers, when a few lights had been turned down, and the last CD had finished without anyone bothering to put on another, and the remaining party-goers had gathered together in the living room, sitting in a circle as if around a campfire, some draped across the furniture, others sitting on the floor, here and there nascent pairs with almost touching hands beginning to feel the weight of the evening in their thighs, Featherstone's book would become the terrible antagonist of grad student ghost stories.

Perhaps one of the post docs would relate how he had heard, maybe third hand, of a graduate student at another school who had read this book, some devout atheist or proud agnostic like themselves, a kindred spirit who had begun the work with an advanced understanding of logic and a smug feeling that he would break this book's presumptuous spine in short order—only to feel, as he flipped the pages, loose distant chains of reasoning draw near and tight—all the reader's ready objections anticipated and disposed of—the central argument of the work circling closer and closer like a hawk, bound to alight on the inescapable conclusion, which began to feel, to our devout atheist or proud agnostic, as inevitable as death and oddly more horrifying: that God not only exists but *must* exist. Or—because, as Featherstone admits himself, there is an escape hatch, a pod in which the die-hards can eject into the void just before they arrive at the divine conclusion—there is simply no such thing as meaning. Nothing means anything. And if you choose that option, Featherstone says, he may pity you, but he cannot argue with you—or you with him, for that matter, since you have just admitted that every term of any argument you might choose to ply is meaningless. So you cannot even say that Featherstone has crammed the idea of God down your throat. All he has done is demonstrated that God's existence is a consequence of there being any meaning at all in the universe. He has only shown you that these—God or total meaninglessness—are your choices, the only two dishes on the menu here in the Café Universe. There are no appetizers of "human dignity," no "lighter" dishes of agnosticism or suspended judgement, no salad bar where you can "construct your own meaning." So choose.

Back in Texas I took it as a point of honor not to weigh in on the question, as if I were a journalist covering an election, proud that even I myself could not be sure what I thought. Later I would have occasion to wonder whether this deliberate abstaining were really a virtue. Occasionally Sothum would needle me on precisely this point in the emails we exchanged— my refusal to commit on "the most important philosophical issue ever framed"—but for the most part our correspondence became more personal and less philosophical as Sothum went deeper and deeper into the study of encryption at MIT.

Besides his usual brilliant tangents on books and films and politics, Sothum's emails from the period were full of finely-drawn portraits of the eccentric geniuses that he was meeting and skillful renditions of their antics. Although I enjoyed reading these letters immensely, I began to see the characters described in them as rivals for Sothum's attention, and I worried that, being neither so brilliant or entertainingly strange myself, I could not possibly compete with them.

So I began to embellish the stories that I recounted in my emails. I never invented wholesale. At first I merely tightened dialogue, heightened mood, edited out inessential actions or rearranged them slightly for drama. But knowing Sothum's continuing fascination with Featherstone I did tend to give the ancient philosopher more of a starring role than he had actually played in many anecdotes, sometimes even reporting actions that I only suspected he might have taken if he were twenty years younger, or not asleep in his chair at the time, or attributing deeds and words to him that were actually performed or spoken by others in his presence.

On a few occasions after sending off a particularly massaged story into cyberspace I worried that perhaps I had finally gone too far, that maybe Sothum's BS meter would light up at what I had written. For example: when I reported that at a college colloquium on atheism Featherstone had become so agitated by some remarks made by a visiting professor that he had stormed the stage, taken the display copy of the interloper's book from its propped-up place of honor, and banged it repeatedly on the table at which the panel was sitting, "like Khrushchev banging his shoe on the table in session at the U.N."

In fact something very close to the incident that I reported had really occurred, except that the firebrand who had used the book as a gavel was none other than my future advisor Professor Dahl, a noted philosopher in his own right and one of Featherstone's protégés. Featherstone had been in the bathroom at the time. Later during the question and answer period he did raise his hand to ask something of the distinguished guest and then, after the entire room had waited with bated breath while he got unsteadily to his feet and made his shuffling way to the microphone that had been set up in one of the aisles, said that he was dying to know where our visitor had found the photograph of the stripped-down grand piano that graced the cover of his book. Featherstone explained that he wanted to find a larger print suitable for framing as a gift for his wife, whose birthday was coming up. I reported this second incident in the same email, word for word, just as it happened.

As Cheryl and I approached the successful defenses of our dissertations, the future brimmed with promise and invigorating challenge—though a bit more of the promise was for Cheryl and a bit more of the challenge for me. She had already found a publisher interested in helping her expand her dissertation into a book, and linguistics departments around the country were lining up to have a crack at hiring this bright young star.

My professional future was somewhat murkier. The dissertation on Featherstone's perspectival logic was received well enough by the department, but it was a bad time—I mean worse than usual—to be looking for work in philosophy, and Featherstone's death had occasioned not a renewed interest in his work but a collective sigh of relief from the establishment so determined to ignore him. Still, the pride and delight that I felt in seeing the world clamor for my brilliant young bride more than offset any disappointment I might have felt at finding no such chorus competing for my attentions.

In the long, hot, Austin evenings we would sit out on our tiny balcony, an ineffectual fan blowing directly on us and the sweating bottles of beer in our hands. We made plan after plan, enough for a lifetime and more than that. I would follow Cheryl wherever she found a job and try for a post doc, or enter law school, or take a cue from Sothum and make all those studies in logic pay real money in computer science. What was important to me was following and supporting my wife, not so much what I did afterwards. This was my chance to show her that I had her interests at heart, that I loved her as much as she loved me, and that I would sacrifice for her future as she had done for mine. Those close nights on the balcony were happy times.

But before we could decide on one of these beautiful plans and put it into action, the campus at Austin was "rocked," as the local paper put it, by "the Peter Stone Scandal." I wondered when seeing that headline whether the newspaper man who put it together understood that "rocked" was a play on both "Peter" and "Stone"—I doubted it.

Peter Stone was a well-known ethicist and distinguished teacher somewhere in his early sixties, and he was also the subject of recent allegations at a school in California— allegations involving a pretty sophomore; an apartment rented in Stone's name; and perhaps, depending on who you believed, an aborted pregnancy. While insisting all the while that he was innocent, Peter Stone had resigned rather than "dignify such malicious nonsense with a response," and had retired to a ranch in New Mexico where he intended to finish his magnum opus: the definitive work on the ethics of voting, which he had been working on for ten years.

But scarcely had he hitched up his proverbial horse at the new ranch when he received a call from Russell Myers, the president of our university and a friend of Stone's. Myers wondered whether the distinguished ethicist might not prefer to continue teaching in Austin while he completed his book rather than hide himself away among the rattlesnakes and scorpions and the occasional tumbleweed, and Peter Stone replied that he would.

Soon the philosophy department was in an uproar. Beyond even the flagrant breach of hiring protocol there was the fact that several of the faculty members claimed to have it on good authority that Peter Stone was guilty of all the allegations that had been made in California and a good many other besides, and that the string of two to three year appointments on his CV was a direct result of his inability to keep his hands to himself. After a night discussing the indignity of the situation in a local pub the nine regular faculty members of the philosophy department drafted an alcohol-fueled memo to President Myers indicating their intent to resign if Peter Stone were hired into any position at the university, including janitorial. The next afternoon President Myers sent each of the nine signatories a copy of his written offer to Peter Stone with salary information redacted and the start date highlighted in yellow. Four of them replied with letters of resignation, and one of them alerted the local press to the matter.

Two days later Peter Stone declined the offer in a response that was leaked from the president's office and published as part of this "developing scandal." Stone cited the "non-academic elements of the environment" of the philosophy department as the major obstacle to his acceptance, but also his new-found love of the New Mexico desert, a "holy and secluded spot" in which to continue his exploration of "how we *should* choose our leaders, instead of how we *do*."

And so it was that a department depleted to nearly half its recent force overnight, unable to staff even the imminent summer courses, nearly tackled me as I exited the classroom where I had just successfully defended my dissertation. Would I, they asked, would I *please* teach one or even two of the introductory survey classes that summer? Dahl pulled me aside to let me know that he would consider it a personal favor, since otherwise he would be forced to cover the class himself and to cancel the Vermont vacation that he and his family had been planning for well over six months.

Cheryl and I talked it over that night, and we agreed that it made perfect sense for me to accept the offer and teach summer classes. She was still deciding where to accept a job, after all, and when she decided I could stay behind for a few months with one of our friends, earning a little extra money while putting that all-important first slug on the CV. It all made perfect sense. But of course that was not how things turned out. Way, as always, led on to way.

The Peter Stone fiasco had given philosophy in Austin a bad name, and as the summer wore on the philosophy department found it extremely difficult, even in such a soft market, to staff their vacancies with quality candidates. Meanwhile Cheryl was visiting this campus and that campus, entertaining endless phone calls and emails, but finding that she simply could not choose between the linguistics departments in Chicago and California, both of which were courting her energetically.

A few weeks before my summer teaching stint ended, the chairman of the philosophy department caught me leaving one of my classes and invited me to his office. He offered me a scotch, which I declined. While sipping at his own the chairman told me that he had heard I was a natural teacher, that I had already impressed Dahl with my serious and exhaustive work on Featherstone, and that in his opinion even my connection to that great departed grand old man was just one more reason why the department would be foolish to cut ties with me just because I had finished my degree—or I with them. He had a roundabout way of getting at things, and a distracting verbal tic that made him preface every fifth or sixth word with what sounded like a samurai war cry, and at first I could not understand what he was driving at. I just sat there staring at him apologetically.

"I'm offering you a real hyah! job, son," he said finally, and he put out his hand for me to shake.

Of course the linguistics department was willing to do as well as and better for Cheryl, and so a few balcony sessions and one celebratory dinner with too many margaritas later, Cheryl and I both shattered one of the unwritten rules of academia and accepted posts in the same departments where we had only just earned our PhDs.

Austin never looked so good as it did that fall. The new crop of freshmen brought a wave of energy that seemed to radiate from the very buildings, a delight in life that was encoded right into the pulsing heat. Cheryl and I waged domestic war against the modest apartment that neither of us had really been eager to abandon, taking down posters to hang up frames, finally installing the extra bookshelves we had long needed, and investing in some cheap but matching furniture to replace the varied hand-me-downs that we had accumulated through the years. We even adopted two powerful symbols of permanence from the local shelter: Chester the marmalade cat, who reached out from his cage and batted Cheryl's head as she passed, thus earning her affection forever; and Novio the Bichon Frise, whose name, given to him by a Mexican shelter volunteer, meant "boyfriend" in Spanish, and which Cheryl refused to let me change to Butch, Spike, or even Snowball.

Those next two years in Texas passed so happily that they seem to me now like some walled garden in time. I believe we had discovered the secret recipe for contentment: take just enough money to get by, add youth, add love, fold in the beginning of two promising careers, and let it all bake in the humid Texas heat. Cheryl quickly became a beloved teacher, even as she threw herself with impossible determination into re-working her dissertation into her first book, and then into finishing her second book only nine months afterwards. She was so happy, almost on fire with her efforts, that more than one of her girlfriends asked her if she was pregnant.

Then during our third year in Austin a pair of disasters struck with stunning swiftness. Two days after Thanksgiving and only one day after we had last seen him, Cheryl's father, who sometimes read while he drove ("only at low speeds and only in town"), finally had the accident that Cheryl and her mother had always warned him about, failing to notice that the light had turned red at a slippery intersection near his house in Winchester and dying instantly as an SUV plowed into the front driver's side door of his compact car.

Pain, like light, comes in different wavelengths. Life's smaller injuries and discomforts, like microwave radiation, inflict their hurt without delay. You feel it instantly when you realize you have been shorted a dollar at the grocery store, or cannot find a seat on the subway, or get soaked by the water splashed up by a passing car. But the great calamities and disasters are in general too large to be experienced immediately. Like massive waves they pick you up and carry you away, and it is not until much later, when you have been set down somewhere distant, that the disorientation clears and you realize what you have suffered or lost. Cheryl was in shock during our trip back to Boston, but she was functional. She helped with the arrangements, accepted condolences graciously, and generally put on a brave front. It was after we returned to Texas, as she had time to absorb how her world had changed, that she became despondent.

She had worshipped her father as well as having loved him, and I had always suspected that some girlish part of her had never stopped believing that one day her mother's practicality and her father's absent-minded bumbling would find a way to reconcile themselves. She was not so naive for thinking so as it might sound at first. Her parents had always loved each other—the way they fought within minutes of seeing each other made that perfectly obvious—but they were not a pair well suited for cohabitation. They disagreed violently on an astounding number of day-to-day details, including some I had never realized people could differ on, such as whether doorknobs should be turned clockwise or counter.

Three weeks to the day after we returned from the funeral Cheryl informed me that she wanted to have a baby. It is a sign of how little I still understood about women that this came as a shock to me. Of course we had discussed children before, several times, but always in the most subjunctive mood, as we discussed getting in shape or achieving financial stability—as one of those things that was always a year or two away. But I could see how desperately Cheryl wanted a child, and I could sense how deeply her desire was tied up with her grief over the death of her father—as if she wanted to show that the forces of life remained uncowed. So despite my nerves I agreed, and we began trying to conceive. From remarks that Cheryl made offhand I gathered that she somehow expected we were going to have a boy, and this made it clearer to me how much she identified this theoretical baby with her father's death. I began to assume that if we did have a boy we would call him Bruce.

Conventional wisdom says that it can take a year of regular attempts for a normal, healthy couple to conceive, but Cheryl insisted on seeing a specialist after only four months. She claimed that she could feel something was amiss, and whether she was coincidentally correct or unusually in tune with her body, our trips to the fertility doctor confirmed her fears. She had a rare internal deformity that made conception difficult, which in her case would have been extremely risky to correct surgically due to the placement of certain veins. The doctor put the chances of her becoming pregnant somewhere below one percent, and indicated that even if she should buck those odds or attempt artificial insemination, the chances were similarly low that she could carry the pregnancy to term.

My once luminous wife fell deep into the grip of depression. Most days she could not even muster the animus to get out of bed. She took disability leave from the university. She stopped reading or doing the crossword. She started turning on the television at all hours without really watching. Day after day she would sit in the same chair, doing nothing but waiting for my return—and I began to push that hour later and later into the evening as days turned into weeks and the weeks became months. These were dark times, and I do not wish to dwell on them, but at some point the situation became unbearable, untenable. I was no longer sure how we as a married couple were supposed to survive what was happening, and I decided to do something, to take action—to resolve this crisis.

All this thought of action was very unlike me. Usually I am almost constitutionally averse to conflict, and prefer to effect change with long siege campaigns of persuasion and cajoling. But I felt unusually confident and self-possessed that night I arrived home determined to pull my wife up from the black hole into which she had fallen. Even the animals noted the difference as I entered the apartment. I greeted them both, but without my usual overflow of love and affection, and they reacted to the slight in manners befitting their species: Novio begging for forgiveness with his wide eyes and wagging tail, while Chester the cat, affecting not to notice at all, retired his wounded marmalade dignity to the bedroom with his own tail held high, having made a mental note that he must act extra aloof and condescending for the next few days, lest anyone start to get ideas. My wife also seemed to have noticed the change in my manner. She spoke before I had the chance to say anything.

"You should see how they wait for you," she said. She was sitting in her usual spot on the sofa with her long hair unwashed in many days, wearing baggy grey sweatpants and one of my old undershirts. "Novio sits right there on the mat in front of the door, chin in paws, and gets all worked up when he hears your keys jingle. Chester sits over by the window, purring to himself and pretending that he doesn't care, but you can tell by the way he points his ears that all his attention is on the door as well. It's hard to say which one is more pathetic. And then there's me." She laughed. I did not like the sound of it. "Forget coming between the animals and the gods, I just come between our dog and our cat."

"We have to talk," I said.

"You have to talk, you mean, and I have to listen."

"You need to see someone."

"I see people all the time. Every time I go out, there they are—people, and I see them."

"If you only see people on the occasions that you leave this apartment, then it can't be very often."

I thought it a sign of how diminished my wife was from her customary bright and formidable self that she had walked so easily into this trap.

"But what I mean," I continued, "is that you have to talk to someone."

"You're making me so tired. First we have to talk. Then I have to see people. Now it turns out I have to talk to them too. Why don't you make up your mind and get back to me?"

"I have made up my mind. This can't continue. You are making yourself miserable."

"No," she said, "I *am* miserable."

"Then you are making me miserable."

My response took her aback—it was not the kind of thing she was used to from me.

"Why don't you leave me, then?" she asked, quietly but not timidly.

"I will never leave you," I said. I was not trying to say it in any particular fashion. It was a simple statement, and I said it as such, but even I could hear the steadiness of voice as I pronounced the words, and even I was a bit surprised by that. But somehow my steadiness only served to make Cheryl attack more bitterly.

"Maybe you should, so I guess that's your mistake. Don't go blaming me for that one."

"I know you're trying to make me angry. It won't work. This has to stop."

"Or?"

"There is no alternative. I am not presenting you with a choice." Whose voice was this? Who was saying these things? "Do you know how long you have been this way?"

"Which unit would you like it in," she asked me, "months since dead father or weeks since infertile womb?"

With that reply she nearly succeeded in provoking a dangerous reaction from me. Even wounded, even with her nimble mind clouded by grief and anger, she still understood that the way to infuriate me was to make me feel pity for her. I very narrowly caught myself from saying something foolish, and instead sucked in my breath.

"I am going down the street to Felipe's," I said with a concerted calm. "I'm going to bring back tacos for dinner. I will be back in half an hour, and then you and I are going to eat dinner together. At the table."

And then, careful not to injure the whimpering dog with the door, I left.

At Felipe's I took my time, drinking a cold Corona at one of the tables of cheap blue plastic before I even put our dinner order in, enjoying despite my nerves the unmistakable fragrance of roasting poblano chiles and listening to Felipe and his brother trade insults that I couldn't understand. I really had no idea what the reception would be like at home, so I dawdled on the way back, swinging the plastic bag with Cheryl's chicken tacos and my own favored tacos al pastor as I walked the long way around the block. But I could not put it off forever.

As I entered the apartment I expected to find Cheryl sitting on the sofa where I had left her, but she was not there, and a sudden fright shot through me. Had she left? Should I be out combing the streets? Then I heard sounds in the kitchen. I walked around the corner and into the kitchen, and saw to my relief that the noises had been Cheryl. She was setting the table with her back towards me, and before I managed to announce my presence and the food's, I saw that she was crying. Huge tears were dropping one by one onto the plates and silverware as she arranged them on the table.

"Cheryl?"

She turned to look at me, her face wet. Dropping the forks she was holding she held her arms out, and I dropped the bag of tacos on the floor and took her in mine. As she sobbed against my shoulder I could smell how sour her hair was, and feel the great heaves as she cried and gulped huge breaths in between.

"Andrew," she said finally, and the word hit me with a force I could not account for, until I realized that it had been weeks since she had last called me by name. Saying it seemed to have some effect for her as well, enough that she said it again. "Andrew, let's get the fuck out of this town."

All these years later in Boston this history was very much on my mind as Cheryl came home later and later each night, saying less and less. I suspected she was thinking about these events as well. And while I was increasingly tempted to put an end to this discomfort between us, I could not shake the hope each evening that the next day I spent with Sothum's papers would be the one to provide the breakthrough, some hint that would lead me forward. But each new day brought as little profit as the one before.

Then one night exactly seventeen days into our spousal stalemate I was shocked awake from a two-thirds slumber. Cheryl was standing above me. She had switched on the light. I vaguely remembered having gone to bed before she had come home, and—less vaguely—I remembered the blow to my chest that had woken me up. As my vision and head cleared I looked down at my chest to see a folder, thick with papers, and Cheryl's hand still on it. She picked it up and whacked me again for effect. There was mischief in her eyes, and she was smiling triumphantly.

"How much do you really know about Babel Investments?" she asked me.

I looked at the folder for a moment, then up at my wife, gloating and beautiful, and then back at the folder.

"Not enough?" I guessed.

CHAPTER EIGHT

Babel Investments and the Thorns of Mildred Rosebush

In fact I had made it almost a point of honor not to know too much about Babel Investments, or any part of Sothum's life that had more to do with money than philosophy. Money had been a sore subject between Sothum and me since that day in the winter of our senior year in Boston when Sothum announced that he would be applying only to computer science graduate programs because, as he put it, "computers were where the money was." Though he appeared to have been experimenting with stimulants again—he spoke even quicker than usual over dinner and seemed not to blink at all—he dropped this bomb casually, almost lobbed it over the table to where Buddy and I were sitting, and I could see from Buddy's lack of reaction that he was not hearing the news for the first time. The combined shock of hearing that Sothum was walking away from philosophy and of realizing that I had been the third Wise Fool to know about it stunned me sufficiently that I did not immediately raise a fuss or ask any questions, but as I considered the situation more clearly back in my dorm room that night I become increasingly angry, pacing back and forth between the bed and window and muttering objections under my breath. By eleven thirty I had worked myself up into such a state that I put on my coat and marched across campus to Sothum's dorm to confront him.

It was a Thursday night in February, and the day before an impressive blizzard had hit the city. Students in varying stages of drunkenness were slipping and sliding along the choked sidewalks, laughing, pushing each other into the huge snowbanks that obscured the view at every intersection, and generally getting in the way and making a nuisance of themselves. Their drunken hijinks impeded my progress and only enraged me further, and it is fortunate that I never quite found the chance or courage to deliver the lecture I was preparing for them on the sanctity of the public way and the lowness of those who would obstruct it, or I might have found myself in a situation from which I was not physically equipped to extricate myself.

I spent so much of my mental energy during the walk composing this lecture for my inebriated peers that I did not put much thought into exactly what I was going to say to Sothum, and when I had slipped into his dorm as another resident was exiting, climbed the stairs to the third floor, and knocked on his door I realized I had no concrete idea of how I was going to begin my speech. Somehow this lack of preparation only made me bolder—or at least desperate—and even before Sothum could respond to the knock I tried the doorknob and found it unlocked.

In our two years as friends I had only seen Sothum's dorm room twice. On both occasions I had been passing by to pick him up with Buddy and had done my best to steal a peek before Sothum had closed the door behind him. I had formed the impression that Sothum lived in a jungle of books ringed by whiteboard cliffs, and as I burst in that night without waiting for his invitation I saw that this impression had been not only accurate but relatively complete. There were no posters or other decorative elements in the room, and besides the whiteboards that Sothum had purchased himself only the standard university-issue bed, desk, and bureau for furniture. The bed was unmade and I took the number of open books spread on it as confirmation of my dinner-time suspicion that Sothum had been experimenting with stimulants again and had not slept in some time. Notes and diagrams covered the three free-standing whiteboards. The only major feature of the room that I had missed during my previous glimpses was the computer hardware graveyard that spilled from the closet along the near wall, arriving all the way to the desk where Sothum was sitting and typing on what appeared to be the only functioning computer left in the room.

"Were you followed?" asked Sothum with more irony than annoyance as he executed some sequence of keystrokes that blanked out the screen where he had been working.

"You can't study computer science," I said. "Or at least you can't desert philosophy."

"Can't I?"

"I mean that you shouldn't. It would be a crime against intelligence. It's beneath you."

"As I mentioned at dinner, I'm going to study computer science instead of philosophy because there's more money in it."

"But..." After this promising beginning I could not think of how to continue.

Sothum rubbed the bridge of his nose with his index finger and thumb. He looked tired all of a sudden—spread thin.

"Why don't you have a seat and we'll hash this out. Just knock those books off the bed. Coffee?"

He stood up and took the coffee pot down the hall to fill it from the bathroom sink. While I was waiting I did not sit down but walked along the whiteboards idly, half trying to decipher the hieroglyphics on them. I had my back to the door and jumped a little when Sothum came back in.

"Where were we?" he said, pouring the water into the coffee maker. "You were about to say something like 'But money should be beneath you.' Right? Well it isn't, and it shouldn't be. You only think that because you misunderstand the nature of money. You think of it as the antithesis of the pure motive. Don't take this personally," he said with such tempo and smoothness that I could not tell what I should not be taking personally: his last remark or the fact that he was now flipping the three whiteboards around so that I could not read what was written on them. "So Andy," he continued, "what is money? What if I asked you to define it?"

"An abstraction of value," I said after thinking for a bit.

Sothum laughed.

"You're hardly putting up a fight. Think about that for a moment: how ridiculous and hubristic would it be for anyone to consider the abstraction of value beneath him? Christ, Andy! The *abstraction* of *value*? The essence of what makes something valuable? Who could be above that?"

"There are different kinds of value," I said, ready to start arguing along these lines. "Worldly, intellectual." But Sothum put up his hand and cut me off.

"Yes, and normally I'd be delighted to work this out step by step with you, but I'm due to crash in spectacular fashion inside an hour or so and I want to make sure we get through this. You're wrong about what money is. It's much more than the abstraction of value."

He paused to finish closing up the coffee maker and switch it on.

"Try a little thought experiment with me. Imagine a man flat broke in the middle of a field. The field stretches around him for miles. He's destitute, without even clothes on his back. Really imagine it—the wind blowing through the grass and the hairs on his naked arms and chest, the loose dirt between his bare toes. You got it? Now answer this: how many options does that man have available to him at that moment?"

"I don't understand the question," I answered immediately. "You want me to list everything he could do to get himself out of this situation? He could start walking to look for help, or start yelling for help, or just give up I suppose..."

"No, I'm asking for something much simpler—not the list of his options but the number, and not just the options that he might employ to better his situation. *All* of them. For example: he might lift his left arm just this high, or his right foot; he might think of elephants or just one elephant; he might start singing 'Daisy, Daisy' in the key of E or F. How many such options does he have available to him standing out there penniless in the waste land?"

"I couldn't possibly count that kind of option."

"Because there are an infinite number of them, right? We agree on that? Great. Now I want you to imagine a man with a good amount of money in the center of a smallish town. Say there's a grocery store and a movie theater and so on, and our hypothetical man has 1000 dollars in his pocket. How many options does this man have?"

"I guess he also has infinitely many."

"Splendid. Just one more question: which of our hypothetical men has more options available to him, the one flat broke in the field or the one in the town center with a thousand dollars in his pocket?"

"That's a trick question. They're both infinite, so neither has more options than the other."

"You're two for three with that answer," said Sothum. "It *is* a trick question, and both of them do have an infinite number of options, but one of them has more options than the other. Both infinities are infinities, but one more infinite than the other, you might say."

He waited and looked at me as I attempted to parse this last sentence. The coffee maker hissed and gurgled in the background.

"That doesn't make any sense," I said finally. "Something is either infinite or it isn't."

"You've heard of Cantor? My main man Georg Cantor?"

"Doesn't ring a bell."

"He showed that infinities come in different sizes—or different cardinalities, as he called them. I think I can prove to you that it makes perfect sense. Imagine you're throwing a formal ball, the biggest formal ball ever thrown. You've invited infinitely many men to the ball, but instead of names these men have numbers: 1, 2, 3, 4 and so on. You've also invited infinitely many women, and they have numbers as well: 2, 4, 6, 8."

"So the men are all the positive integers and the women are all the positive even integers?" I said. I did not feel like being babied with analogies when discussing something as important as Sothum's departure from philosophy, and I made a point of using what I was pretty sure were the correct mathematical terms.

"If you like to think of it that way. Here's the question: when it's time to dance, will every man find a partner? Will every woman?"

"All right, I see your point. The positive integers include all the even positive integers, so there are more men than women. Half the men won't have dance partners—the odd half. Just like in life, come to think of it."

The coffee maker beeped and Sothum poured two mugs. He did not ask if I wanted milk or sugar. We had remained standing so far, waiting for the coffee to finish, but now Sothum returned to his chair and indicated the bed again to me.

"You might want to sit down for this part," he said. "I know I need to, because you've made me dizzy. Just a minute ago you were claiming that there was only one size of infinity. Now you're saying there are twice as many infinite men as infinite women at our ball. You're wrong, by the way. Every woman gets a dance partner, as does every man. Imagine you're one of the men there, you're number 50. There's a social co-ordinator who starts shouting out dance assignments as the band is warming up. Man 1 with woman 2! she shouts. Man 2 with woman 4! Man 3 with woman 6! Who will you, as man 50, end up dancing with?"

"Woman 100, I guess."

"Correct. Now give me the number of a man who the social co-ordinator will be unable to pair off? You said half of the men wouldn't have dance partners, so it shouldn't be too hard to find at least one."

"I can't," I admitted after some thought. "You're right. They all get dance partners. But doesn't this just prove my original point? That it makes no sense to talk about different sizes of infinity?"

"No, what we've just done is shown you how to tell whether two infinities are the same size or not. This was one of Cantor's great insights. If you can map all the members of one infinity to another—mapping a man to a woman by doubling his number, for example—then the infinities are of the same size. You can pair everybody off. But if you can show that you can't pair them off, then one infinity can be larger than another. So our man flat broke in a field..."

"Wait," I said, and Sothum did, sipping at his coffee while I tried to work it out. "I sort of see it, but I don't get it. Are you saying that—because the man with money in the town could afford to give away everything and drive out to a field—you can't pair his options off against the options of the man who's already flat broke in the field? The man with money in town will always have more?"

"Bravo, and not exactly. Seeing it is so much more important than getting it. There are some mathematical subtleties you've just glossed over, but it's good enough for government work and we'll run with it. What you've just shown, my friend, is that money represents an increase in free will. Even though free will is infinite in any circumstance, money *increases* the size of that infinity. As do health, strength, intelligence, imagination, by the way—any form of power. Power is something good in and of itself—power is the cardinality of free will. So Andy, I ask you again: if power is the cardinality of free will, and money is a form of power, can you really imagine money being beneath anyone?"

I had to admit that I could not.

"This might be my favorite of your qualities," said Sothum, with genuine affection in his voice. "Your capacity to be convinced. To *see* even when you might not fully *understand.*"

For a moment I thought about trying to object that merely by demonstrating the nature of money as he had just done Sothum himself had shown more clearly than I ever could have why he must on no account abandon philosophy. But, as so often after having just experienced one of his arguments, I found myself shocked and awed, unable to object, to raise questions, or to do much more than mentally replay the steps by which he had arrived at his conclusion.

"This has been interesting," Sothum continued, "but even the combination of coffee and such a fascinating topic aren't going to keep me awake much longer, and there are some things I have to take care of before I crash. We'll talk more tomorrow."

I allowed myself to be ushered out the door.

I took the long way home that night, trying to decide what had just happened. Had Sothum just pulled me kicking and screaming up another rung of the ladder to enlightenment? Or had he merely dazzled me with his superior intelligence, putting me in a maze that he knew I was incapable of navigating in order to get me off his back? I kept swinging from one conclusion to the other, reworking the same evidence at each turn, and by the time I arrived home I was thoroughly in a muddle and unable even to decide on which side my suspicions lay. I was so engaged in wondering whether I had been tricked or not that it was not until the next morning when I even wondered what could possibly have been on those whiteboards that Sothum hadn't wanted me to see.

When Sothum began his study of computer science at MIT I still held out hope that he would quickly realize his mistake and return to philosophy. As that hope faded I began to dream that upon receiving his degree he would declare how he had gotten computers "out of his system" and would now be pursuing a second degree in his proper field. But these were my dreams, not his, and I was disappointed but not shocked when it turned out that after graduate school he would be moving to California to work for a startup called Machine Translation Technologies. Their natural language translation software had already earned a reputation for unusual accuracy, especially translating between English and Chinese, and many of the industry pundits were writing that the company could turn out to be the next Google.

Reginald Reginald, the founder and CEO of MTT, recruited Sothum personally. Somehow one of his scientists had gotten ahold of an early draft of Sothum's dissertation, "Translation as Encryption," and Reginald Reginald wanted to know if Sothum would like a chance to put some of those promising theories into practice. Sothum made the trip out to the west coast the following week, all went swimmingly, and on his last morning in California the CEO mentioned some exciting numbers around base compensation and equity.

By this point I had pretty much reconciled myself to philosophy's loss and technology's gain, but Sothum surprised me once again. In the same email in which he announced his acceptance of MTT's offer he attached a Word document. He made no reference to the document in the body of the email—I just happened to notice the paper clip icon indicating its presence and click on it, only to discover that the attachment was a two-hundred and fifty page manuscript for a philosophical work entitled *Degrees of Freedom*.

Though Sothum's name was nowhere to be found in the manuscript I recognized the writing style instantly, and after reading a few pages I recognized the subject matter as well. I was reading a book-length expansion of the argument that Sothum had made to me about money and power that night in his dorm room, complete with the man flat broke in the field, Cantor's classification of infinite sets, and many supporting tangents and ancillary arguments besides. I read the entire thing in one sitting, and was delighted when Sothum responded to my ecstatic email with the news that he had been "shopping it around" at various academic presses and had some nibbles there.

I think the two year wait to see Sothum's book in print was longer for me than it was for him. He was kept pretty busy during that time, becoming as he did the darling of Machine Translation Technologies. Within six months the CEO was referring to Sothum as "Futureman," and even gave him a business card with that name embossed on it in raised Helvetica, below which appeared Sothum's new job title: "Secret Weapon #1." Meanwhile I had managed to convince myself once again, with no real evidence, that there was a chance Sothum would return to philosophy. This time I was sure the publication of his book would do the trick. The philosophical establishment would praise it to the skies, Sothum would realize that he was squandering his talents with this pointless shuffling around of ones and zeroes, and all would finally be right with the world.

I could not have been more excited seeing my own book in print than I was the day that my copy of *Degrees of Freedom* arrived on my doorstep. Here it was in my hands—an actual published book with a stiff blue cover and Sothum's real name on the spine! Just riffling through the pages and feeling the intelligent breeze they stirred up gave me pleasure. And I was overwhelmed to discover upon opening my copy that Sothum had dedicated the book to "A.W., for the nudge." I did not even mind that he had not spelled out my name—everyone who mattered would understand the initials, and here was proof that Sothum did not resent my determination to bother him back into philosophy, but understood and appreciated it. I resolved to double my efforts.

I read the book again in a single sitting, and for months it was always on my nightstand while I slept or in my backpack while I traveled. I was so ecstatic that Sothum had finally written something of such substance that I didn't care when a few of the academic reviews were indifferent, or that the Amazon sales rank looked like the jackpot for a state lottery. I knew in my heart that this was an important book, and I trusted that someday it would become famous accordingly. It had to. If Rilke was correct in defining fame as "the sum of all misunderstandings about you," then I suppose I was right.

It was just around this time that Congressman Harms, the embattled Republican from New Hampshire, was vacationing on the Outer Banks of North Carolina with his extended family. His family included one niece Leslie, who was a lobbyist for technology firms and a former classmate of Sothum's at MIT. To hear Sothum tell it Leslie had always been a little bit in love with him, and whether because of this supposed infatuation or simply because she found it interesting that one of her old classmates had published a work of philosophy, Leslie had brought a copy of *Degrees of Freedom* along with her to the shore. Congressman Harms must have seen the book sitting around and picked it up, and against all odds he read through all 250 pages—or at least enough of them to give him an idea how he might try a new appeal to his economically troubled and anti-intellectual base.

Before his vacation was even over this distinguished gentleman had mobilized various aides and speechwriters, and the following week he was waving around a copy of *Degrees of Freedom* and giving slight variations on the same speech to whoever would listen to or broadcast him: that the financial crisis in which we found ourselves was certainly not the fault of the common American on Main Street, and perhaps not even the fault of the bankers on Wall Street, but rather the fault of all those eggheads spewing their hot air over on Academy Lane. Why he had right here—*right here in his hand*—a book that claimed to be a work of philosophy, but which only had one disgusting message once you got past all the highfalutin talk and fancy words: greed is good. Money is freedom. Forget about the other kind of freedom that our sons and daughters were fighting for over in Iraq and Afghanistan—apparently that didn't count. There was even a whole chapter in this offensive book called "Freedom Isn't Free"—a chapter that had nothing at all—*at all*—to do with veterans, and if that wasn't the biggest slap in the face to the men and women who put their lives on the line for our real freedoms, well then he didn't know what was.

He went on the talk show circuit, and the private lecture circuit, and every other circuit he could find, waving Sothum's book around at every opportunity, and overnight sales of the book went through the roof and stayed there through an emergency printing. A lot of people bought the book to hate it without understanding it, and a lot of people bought it to defend it from roughly the same position of ignorance, and I think here and there a few might have even read the damn thing.

Sothum was disgusted enough with the initial fanfare, but after the New York Times carefully edited his letter down from an intelligent and reasoned response to a few inflammatory soundbites, he became despondent. His emails shortened from pages to lines and when we spoke on the phone he sounded lower than I had ever heard him. Nothing seemed to interest him—not the royalties flowing in or even the breaking news that Machine Translation Technologies was going to be acquired by Google. When I made the mistake of suggesting to him that he might try to retire from software and write another book he nearly took my head off through the phone line. I became more worried about his immediate state of mind than his future contributions to philosophy.

So I was relieved when after the acquisition had gone through successfully he did not stay at Machine Translation Technologies until all his options had vested, but cashed in those he already had and moved back to Boston. I was less than thrilled with his decision to hang out his shingle as an independent quantitative advisor and investor—I had to look up what it meant exactly, though I understood it had to do with money and stock—but at least some of his energy and purpose seemed to be returning. And of course I was delighted that he would be in Boston again, as after the death of Cheryl's father she and I had moved back to the area ourselves to be closer to her mother.

Buddy was not far away either, still climbing the ranks in the New York literary world, publishing his own work in prestigious magazines and basking in the favorable reviews of *A Friend Indeed*. He would come up from New York to visit Sothum one or two weekends a month, and the three of us would often meet for an early dinner on Sunday at Huanchen America's before Buddy took the shuttle back. He would generally stay with Sothum, though I can recall at least two occasions on which he condescended to grace our couch instead—once because Sothum's mother was visiting him shortly after Big Stan's death, and once because Sothum said he was entertaining clients at his home.

Babel Investments became successful very quickly. Sothum made it clear to me at one point that he no longer had to worry about money, though he did not elaborate further than that. I was even less interested in the details of his financial adventures than I had been in his work with computers, so I never asked many questions and Sothum never offered details, except to remark more than once that his clients were entrusting him with vast sums of money, and in return he intended to honor both the spirit and the letter of his confidentiality agreements. Sothum even refused to dine with Buddy's father when he came into town for a night, citing his desire not to give even the appearance of an inappropriate connection with an industry insider.

Sothum worked crazy hours, he made a lot of money, and past the most guarded descriptions he would not say how—and that was about all I really knew about Babel Investments until Cheryl tossed that plump folder down on my chest and woke me up.

"Four companies," Cheryl said. "At least. I wouldn't be at all surprised to find out that there were others. All of them owned by the same umbrella corporation—Parasol Ventures, isn't that just like him?—all of them making daily trades and nothing else, no products of any kind, and all of them clients of Babel Investments. The *only* clients of Babel Investments, as far as I can tell."

Thanks to the coffee that Cheryl had generously prepared for me while I had started flipping through the results of her extracurricular research project, I was alert enough to make at least some of the obvious connections that my wife was leading me to.

"So Sothum was his own and only client."

"As far as I can tell, he didn't even have any employees. Oh, except for the law firm that Parasol Ventures owned, and whose services were retained entirely for Parasol's taxes and other legal needs. Care to hazard a guess?"

"The Law Offices of X, Y, and Z, by any chance?"

"The very same."

"How did you find all this out?" I asked with something between admiration and bewilderment. "I wouldn't even have known where to start."

"I have my ways, Andrew. In this case they consisted of plenty of shameless flirting with one of the business school professors and..."

"Wait," I said, "not *the* business school guy? The one who hits on you right in front of me at every university event? The one with the hairy chest?"

"And the black glasses, yes. Professor Sandwich is his name. For real. You can stop making that face, my virtue is intact."

"It wasn't your virtue I was worried about. I just felt bad that you had to flirt with him."

"It's sweet of you to be concerned, but he's actually quite a nice man. He's just lonely. And I must say he knows quite a lot about his subject—all about what information companies must file publicly and with whom. He also has a shadowy network of unnamed and well-connected friends who can find out the things that companies don't have to file publicly. So it is he, I must admit, who is responsible for providing me with most of this information, or at least pointing me in the right direction. He called the corporate structure that Sothum had constructed 'masterful,' by the way, and said that Sothum had thrown up some red flags recently—'almost as if he wanted to be found out.' So you can thank Professor Sandwich for all that the next time you see him. But this, on the other hand..."—she paused to reach across the table and pull out a few sheets from near the back of the folder—"this was all me. What was the name of the town that Buddy's mother said the journal was mailed from? The one that the cops supposedly looked into, but never found anything?"

"Eldred."

"That would be Eldred, New York, correct? Then take a look at these."

She handed me the papers, but then proceeded to summarize the contents before I could properly examine them.

"Golden Holdings—one of Sothum's companies—bought some real estate in Eldred. You see the date? Not long at all after Buddy vanished. And then this is a record of the next sale of that property, when Golden Holdings let it go to one 'Mildred Rosebush' for the princely sum of?"

She reached over and pointed at a line on one of the sheets.

"One dollar," I read.

"Quite a bargain, wouldn't you say? Though I suppose that if one meets a woman named Mildred Rosebush, one does what one can to help. What do you think about that, by the way? Alias? Invented name?"

"Let's hope so," I said. We sat for a few seconds in silence while I tried to wrap my head around all this new information. "So," I said finally, "what's next?"

"Seriously? Man up, Andrew. Finals are next week. Grades are in by Friday. Then we're going to Eldred."

As much as I liked this idea, and as much as I simply wanted to accept that my wife had taken this investigation over and was doing a much better job with it than I had managed to do, I still felt the need to clarify one thing.

"So now you think that there's actually something in that envelope?"

Cheryl had to think for a moment how to answer that one.

"I still don't think there's anything in there worth ten million. I still think you should take the money. I'd like us both to feel that way, though. Or—another way to put it—I still think this is Sothum's joke, but I want you to be in on it rather than the butt of it. But Andrew—since we're talking along these lines—I've met you more than halfway on this thing, wouldn't you agree? So if we get down there, and it turns out that Mildred Rosebush is a nice old lady puttering around her garden, and that her dog saved Sothum's life and he bought her a house to repay the debt or something like that—or if we get down there and we just don't find anything—or even just don't find anything that's particularly compelling evidence with which to continue this wild goose chase—can we agree that we're done?"

She put out her hand for me to shake.

"Fair enough," I said, brushed aside her hand, and stood up to kiss her across the table.

There was a frustrating amount of traffic on the drive down to Eldred, even though we left as early that Saturday morning as we could drag ourselves out of bed and into the car—which, in my case, turned out to be about 11:30. I had left my grading until the very last minute as usual, and had pulled an all-nighter Thursday and worked straight through Friday to get everything in just before the bell. By the time I woke up on Saturday Cheryl had already dropped Novio and Chester at the kennel and finished the crossword.

She drove most of the way, except a brief stretch after lunch, and as we were the last couple in Boston to refuse to buy a GPS or a smartphone I navigated from the directions we had printed off the Internet. At first we talked a lot and played with the radio, chasing the next classic rock radio station as the last one would fade into static, but as the afternoon light deepened and the roads emptied out, and the towns got fewer and farther between, I switched the radio off and we drove the rest of the way without any more conversation than was needed to call out exits and turns.

When we finally pulled into the gravel driveway of what we believed to be the correct address, the sun was just falling into the young leaves of the tallest trees. The property was set a good quarter of a mile back from the main road, with only a crudely numbered mail box to mark it, and both that main road and the neighboring houses were completely invisible behind a thick set of maple and pine trees. The house itself was not quite white, not quite large, not quite kept up. A wooden porch wrapped from the front around to the right. Most of the boards of the porch had weathered grey, but here and there some obviously newer replacements stuck out, still blonde and glossy from the varnish. To the left of the house a solarium sloped down ten feet or so from the second story, but pine needles and cones had covered at least half of its glass roof. The grass in the yard was bright and thick in the center and practically non-existent towards the shady edges. There was a grimy Subaru parked in front of us in the driveway.

"Well," said Cheryl, and she managed to accent the word halfway between a question and an exhortation.

I did not know what to expect as we crossed the yard and the porch and arrived at the front door. No answer? A butler, stiff and spooky, who would say that he had been expecting us and offer us some refreshment? What we actually got, after ringing the bell, was an excited squeak of a voice—"Coming! Coming!"— heralding a small and bustling woman, easily in her sixties, who opened the door and looked at us as if she were very pleasantly surprised that company of any kind should be knocking at her door, even two complete strangers who must have looked quite out of place in those environs. She was dressed as if for Thanksgiving, with neatly pressed slacks and a red, buttoned sweater over a white blouse. Her grey hair looked and smelled strongly of a recent perm, and her false nails were painted Corvette red. I was pretty sure we had found Mildred Rosebush, and when I told the woman that was who we were looking for she confirmed with delight that we were in the right place. I introduced Cheryl and myself, and then fumbled around for a continuation before adding that this was a bit awkward, but we were friends of Stanley Riordan, and...

But no sooner had I said that name than Mildred Rosebush grabbed Cheryl's wrist and mine and was dragging us bodily through the door and into the hall.

"You must come in, please, you must come in! Oh," she exclaimed when Cheryl winced, "I'm sorry about the nails, those are my thorns, ah-ha-ha-ha." She released us just long enough to close the door and then took our wrists again. "Friends of Stanley's, how exciting, he will be so pleased! Stanley! Stanley, you have visitors! Come and say hello!"

My ears filled with a rushing sound, and my mouth went dry and bitter as quickly as if I had been threatened with a knife or a gun. I could not even think to look at Cheryl—I could not absorb what appeared to be happening.

"Stanley," Mildred continued, "don't be rude, come out and say hello! I'm sorry," she said, turning to us and dropping her voice, "I think he's just shy. He never has any visitors, you know. Stanley, look who's here!"

As she continued to develop on this theme I let her lead me down the hall and into the kitchen, where the setting sun streaming through the window made me blink a few times before I could make out the scene. A man was sitting at the small kitchen table, wearing a light blue bathrobe. It seemed that we were interrupting him—he was engrossed in writing something, hunched over his work so I could only hear, not see, the scratchy pen. His big bald head gleamed in the sunlight.

"Stanley!" said Mildred Rosebush, "say hello!"

The bald head raised up to look at us with absent eyes, entirely empty of annoyance, recognition, or even interest. Cheryl let out a little gasp and clutched my hand, and I felt my knees buckle.

"Buddy!" I said.

He blinked a few times and went back to his writing.

CHAPTER NINE
Another Envelope

When Cheryl left Eldred she left a note, which so far I have
refused to read. It is still there exactly where I found it in the
sealed envelope addressed to me, leaning against the lamp on
the bedside table of the guest room. I prefer to be able to tell
myself that Cheryl's departure was communicated,
unremarkable, no cause for alarm. I tell Mildred the same thing.
She is not fooled, of course—if all were well, why would Cheryl
have left without saying goodbye?—but even such manners as
Mildred Rosebush possesses do not allow her to contradict my
official position on the matter. And by not reading the note I find
that I allow myself to remain similarly unable to address the
issue.

On the morning Cheryl left I sensed no unusual activity
before I awoke to the alarm. Since I have not slept soundly since
arriving in Eldred, she must have extricated herself very quietly.
She must have written the note the night before so as not to risk
switching on the light in the guest room, or an extra trip up and
down the stairs to write in better light. Since the alarm is on the
same bedside table as the lamp I saw the note immediately upon
awaking, and I knew that her clothes and books would be gone,
as well as the car. You don't address and seal a note that says
you've gone for coffee, after all. And if you've gone for coffee, you
come back.

I rose as usual that morning. I prepared my own breakfast, walked with Buddy down to the haunted house, and made the observations as I usually do. All day I kept my habits and routines so regularly that it was not until Cheryl failed to show for dinner that Mildred even asked me what was going on.

Habit and routine are what make my life possible here. My stepfather used to say that the difference between the two was that routines were hard to get into and habits were hard to break. He may have been right, but these days I can't notice much that distinguishes them. I would sooner break my leg than one of my routines, and my days are so fully planned that they leave little room for new habits to creep in. That is not to say that I do not endeavor to remain flexible. Sometimes tweaks and adjustments prove to be necessary. For instance: I used to continue making the observations while I shopped, especially in the produce section. I would pull out my small blue notebook and jot down a few impressions of the green peppers or the red onions. But as the summer wore on I abandoned this practice, and now confine the observations to my morning walks with Buddy. I could feel the other customers looking at me while I wrote, wondering whether I were a health inspector recording violations or just an eccentric with an unhealthy interest in fruits and vegetables. Even when I happened to find myself alone, the observations themselves felt forced and unnatural in the controlled climate of the produce section, with its artificial chill and regulated mists. And I discovered that I was buying inferior produce.

Although Cheryl had been making it clear for some time that she was not happy, her departure still took me by surprise. Then again I had been shocked when she had agreed that we could stay in the first place. I had seen the disbelief on her face that first afternoon as we walked into the kitchen to find Buddy sitting there, the confusion that played across her features as she tried to reconcile what she saw—Buddy—with what she heard—Mildred calling him, too many times to be mistaken, "Stanley"—with what she had long assumed—that he was dead. I had seen that confusion resolving to relief as she convinced herself that yes, this man in front of us was really Buddy Johnston, in the flesh—and then relief turn to puzzlement as Buddy did not answer either of the names by which the three of us were calling him, in fact did not appear to be aware that we were present, but only continued writing at the same even and unflappable rate in the notebook on the table there in front of him. As she realized by degrees that Buddy was not just being inexplicably rude, but that he was somehow wrong, that something was terribly wrong with him, I saw the blood drain from her olive face. She began to sway, as if she were debating whether or not to remain upright and conscious, and I put my arm around her waist to steady her while Mildred whisked us out of the kitchen and into the living room.

"Let's go in here for a few minutes and give him some time to get used to the idea," Mildred had said. "This is a lot of excitement for him."

"What's wrong with him?" Cheryl asked her, and then, turning to me, "What's wrong with Buddy?"

"Your buddy is fine, don't worry," said Mildred. "Why don't you sit down? Here, I'll help you sit her down, right here on the sofa, the poor thing."

I could feel Cheryl recoil slightly as Mildred reached out to help me lower her onto the sofa.

"I thought you were friends of Stanley's," she said. "Oh! I understand, you must have known him before he got quiet, that would explain it, that would be a shock for anyone. I'll bet that you could use some tea, you rest here for a moment and I'll make some tea."

So saying she picked up a scratchy afghan from one of the sofa's arms, unfolded it, and laid it over Cheryl's chest and shoulders. Then she clapped her hands as if in appreciation of her own work and went back to the kitchen, where I could still hear the murmur of her continuous stream of speech. I supposed that she was giving Buddy some sort of calming lecture about our presence. I was happy to see that as soon as Mildred left the room Cheryl seemed to recover some presence of mind.

"Andrew," she hissed, punching and wriggling out of the afghan, then pulling me towards her so that she could whisper, "what the hell is going on? What's wrong with Buddy? Who is that woman? And why does she keep calling him Stanley?"

As I had answers to none of these questions I could only promise her that we would find out as soon as Mildred returned. I myself felt unaccountably calm. Perhaps Cheryl's reaction had allowed me to focus my worry and attention on her, so that I could simply accept what I saw in front of me as bare fact without any grasping for explanations—or perhaps, as I had always been more inclined to think that this investigation was something more than a wild goose chase, I was simply less susceptible to surprises along the way—even one of this magnitude. I tried to put my hands on my wife's, to calm her down, but she refused to let me.

"Here she comes," I said. "Now just be calm and let me ask her some questions."

Cheryl did not exactly agree to this plan, but she did not protest either, and I was glad to see that she did not burst into interrogation as Mildred came back into the living room carrying a plate of muffins. Mildred set the plate down on the coffee table in front of us and went to sit herself in a wicker chair against the window. The late afternoon sun caught in her thin hair, and as she smiled at us with great pleasure she looked like some matronly angel crowned with a teased halo.

"The tea won't be two shakes," she said, "and I've brought some muffins to start with, those two are carrot and the other is blueberry. Don't be afraid to take blueberry if that's what you want, even though there's only one, because I already had one of each this morning and I'm not even going to have one now."

"Mrs. Rosebush," I said, "would it be all right if I asked you a few questions?"

"I won't answer unless you call me Mildred. Mrs. Rosebush was my mother, and she hated it when anyone called her Mrs. Rosebush."

I had trouble following the logic here.

"All right then, *Mildred*..."

"You have to have a muffin, I made them myself this morning, they're not dry like store-bought muffins are, but they don't keep well, probably because I don't put any preservatives in them like they do in stores."

I realized that I would get no further without eating a muffin, so I picked up the one that was closest to me, which happened to be carrot, and made a great show of enjoying my first bite.

"You see? Not dry at all."

"There's nothing dry about these, that's for sure," I said, and in fact the muffin contained so much butter that I could hardly keep it from crumbling out of my hand as I ate it.

"I'll give you the recipe, that's the secret, you know, is to have a really good muffin recipe, this one calls for... Oh! I can't remember, but I'll get it for you. That's the kettle! I'll be back in two shakes with the tea."

"Nice work," said Cheryl, as Mildred shot from the room.

"You think you can do better?" I asked her.

She only shook her head, and we sat silently until Mildred returned with three steaming mugs, distributing two of them to us and taking the third back to her station by the window.

"I hope that Earl Grey's all right, it's all I could find, I'm more of a coffee drinker than a tea drinker, I think because coffee gives me more of a boost and I really need that oomph in the mornings, you know what I mean?"

"It's our favorite," I interjected, taking advantage of the brief pause where she had drawn breath, "but I'd really like to ask you some questions. What's wrong with Stanley, Mildred? When did he—how did you say it?—'get quiet?' What happened to him?" Although I had been preparing myself to say Stanley and not Buddy, I nearly slipped.

"Oh!" she said, and her voice dropped, as if she were concerned that Buddy might hear her speaking about his condition. "I'm not a doctor or anything, so I don't know the names, but the way Norman explained it to me was that he just got quiet because he's a great poet and sometimes this happens to great poets, they just go inside themselves, like any of us might sit and daydream and lose track of time, only sometimes great poets don't come out of it for years and years and sometimes they don't come out of it at all, but Norman said it was the price that Stanley pays for writing like he does."

It was clear as she spoke that she had a tremendous amount of respect for this odd affliction that was so peculiar to great poets, and was almost in awe to think that just down the hall from where we were sitting at that very moment one such great poet was working his way through some inner darkness. I took advantage of the pause that this awe inspired in her.

"I'm sorry, Norman is?"

"Norman Riordan. Stanley's brother! I thought you said that you were friends of Stanley's?"

"Norman, of course," said Cheryl, with a significant look in my direction. "You remember Norman, Andrew—very tall and thin, with bright blue eyes?"

I had the feeling that she was not interested in rescuing me so much as showing me up, or implicating Sothum.

"Oh!" said Mildred, "that's him! Just the brightest blue eyes I've ever seen. They say that Frank Sinatra..."

"Mildred, how do you know the Riordans?"

"Oh! Well, I take care of Stanley."

"Yes, I see, but how did you meet him? When did you start taking care of him?"

"I see—do you mean, who hired me?"

"Sure," I said.

"Norman, of course! I don't think Stanley could have hired me himself, do you ah-ha-ha-ha?" Again she had dropped her voice when speaking of Buddy's limitations. "Norman hired me to take care of Stanley after he got quiet, and I got to live here, too, that was my arrangement with Norman, he was always so generous. But then he got sick, the cancer, isn't that just awful, and he said he was worried about what would happen to Stanley when he was gone and I told him I would always take care of Stanley, and he said let's make a deal, if you will stay here and take care of Stanley I'll make sure you still get your salary and I'll give you the house for free, can you believe that? Well really it wasn't free, I did have to pay him one dollar, he said to make it legal, but then he gave me the dollar back, he was a nice man."

She stopped speaking and looked suddenly very concerned.

"Maybe I shouldn't have told you that. Do you think they could take the house away from me if they found out he gave me back the dollar?"

"I wouldn't worry about it," I said.

"But you won't tell anyone, will you?"

I promised that our lips were sealed and Mildred seemed mostly reassured, though before she went on she did glance suspiciously at Cheryl, who had not taken her own pledge of silence.

"I could tell just by looking at you two that you were nice people. Right when I saw you standing there outside my door I said to myself 'These are nice people!' Oh!" she exclaimed, jumping up from the wicker chair, "would you like the grand tour of the house?"

Though the look that Cheryl gave me made it very plain that all she wanted was a word alone with me, I played dumb and endured her frozen smile as I said how much we'd love a tour.

Mildred led us through every room on each of the house's two stories, giving us the history of nearly every object we came across—how much it had cost her and where, if she had bought it, or who had given it to her and when, if it had been a gift. In her bedroom she walked us down the long wall of framed photographs that she had hung there, stopping before each one and identifying the subjects for us, giving us the year and manner of their deaths and some unique fact or anecdote about each of them. Usually the anecdote involved some mistreatment or injustice directed at Mildred herself, and Cheryl made no attempt to hide on her face how much these injured remembrances rubbed her the wrong way.

"This is my youngest brother Jack, but we called him Jack-Jack. He got drunk and drowned in the lake down by the Preserve in '84. He used to call me 'mildewed rosebush' when we were little.

"This is my father. He died of a stroke in '88. The doctor said that it was so big he wouldn't have felt a thing. He paid for all my dresses but he didn't like it when I wore my nails this long. My mother made me cut them for his funeral but then I started using false nails right after it was over."

As she progressed along the wall it became clear that she had never married, had no children, and no surviving relatives to speak of, and despite Cheryl's obvious dislike I began to feel a pang of tenderness for this batty, chatty old woman, all alone in the world, passing her days in this remote house with no company but these photographs and her mute, damaged house-mate.

"Come on downstairs," said Mildred when I thought we were finally finished, "you folks have to see the finale."

At first "the finale" appeared to be the basement, which had been finished into a guest apartment with an attached bathroom and a private entrance in the back. The air was a little humid and the temperature a few degrees lower than the first floor, but overall it was a pleasant, livable space—if a bit thin to serve as the finale of our tour. But it was not the entire apartment that Mildred intended to show off.

"This is the guest apartment where Norman would stay when he visited. And here," said Mildred, opening a door off the bedroom, "I have saved the best for last. I always dreamt of having a trophy room, so that's what I call this, ah-ha-ha-ha, the trophy room."

The trophy room was really more of a walk-in closet than a room, but at least it didn't contain any trophies either. What it did contain, as revealed by the bare hanging bulb that Mildred switched on, were several huge stacks of leather notebooks against the right wall and several shorter stacks against the left. There were many hundreds in total, perhaps more than a thousand.

"Are all these..."

"Not all of them, not yet ah-ha-ha-ha! Those on the right are the empty ones and those on the left are the ones he's already filled up. Norman always brought a bunch of them when he came to visit, and he ordered up a whole truckload when he found out about the cancer.

"These are the only things he'll write in. I used to try to give him something with bigger pages so he could spread out a little, or something a little cheaper, you nice folks wouldn't believe what one of these beauties costs, but he just wouldn't use them. Our Stanley has to have this color, this size, this brand, or he won't write his poems. Are all great poets like that? You want to know what's funny though, he's not picky at all about the pen. He'll use whatever old thing you throw at him, whatever color, sometimes he even uses my Sudoku pencils when I don't have a pen handy. I guess if I put some ink in a turkey baster he'd probably use that! Not really, I guess. But for the paper, it always has to be one of these notebooks."

As she spoke, unexpected tears came to my eyes and I began to choke up. Somehow this fussy detail, his continued refusal to commit his precious words to any but the most elegant of media, brought home to me that we were actually talking about Buddy. I realized that since we had arrived in this house I had behaved as if I were within a dream, reacting viscerally to nothing, accepting the rules and conditions of the world around me immediately and without question, no matter how insane they might appear.

"How much does he write?" I asked, my voice still thick. I saw Cheryl notice the emotion that I had betrayed, and she seemed to feel it as some relief—as if she approved that I was finally absorbing the seriousness of the situation in which we found ourselves.

"Oh! It depends. Some days he goes great guns from the minute he wakes up until the cows come home, and it's hard to even get him to eat. Other days he doesn't write a word. But usually he fills up one of these every couple days, or a week at most if he has the writer's block. Norman said that even great poets get the writer's block. That reminds me, do you mind if I ask you folks a question about poetry? I don't know a lot of poets, well, to be honest, I just know the one, but it always seemed to me like Stanley wrote an awful lot for a poet. I went to the bookstore over in Liberty, and a lot of poets can fit all their poems into a book that's only this thick. I guess I always imagined a poet writing a little bit, then maybe thinking for a while, or waiting for inspiration, like looking at a river or a flower for a while, and then writing a little more. Also I imagined they would change things they wrote. You know, go back and change a word here and there, or toss around in bed looking for the right word and then jumping up and crossing out the old word and writing in the new word, like you see in films. But Stanley never changes anything. Look," she said, taking one of the finished notebooks and showing us, "no changes. Is that normal? Or just because he's a great poet? Also, you folks probably already knew this already, but I didn't, when I first saw these notebooks I didn't even know they were poems at all because they didn't rhyme at all, and they didn't even look like you see normal poems with lines and paragraphs and everything. Look, these are just like big hunks of writing. But then Norman explained to me about prose poems, so now I know these are prose poems."

As Mildred continued her discussion with herself, not requiring or even allowing an answer from either of us, I noticed something propped against the wall in the back of the trophy room, and it excited me so much that I interrupted her to ask about it.

"What about that laptop? Is that Stanley's as well?"

"Good Heavens, no, ah-ha-ha-ha! Stanley can't use a laptop, bless your soul! That was Norman's, he asked me to keep it here with the notebooks because he said they went together. Oh! You don't think Norman was a poet too, do you? Secretly, I mean? Like a whole family of poets?"

The prospect of having discovered another great poet's work hidden right there in her own trophy room seemed to tantalize her sufficiently that this time she actually did stop speaking and wait for an answer to her question.

"No," I said, "Norman was a philosopher."

"But he was a genius though, right? I always thought he might be with those eyes of his, they looked right through you."

"Yes," I said, "he was a genius."

"So they were a family of geniuses then, at least."

"Yes," I agreed, "they were a family of geniuses."

"Well," said Mildred, "I think Stanley must have had plenty of time to get used to the idea of visitors by now. Why don't we go and try saying hello again?"

At the mention of seeing Buddy some of the blood drained from Cheryl's face again, and I was ready to make some excuse, both for Cheryl's benefit and to steer the conversation back to that laptop, but then Cheryl spoke up.

"Yes," she said quietly. "I would like to see him again."

As Mildred led us back to the kitchen and our afflicted friend, my brain was racing furiously, turning over various plans for how to get my hands on that laptop. I had no doubt whatsoever that Sothum had left the clues that had led us here, and I was quite sure that he had intended for me to find that laptop. I felt confident that somewhere on that hard drive would be the answers that I was looking for—not just what had happened to Buddy, but what was in the envelope that was still awaiting me in the Law Offices of X, Y, and Z.

Buddy did not look up from his writing as we rejoined him in the kitchen, though Mildred exhorted him to greet us repeatedly and with great energy.

"Does he ever say anything?" asked Cheryl.

"No, not yet," Mildred said, "but I keep trying, I talk to him all the time, I keep thinking that one of these days I'll be talking

talking talking, and he'll look up and say 'Please be quiet!' and go back to writing poetry ah-ha-ha-ha!"

Cheryl and I had stopped just inside the door to the kitchen, as far as we could be from Buddy while still remaining in the same room, and Mildred slipped behind us and, putting a hand on each of our backs, began to guide us to the table.

"Sit down with him for a few minutes, he'd like that, there's nothing to worry about, he doesn't bite! Stanley, your friends are going to sit down with you now, don't you want to be polite and chat with them?"

As we approached him Cheryl's apprehension and discomfort seemed to give way to more tender impulses. She even reached out, tentatively and with much encouragement from Mildred, and took Buddy's left hand in her own. He did not react, and she withdrew quickly, but touching him seemed to have had a profound effect on her, and I noticed some tears. I could not react with such tenderness. The closer I got to him myself the more my skin tingled and my hackles rose. Each physical detail that I noticed made his silence seem more alien and terrible: the thinness of his white legs, crossed beneath the light blue robe; the twinned moles at the base of his neck, just where they had been the last time I had seen him; the whisper and slight whistle as he breathed deeply and regularly, always in through his nose and out through his mouth.

Mildred had kept him well, that much was plain to see. His skin, while pasty from lack of sun, was clear and clean, and the sides of his bald head, where hair could still grow, looked freshly shaven. The nails and cuticles of his fingers were so short and well tended that I wondered idly whether Mildred might have been a manicurist before she had become a caretaker. He smelled very faintly of coconut soap.

"Mildred," I said, "I have been thinking a lot about a comment that you made down in the basement just now."

Mildred had been talking to Buddy as I spoke, reminding him that not everyone had friends who came to visit, but she fell silent immediately. She appeared baffled by my remark—I do not think that she was accustomed to people thinking about her comments.

"You called Stanley and Norman a family of geniuses. I think that was a very insightful remark."

This seemed to captivate her even more.

"And I started to think that maybe there was a book to be written about this family of geniuses. You know what? That might even make a good title—'Family of Geniuses.'"

"Andrew!" said Cheryl, horrified.

"So...you would write about Stanley's poetry?" asked Mildred.

"Yes, absolutely. Maybe we could even get some of it published."

"Oh!" said Mildred, but she said it very quietly and seriously, as if a man she had long adored had just confessed his love for her.

"Andrew, could I speak to you in private for a moment?" said Cheryl with ice in her voice. I ignored her studiously.

"I don't want to focus on just the poetry though," I continued. "That will stand on its own, with or without my help. I want to tell the human interest story, too—the whole story of this family. How Stanley 'got quiet.' How Norman was such a brilliant philosopher. And all the things that he did to help his brother, too—including finding you to take care of him. Because you are kind of part of this family now, aren't you, Mildred? This family of geniuses? So what do you think? Isn't that a book that you would want someone to write?"

I could sense that beside me at the table Cheryl was gathering herself up for an atomic detonation of reproach, but before she could reach critical mass Mildred burst out with such a squeal of delight that even Buddy glanced up at her for a second.

"Oh! I think it's just a wonderful idea, and maybe you won't believe me but it's 1000 percent true, I've always thought that someone should write a book about Stanley, because don't other great poets have books written about them? Oh! I never thought that I would be in the book though, I think it's a wonderful idea, when can I read it? Oh! I could read it aloud to Stanley! He would just be tickled pink about that, wouldn't you, Stanley?"

"I would have to borrow some of the notebooks," I said.

"Yes of course, how many would you need, we have hundreds of them, don't we Stanley?"

"And I would need to borrow the laptop as well."

All of Mildred's enthusiasm vanished instantly, and a pained and troubled expression occupied her face.

"I don't know," she said. It really did seem to be the lack of some knowledge that was responsible for her hesitation, as if she were clear on the protocol for lending leather notebooks but not laptops. "Do you think you need to? I told you Norman wasn't a great poet, didn't I? Or did you tell me? I just don't know—there are so many of the notebooks, but there's only the one laptop, and I'm not even sure how to turn it on."

"Every author needs access to what is called his 'source material,'" I said, sounding as reasonable and authorial as I was able, "and the notebooks and the laptop are my source material. If I can't look at both of them then I really can't write the book. I think that would be a shame. Don't you? It could be such a wonderful book."

As I had been speaking, Cheryl had finally had enough. She stood up and put her hands on my shoulders, trying to push me, first gently and then less so, out of my chair, remarking to Mildred meanwhile how much we had enjoyed our visit and her hospitality. But Mildred had not been listening to either of us.

She had been standing there in front of the table, her brow so furrowed that her eyes were almost hidden, shaking her head a little back and forth as if she could not quite believe the perplexity of the problem before her. Then she gave a ragged gasp and clapped both hands over her mouth, as if she had been watching a murder mystery and the killer had just stepped from the shadows, revealing himself to be the one person she could not have suspected. Her eyes grew so wide and so alarmed that for a split second I feared that all the excitement had been too much for her, and that she had just suffered some cardiac or neurological event. In fact it was only her own genius that had rattled her so.

"I've just had the most wonderful idea," she said, delivering the words in a gear which we had not yet experienced, and which was impressive even by her standards, "we've got the guest apartment in the basement and it's empty and I could make it up in two shakes, really in two shakes, and you could stay a day or two and visit and look at the notebooks and the laptop here and we could play gin rummy and you could write your book!"

"Andrew!" said Cheryl, almost shouting. "Car! Now!"

"Would you give us just a minute to chat about it?" I said to Mildred as Cheryl practically dragged me out through the solarium.

"We're getting out of here," said Cheryl as soon as we were safely out of earshot.

"Wait," I said, pulling her to a stop before she could reach the car. "Just wait! Can we talk about this for a second?"

"What is there to talk about? We should be calling the police right now. And Buddy's mother!"

"Right, sure, but don't you want to find out what's on that laptop first?"

"I don't care what's on that laptop. Have you lost your mind?"

"Well I do care what's on it. We've come this far and it doesn't make any sense to stop now. Not when we're so close."

"This isn't a game, Andrew. That vegetable in there is Buddy, and there's something very seriously wrong with him."

"If you'll remember," I said, drawing myself up, "I was the one who never thought that this was a joke or a game or anything of the sort. It's always been serious to me."

"Is it serious enough to you to do the right thing now?"

"What's that?"

Cheryl looked at me skeptically and thrust her hands out in a ta-da pose, insisting that I be the one to say it.

"Call the cops?"

"And Buddy's mother."

"You're so sure that's the right thing? Do you think Sothum would have left Buddy like this all this time without taking him to a bunch of doctors? You think he wouldn't have tried to help him?"

"Let's not get started on what Sothum would and wouldn't have done. He clearly didn't want the word getting out about what had happened to Buddy. He even covered him up under his own name. You don't think that's sick? What makes you so sure that Sothum would have risked taking him to a doctor?"

"Let's remember this is Sothum we're talking about—one of our oldest friends—and not some monster."

"I'm not so sure what I think about that statement, Andrew, now that I've seen what he did to Buddy. And then dumping him with that lunatic woman! She can't stop looking out the window at us, by the way."

"Wow, talk about jumping to conclusions. So now Sothum made Buddy this way, too?"

"What other conclusion am I supposed to reach? Sothum clearly knew what happened to him, and he clearly went to great lengths to keep it hidden. Doesn't that sound like guilty behavior to you?"

"I know Buddy has always had a special place in your heart," I said nastily, "but I, for one, intend to suspend judgement until I see what's on that laptop."

"I'll tell you what," said Cheryl, with great calm and gravity. "Screw that laptop, and screw you."

We fell silent after that and stood there, Cheryl with her arms crossed, me with mine awkwardly useless in front of me, not looking at each other. All around us the woods were filled with the calls and rustle of birds finding a place for the night. The sun had fallen behind the western trees, and long fingers of shadow stretched across the scraggly lawn. I could feel the cooler air stealing out of the woods as if it had been waiting for the cover of darkness to advance.

As we stood there at odds I began to worry exactly how we were going to move on from this standoff. Cheryl did not seem inclined to retract her last comment, or even to elaborate on it, and I did not intend either to give in or to be the next to speak. I wondered whether physical stamina might not finally decide the issue, and I even flexed my toes in anticipation of a contest of endurance. Then I heard a sound over my shoulder, in the woods behind our car—the hesitant snap of a few twigs, a whisper of dead cones and needles being disturbed. I turned and saw a deer stop stock still, its liquid black eyes huge with concern and entirely focused on us, its ears arrayed perfectly forwards. For at least a minute we all three hardly breathed, and it seemed that everything was holding its breath, as if the entire woods had grown quiet, until the deer, sensing either an opportunity for escape or some slight movement one of us had made, wheeled around almost in place, and with a great forward bound vanished back into the woods.

Without even thinking I turned to look at Cheryl, and as our eyes met I wondered if I looked as bewildered to her as she did to me. The stalemate between us had ended in a fashion that I could not quite understand—but somehow I did understand, just from the look in her eyes and the feeling in the air between us, that she was agreeing to stay—with conditions. And though I felt that we were in unspoken agreement about what these conditions were, it still felt necessary for some reason to follow our conversation through to its conclusion.

"I know it's a lot to ask," I said.

"No it's not," she answered, but her voice was calm. "It was a lot to ask a month ago. This is way beyond a lot to ask."

"All I need is one night, maybe two. Just a chance to see what's on that laptop. I know I'll figure out what's in that envelope, Cheryl. I know it."

"And then what?" she asked.

"Then we do it your way. We call the police, and Buddy's mother, and whatever else you think we need to do."

Cheryl looked away from me a moment, out in the direction where the deer had vanished.

"One night," she said finally, turning back to me, and holding up her index finger for added emphasis.

"Maybe two," I replied, and I reached out my hand to her, which, after a moment, she took.

Our decision to stay delighted Mildred, and she launched into the preparations necessary for our room and board with such a scattered, puffing urgency that at times it seemed as if half of her body would attempt to dash off on an errand to the left while the rest of it had decided firmly on a project to the right. The only cloud marring her perfect happiness was that—as she had not expected us—she had not had the chance to buy ingredients for a special dinner, and we were going to be stuck with meatloaf, which was bound to be too small, and pasta as a "filler."

Her endless reversals and twists and developments of the theme—there was no excuse for serving such a dinner to company, but really what was she supposed to do since we had arrived unannounced, not that she was blaming us, luckily she made meatloaf so good we would swear it was better than our mothers', unless our mothers actually made meatloaf, she didn't mean to cast aspersions, and pasta really didn't go with meatloaf, but it was all she had, because we hadn't announced our visit—exhausted me and exasperated Cheryl, who gave up trying to help pretty early in the process, instead fetching a book from the car and hiding in the living room. Meanwhile I could think only of the laptop, but when I tried to suggest to Mildred that perhaps I too would spend the time until dinner reading, she began to shepherd me away from the door with such energy and desperation that I found it impossible to challenge her.

And I did feel very sorry for her, and even touched in some way by the machine gun line of speech that she laid down to keep the isolation away. As the sun had fallen the house had become a lonely enough place even with all of us in it—I could not even see the lights of the nearest neighbor through the windows of the kitchen—and I imagined that for an old woman with only a haunted and silent "great poet" for company each evening had the potential to turn into a severe test of her resistance to loneliness and paranoia.

Still I found myself wishing mightily that if she were going to talk so much, we could have at least talked about *something*. In general she seemed to like to narrate her own activities, complete with both foreshadowing and recap, so that dropping a few eggs into the mixing bowl for the meatloaf might turn into "Now I have to add the eggs, because you need eggs in a meatloaf or it will be dry, there they go, and now our meatloaf will have eggs, just like a meatloaf should."

It was very clear that she had no interest in finding out anything about these guests that she had been so delighted to invite to stay with her, so any normal conversation with real back and forth was out of the question, but it frustrated me to discover that even if I asked her questions about herself and her family she could not stay on point long enough to turn her initial enthusiasm into a cogent vignette. I might find out that two cousins of hers had married, but before she managed to relay who these people were or why I might find them amusing, she would be reminded of a wedding she once went to that was so scandalous, so unspeakably beyond the pale, that it reminded her of an aunt who had always been the black sheep of the family. And so on. It was quite a relief when the meatloaf was in the oven, the water for the pasta boiling, and Mildred proposed that we bring some cheese and crackers out to Cheryl "who must have been lonely."

Dinner was an uncomfortable affair. I found Buddy's presence at the table disconcerting, and the mechanical, methodical manner in which he ate—the square route his fork took from plate to mouth each time, and the square trip back, each time lifting a single piece of rotini or of the meatloaf, which Mildred had cut into small squares for him. He seemed to chew the two in exactly the same fashion, and his face never betrayed any evidence that he enjoyed the flavor of one over the other, or even that he could discriminate between the two. Mildred nattered on, and Cheryl shot me occasional disparaging looks when her stories turned especially boring or incomprehensible, or when they presented some thinly veiled criticism of a member of her family. Meanwhile I was unable to enjoy my own food any more than Buddy appeared to be enjoying his. I could pay no attention to the stories that Cheryl was reacting to. I simply wanted dinner to be over. I could not wait to get my hands on that laptop—to see what Sothum had left for me here at the end of my treasure hunt.

When we had finally finished eating, I took Mildred's protest that she did not need help with the dishes at face value, ignored Cheryl's disapproving glance, and excused myself to the basement apartment, where I went right for "the trophy room" and pulled the laptop out for examination.

It was a strange model: futuristically thin, made of some lightweight metal with a scratchy matte finish. I had the entirely unfounded impression that it might be titanium. There were no brand markings of any kind on the surface, and none of the plugs or sockets or connections that I was used to seeing on a laptop. Apart from the round opening for the power cord it appeared impossible to connect the laptop to anything. The casing was so regular and the seams so tight that at first it was not clear to me which half would be the screen and which would be the keyboard. When I had eased it open the laptop appeared less unusual than it had closed—a standard-sized keyboard with raised, spaced keys and a dull, smallish screen. Flush with the surface of the keyboard in the top right corner was a power button, which I pressed.

When it comes to computers I am pretty quickly out of my depth, but years of performing standard academic tasks have forced me to acquire at least a basic competency with the electronic beasts. So while I did not recognize the exact screen that was presented to me, it was similar enough to my standard Windows setup that I could recognize it as some kind of desktop, and the white rectangle in the middle of it—README.TXT—as a file. Double-clicking on README.TXT opened it, and I began to read.

When Cheryl came down a few minutes later, she asked me what it was like.

"Hard to describe."

"Can I read a few pages? I'll give it right back."

Reluctantly I handed the laptop to her and waited, drilling holes in it with my eyes, while she scrolled through a few pages.

"I don't like it," she said, handing it back to me. "It's creepy. It's like you can feel when he's in pain and when he's not. You can hear him running out of breath. And I don't like at all how he puts words in your mouth. It's not polite. If I were you, I would be insulted by that. You're not going to like what you find in there—you're not going to like what he makes you say. I know that won't stop you from reading, but remember I said it all the same. I'm going to take a shower."

She gathered her things and left, and as the pipes started to squeak and bang with water I moved upstairs, where I would not be bothered when Cheryl came out of the shower, and found where I had left off reading.

CHAPTER TEN

README.TXT

Funny thing about constant pain: it shortens you. Everything about you. Breath, attention span, posture. Sentences. Your life, usually. You know Pollyanna and I are like oil and water. Cats and dogs. No one enjoys pain, not even masochists. We've worked this out together. What we call pain they must experience as pleasure, or at best cessation of worse pain. Pain is something you don't enjoy, defined that way, end of story. But I wonder if maybe it isn't good to write a memoir in pain? Not fun, not helpful, not pleasant. Good. For the memoir, not you. Keep it focused, sharp, economical. Cold comfort maybe? But the memoir is going to be around longer than you are. I do not mean to say no pain meds were harmed in the composing of the below. Vast armies gave their lives for it.

A memoir shouldn't be written like a journal. Journal-keeping isn't an honest practice. Where does a man find a more gullible audience than in his journal? Or one more inclined to think well of him? Any memoir worth writing is not a journal but an apology. Not "I'm sorry." The apology of Socrates. A defense. In your memoir you are not really remembering. You are trying to convince someone of something. Usually someone who has some reason to think badly of you. Trying to convince him you are better than he thinks you are. That's the truth. That's honest. Your view versus his. Persuade him if you can. So maybe write your memoirs like a letter? I tried that at first. Dear Andy. But I couldn't get too far.

You know the troubles I've always had writing things down. A small miracle I even finished the one book. I drift into tangents. I always intend to loop back. Usually I fail. There are so many interesting paths to go down. So many things to say. I prefer the back and forth of talk, discussion, argument. Midwives for each other's ideas. Someone to join you on the tangent when it is interesting. Yank you back when it is not. But a phone call to you was out of the question. Let alone a visit.

You remember the argument we had a few years back? When I was angry at you for calling Reagan an idiot? You kept telling me you'd never said any such thing. You were very careful not to claim you'd never thought it. But you'd never said it. You swore up and down. Maybe I was thinking of someone else? Not a chance. Maybe you had called someone else an idiot, and I had confused the two? No, it was Reagan, I was sure. Maybe I'd had this conversation with you in my head, you said finally. Not really a serious suggestion on your part. You just wanted to move on. To get me off your back. But as it turned out you were right. As soon as you said it I realized that was exactly what had happened. I wouldn't admit it to you at the time. It seemed tantamount to admitting that there were marbles unaccounted for. But it was not the first time or the last that you and I would argue in my head. I realized that I had engaged in many imagined conversations over the years, with many partners. My own thoughts had been so conditioned to dialogue that when no interlocutor was to be found I conjured one up. Out of my impressions and memories. Someone to convince. Imagined responses. Assumed objections. Some of these conversations were with you. Some of the best in fact. I wish you could have been there for them.

So. There are some things I know you want to know. Some things you wouldn't ask me and I wouldn't tell. And now I'm running out of time. Writer's block and endless tangents are luxuries I can't afford. So we're going to hash this out in dialogue. You and me. In a philosophical form sanctioned by long tradition. Or if you prefer to think of it differently: you'll take my confession. You'll consider my apology. You'll make your judgment. It's true I'll have an advantage. The entire conversation taking place in my head and all. I'll probably end up doing most of the talking. My impression of you is bound to be flat. Compared to the real thing. And your questions will be serving my purposes. Not really your own. Helping me move forward. But I'll be as fair as I can within these constraints. More than fair: I'll help you ask questions you never had the guts to ask me in life. In real dialogue. I'll even let you start.

A: All right. Since we don't have much time, let me ask you straight out. What happened to Buddy? In particular, the points I would like you to cover are these. How did he end up a vegetable in upstate New York, attended to by a caretaker who wears press-on nails and is constitutionally incapable of silence? How long have you known what happened to him? Why didn't you tell me about it? How involved were you? Did—I have to ask this—did you do this to him?

S: A good starting set of questions. But there's nothing else you want to know? Nothing else you're wondering about? This is your chance to ask. Your last chance.

A: If we're putting everything on the table right at the start then yes, I have one more question: what's in the envelope? And why did you set it up so I had to choose the envelope or the money? Is this your idea of a joke? Or is there really something in the envelope worth renouncing a fortune for?

S: All reasonable questions. Questions I'll answer. But these aren't simple answers you want. If I were to answer you now straight out in "simple" terms you wouldn't believe me. Forget "believe." You wouldn't even understand. You'll need background to understand the answers. There are whole areas of my life I've kept carved out and private. Secret from you and everyone else.

A: So that's what I'm in for? Your life story?

S: That's the price you pay. That's the ticket. That's the trade. My apology for your answers.

A: All right. It's a deal. Let's get started. The clock is ticking.

S: Done. We have to begin early. You know how much I have always loved puzzles. The harder the better. Philosophical conundrums. Logical teasers. "The professor who wears green lives next to the professor with a cat." Mathematical mind-benders. This love has been with me since childhood. I can even remember my first experience of the puzzle. The first time I felt an artifact from another consciousness in direct opposition to my own understanding. It was the latch on the gate preventing my two-year self access to the stairs. I was not interested in the stairs. Not really. I was only interested in the fact that they were forbidden to me. And especially fascinating was the method of the forbidding. The scissoring wonder of the gate, taller than I was. The gleaming workings of the latch. I sensed a gauntlet thrown down, or the two year old's equivalent.

For two days I examined the latch, pretending disinterest whenever I heard my mother approach. For two nights my dreams were haunted. Even while asleep I turned it over and over in my head. Trying to understand. All my daytime pawing and poking at the latch had translated into a reliable mental image of the mechanism. Which I could manipulate and explore in any state of consciousness. My dream fingers grew tired those nights trying to open the dream gate.

One other odd detail: I refused to watch my parents operate the latch. My mother sensed my interest and guarded her technique with her body. But I averted my eyes intentionally when my father opened the gate. He made no attempt to hide its operation. He was annoyed he had to open it just to use the stairs. He made a big production of it. A lot of muttering and exaggerated movements. At that time I lacked the word. But I felt discovering the secret of the latch through espionage would have been cheating. A defeat in victory. I was not willing to settle for that.

Then finally: the feeling of glory, of triumph, of fulfillment! The moment when my clumsy fingers first worked the latch. It didn't feel as if the puzzle had been resolved. It felt as if *I* had been put together properly! For the first time. As if I were working at a task that was proper to me. I never forgot that feeling. The feeling I would spend most of my years chasing. I never forgot either how quickly the feeling faded. A warm bath gone cold. An emptiness. The dullness of closing and opening the latch. Just to prove I could. And still could. How terrible to see this once-mighty mystery reduced to something trivial. I closed the gate and never bothered to open it again. Now that the stairs were available there was nothing about them that interested me.

My thirst for puzzles only increased as I grew. But natural mysteries held no wonder for me.

A: Pardon the interruption, but I find this hard to believe—I have heard you converse with geologists about geology and meteorologists about the weather, almost as equals—you used their argot and were comfortable with their concepts. In every conversation I had with you I knew that eventually you would find some way to mention the second law of thermodynamics. Buddy and I used to give each other an amused look every time you said "Remember: the entropy of a system tends to increase." Clearly at some point you took a naturalist or scientific turn.

S: That all came later. When I was a child the fact that the sun was a ball of burning gas was as trivial to me as the names of the other children in my class. Some of these other children were fated to be botanists, physicists, naturalists. They wandered around and played with flowers, watched clouds, chased squirrels. I pestered my mother to tell me riddles. Once I could read I pestered her to buy me books of riddles and puzzles. For my seventh birthday she gave me an incredible gift. A book that explained to children how to create their own codes and ciphers. Also how to break the codes and ciphers of others. Much more interesting to break them than make them. I struggled with the first code-breaking exercises in the book. But then I learned the tricks. I conquered the later exercises too easily to enjoy them. I was unsatisfied. Also contemptuous of the adults who had put these simple puzzles together. It never occurred to me that they might have pitched the puzzles to my age group. Made them easier for my benefit. I assumed they had done their utmost to foil my understanding. As I would have done to them. As the makers of the gate had done. When I began to create my own codes my mother was delighted that I was doing something "creative." She did not understand I was putting these codes of my own together only to learn how better to take other codes apart. Nothing creative about it. I began to take other things apart in order to solve them. Radios. Toasters. Not really so interested in putting them back together. The greatest pleasure I found was in a peculiar form of destruction. And it was a fleeting pleasure. Riddles obey their own variation of the second law of thermodynamics. They have their own form of increasing entropy. Once you have solved the puzzle it is broken and cannot be put back together. It will never fascinate or delight you again. It is a discarded affair. A drug to which you become resistant after a single use.

A: You said the names of other children were trivial to you. You can't be suggesting that you had no friends.

S: Before she died my mother told me she had spent my early years worried I might be autistic. "On the spectrum," she said. But she was backporting later terminology into those memories. Autism was not yet a fashionable diagnosis when we were young. People didn't go around talking about the autism spectrum. My mother only suspected that I had social problems. She wanted to take me to a specialist. My father nixed the idea. He wouldn't pay for such crap. I was obviously fine. I could walk, talk, eat, sleep. What was the problem? My mother's point was that I showed no interest in other children. Or people in general. She did not understand how deeply interested I really was in other people. How I was dependent on them for the primary pleasure in my young life. I was just not interested in them socially. Not in the way she understood. Rather as opposing minds. As sources of new riddles and puzzles to be solved. I needed and loved people because they created the only conundrums worth solving. I didn't care why the sunset produced those colors or the ocean was blue or the grass green. A puzzle with no author was not interesting to me. If human beings went around spouting riddles and brainteasers all the time no child would have been more social than me. But people who liked riddles didn't do that. They wrote books. So I spent more time among books than people.

A: Surely you must have had *some* friends?

S: I looked down on my peers. The ugly truth of the matter. They were not interested in the pure exercise of the intellect. They were interested in plastic cars and trucks, then robots and ray guns. When I tried to give them any but the easiest riddles they lost interest quickly. They mocked me. By the time I was ten my arrogance was palpable to them. It would have made me insufferable to adults as well. If they had been able to sense it. But I thought myself so far above my elders that I did not feel the need to remark on or demonstrate my superiority. In fact I somehow acquired a reputation among my teachers for being a brilliant but modest boy. Undeserved in the extreme. I still had not grasped the concept that the problems adults gave me had been tempered by their authors. In consideration of my tender years. And my teachers did not understand how I considered each test they administered as their best effort to stump me. I found their pride and delight in the fact I could ace these tests almost pitiable. Like the victim of a bully fondling the biceps of his tormentor. Cooing over them. Disgusting. I said nothing when they gave me praise except "thank you." And they took my hot ears as a sign of embarrassed modesty. I was embarrassed, but for them. None of them ever understood. And I would no sooner have said anything about it than I would have kicked a dog.

A: You sound...

S: Hateful? Because I was a hateful child, Andy. A misshapen soul and mind. Unusually strong in one area and atrophied in all others. We would not have been friends back then. I had no friends. That was a dangerous time. If nothing had shaken me up I might have hardened in this unpleasant mold. I might have lived a miserable life. Gloating emptily that I excelled above all others in a game that my opponents did not realize they were playing. Also terrified night and day. Terrified that at any moment I might run across someone better than me. Someone who could humiliate me effortlessly in the only arena I cared about at all. Luckily something did shake me up.

My mother took me to church every Sunday. For this reason I dreaded Sundays. Forty-five minutes of torture. Uncomfortable pews and irrelevant company. The tired singing dying in the corners. The muttered prayers. I believed in God of course. Because I had been brought up to believe in Him. Because not believing in Him had never been presented as an option to me.

But at the time I didn't care much more about Him than I cared about ragweed or sunsets. He was an external fact that I accepted without interest. Offering Him such dishwater worship as I witnessed each week seemed ridiculous. A waste of time. I tried to invent excuses not to go. I had too much schoolwork. I was not feeling well. But only a fever ever excused me.

Our usual priest was old and so boring that he bored himself. He recycled his homilies on a criminally short cycle and once he fell asleep blessing the bread and wine. If his essence could have been bottled and sold as a sleep aid the church's financial woes would have been over forever. But one week when I was ten a visiting priest delivered the homily. A Jesuit. An African. He had the small wiry build that wins marathons. A head shaped like a teardrop falling upwards at an angle. Covered with short curly hair. He kept his left foot forward and rocked back and forth on it as he spoke. Theatrical gestures with his small perfect hands. Displaying to good effect the cut of his robes. He had a soft, lilting way with the English language. A hushed delivery. As if what he was saying were important and maybe dangerous. It was the difficulty hearing and understanding him that first made me pay attention. But then he said something I found interesting in its own right. Something I would find unforgettable.

"He has scattered His messages upon the waters, secret intelligences in the glints of sunlight off the river and consolations in the wavering moon upon the ocean. He has buried maps of His intentions in the paths of roots and branches. In mathematics, we hunt for His hidden music. In poetry, we seek the keys to interpret His dreams. For He has ciphered His own mighty essence into everything, into you and me and all that we can sense or apprehend."

A revelation, no less. I looked around the church, on fire as it seemed. A minute ago I had seen nothing but an unpleasant delay in my day. An obligation that I could not dodge. Now everything was buzzing with interest. A shaft of sun illuminated dust motes caught in contrary motion. One woman had brown hair, another blonde. In the back pew a child coughed. I understood now: these were not trivia. The visiting Jesuit had made me understand. He had opened up the largest book of riddles ever authored and handed it to me and said "Take it, read it." Behind all these everyday phenomena there was a challenge. An intellect calling out to my own. I felt it now. Looking around I even experienced my first pang of humility. No one else looked as shocked and stricken by these words as I had been. What could this mean except that they had known already? Was I really so late to the party? I resolved right there to become interested in everything and everyone. From that point on all things would be riddles in themselves. Potential objects of understanding. I guess that was the moment I became a philosopher.

A: I suddenly feel as if I were interviewing you for television. "Tell me, what was the moment when you knew you wanted to be a philosopher?"

S: One point for you. But you missed the second free throw. You fell into one of your imprecise statements. There was no moment when I knew I wanted to be a philosopher. There was only a moment when I became one. I believe I have pinpointed that moment. I became a philosopher in the moment that I became aware of God as an adversarial intellect. I had not really become religious. I did not worship. Church *qua* church was no more interesting to me after that than it had been before. The visiting Jesuit left and did not return. I did not start to read the Bible or ask forgiveness for my sins. I was still ambivalent about Jesus and the Trinity and the details of the Christian God-view. They were uninteresting to me. But I had formed a personal connection with God. In that with God I had found a fountain of infinite and diabolical riddles. Real riddles. Riddles with an author.

My desire to solve, to break, to take apart, was redirected. Away from trivial tricks of human logic and towards the universe at large. He had invited me to a banquet, he had set a place for me at an overflowing table. I launched into voracious study. These were riddles of a different sort. They did not snap shut with their own solution. They opened further. These were riddles of discovery. An attempt to work your way into the mind that had devised them. Now that I understood that the secret of the honey bee's habits had been hidden from me, I lusted after the habits of the honey bee. Now that I felt in the triangle a quandary more subtle than any of the wrought-iron puzzles I had found in my Christmas stockings, I thrilled to geometry. Even people began to interest me. Not only as the authors of riddles but as riddles themselves. I did not always seek out the company of others. There were enough objects of wonder now in any unremarkable room to hold my interest. But I did not avoid people either, or ignore them as I used to. My mother was relieved at the change. Relieved but not fully reassured. I think she sensed the strangeness of my interest. The way I still looked at people. Not that much differently than I looked at a book or a tree. She still pushed me to invite friends to the house. To "get outside" as well and "take some fresh air with the other children." But it was not with the same tone of concern she had used before.

A: There must have been some other children who were important to you back then? I keep harping on this, but you are such a social creature now that I still can't believe that you had no friends. And it's an open secret that you're a womanizer. Don't think because I've never mentioned that you always have a different woman on your arm that means that I haven't noticed them drifting in and out of your life. "Drifting" isn't even the right description—they enter and exit in a timely and ordered fashion, as if you started a stopwatch at the first kiss. But you clearly discovered women at some point.

S: Yes, and my mother would have been more relieved still to know when I made that particular discovery a few years later. But I did not let on for some time that I had become aware of girls. In part because of the normal shame of a young boy. But also because the discovery of women led me quickly to grief. To doubt.

I had already noticed girls in one sense. I knew they were different than boys. They stood in larger groups and talked more. They behaved more strangely. They took roundabout paths to things. They flitted. Some of them were prettier than others. I could tell. But this did nothing for me. Some houses were prettier than others too. Some beetles. I could tell this was the case but I didn't spend much time worrying about it. Why should girls be any different? It must be the same for every young man. You don't notice girls until you notice the one girl. *The* girl.

I was thirteen. As was she. Her name was Selena Elizabeth Morton. I wanted to tell her about her names. That she shared one with the goddess of the moon and another with a queen. How well she wore them. But my tongue broke in her presence. Her house was two bus stops after mine. She sat in the same seat every day. I started to sit one row back, to have the best and longest view possible as she boarded the bus and walked to her seat. Her skin was silver. Flesh mixed with pearl silver grey. Like the moon. I remember her hair as silver too, like my grandmother's. But thicker and straggly, a little greasy. I guess she didn't wash it as much as she should have. I didn't care. I loved the way it fell flat and limp around her face. I loved when she brushed it back behind her shoulder or twisted it around her finger. I dreamed about these things while I was asleep and awake. I knew I wanted to touch her hair. Though I couldn't say why. I also knew I didn't want anyone else to touch it. Not anyone. Not ever.

So I noticed one recess when Bobby Drake walked up to Selena. He was a large good-looking boy with red hair. Occasionally with red knuckles as well. She was surrounded by giggling, whispering friends. They giggled and whispered louder as Bobby approached. Then fell silent as he solemnly presented Selena with a flower. A field daisy. A hush spread over the entire playground. None of us had ever seen such boldness. Selena's friends melted away from her. They recognized she would need some time alone to absorb what had just happened. As if a wrinkle of force emanated from her. All the spectators in her path turned and moved away as she walked off the asphalt playground and onto the soccer field. As if she were driven back to the birthing ground of the daisy in an effort to understand it. No one followed her. I mean no one followed her except me.

What a memory to have at one's disposal. One to take to the grave. The mid-day sun pale and yellow and bright. Perfectly balanced by a spring breeze. Patches of new grass. Patches where it had yet to re-appear. All this seemed to exist only to frame the girl walking there, taking small steps in her leather oxfords. Her skinny silver legs at odds with her knobby knees. Red shorts with white trim. Slim body, yellow shirt. Not a flower herself but a bud. A look of furious concentration on her face as she contemplates the modest daisy. Twirls it by the stem. As if the moon were frowning.

I wasn't attempting to behave boldly by following her. I wasn't attempting to behave at all. I could neither leave her or approach her. I matched her pace and kept a respectful distance. Until I saw her begin to pick the petals of the daisy. She picked them one by one. With a great and hopeful gravity. She was playing "He loves me, he loves me not." I knew she must be hoping for a particular answer. Somehow this unlocked my tongue.

"You shouldn't do that."

She looked up at me. Blinking with indignity that I had interrupted her adolescent pastoral.

"What?"

"That daisy has 34 petals. That means you'll end on 'He loves me not.'"

I had not planned what I was going to say. My heart was beating very fast and I did not feel in control of my speech.

"I would have pulled one off before I gave the flower to you, and then counted just to be sure."

She did not seem to have heard this last part. Or maybe she had just not made the inference I was looking for.

"How do you know it has 34 petals? You couldn't count from there. Are you, like, some kind of flower freak? Like you know the number of petals on every flower?"

She laughed at me. But it was not hard for me to laugh with her. I was equally contemptuous of the kind of person who would memorize the number of petals on every species of flower. Unfortunately the nature of my contempt was different than hers. I didn't realize this then.

"No, who memorizes that?"

"Then how did you know?"

"It's simple. Different kinds of daisies have different numbers of petals, but the number of petals is always a Fibonacci number. Well, almost always. You can see just by looking that your daisy has way more than 20 petals and less than 40. The Fibonacci numbers in that range go 21, 34, 55. The only one that makes sense is 34."

I was sure that my explanation would clear things up for her. She would understand I was not the kind of boy who would commit to memory something trivial like the number of petals on every kind of flower. But she looked at me for a few seconds, more strangely than before. Then she started to count the petals left on the daisy. I thought she was verifying what I had told her. I liked that about her. I took the opportunity to explain further.

"God hid the Fibonacci numbers everywhere. In pine cones, the nautilus, artichokes. Come here, I'll show you."

I knelt down to draw some examples with my finger in one of the patches of dirt.

"There is no God," she said. "He's just a fairy tale. Mary Browning told me so."

She said it without rancor. A little exasperation, maybe. But she said it gently and simply. How she might have told one of the younger children that his classroom was on the other side of the building. Then she turned around and took herself deeper into the field. Still littering her path with daisy petals.

A: And? You've stopped talking.

S: I'm trying to think of a way to explain to you how significant this event was for me. It will help you understand what happened later.

A: You're not suggesting that this experience actually shook your faith? You just testified to how hateful and contemptuous of others you were as a child. Why would you care what Mary Browning said about God, or even Selena Elizabeth Morton, who was apparently beautiful but not even acquainted with the Fibonacci series?

S: You don't seem to be interviewing me any more. That sounded more like cross examination. The experience did not shake my faith because I had no faith. Faith implies resistance to doubt. I had never doubted. Suddenly I required faith that I did not have. Because I had acquired doubt. And more than doubt. It is difficult to explain, but this may help you understand. Three years before the incident with Selena Elizabeth Morton, when I was ten, my mother took me out for an ice cream before dinner. Very unusual. It was the stretch between Thanksgiving and Christmas, but I was not on vacation. It was a school night. She had even dressed up. She was wearing her seasonal red pants suit and the big swinging silver earrings my father had bought for me to give her the year before. She sat in the booth fidgeting as if she wanted a cigarette. I remembered the behavior from when she had quit. I tried to order a single scoop of vanilla. To reduce the sense of fantasy. But she changed my order to a banana split. Then she sat and watched me eat the whole thing. I was now sure bad news was coming. I thought my father had died. But when she cleared her throat and began to speak seriously it was only to tell me that she and my father had decided I was old enough to know the truth about Santa Claus.

She kept justifying herself. Not for dispelling the illusion. For having lied to me in the first place. She asked me a few times to think about how much magic my belief in Santa Claus had brought to my childhood. She paused each time she asked it. Until I got the feeling she wanted a number. A metric of some kind. She kept asking me if I had understood what she had told me. She mistook my silence for confusion. I told her yes. I understood. I was fine. She made me repeat this a few times. Then capitalizing on my fineness she added breathlessly that she and my father were also the Tooth Fairy and the Easter Bunny.

"That's a relief," I said.

She laughed, relaxed. She said how adult I was becoming. But what I had said was not a joke intended to break the tension. It was the truth. I was relieved. All three magical beings had always horrified me. Offended my sense of the world. I accepted their gifts and chocolate eggs and dollar bills, but with suspicion. Why were all these delivered under cover of darkness? Each of these creatures had magical abilities. Powers. Did they really exert these powers only to make children happy? Why? What if they changed their minds some day? The nibbled cookie and half-drunk glass of milk on Christmas morning. What message could have been more terrifying coming from a man who could enter and leave locked houses without detection? "I take what I please, I leave what I please." At least he stayed in the living room. Of course I spent every dollar bill that appeared under my pillow. But I did not like thinking how they got there. A fairy so subtle she could reach her hand beneath my pillow and I would not wake up? And where did she get the money? Why did she want the teeth? Even then I knew something about economics. Chickens and goats, supply and demand. If every tooth was worth one dollar year after year then there was no market for them. That meant only the tooth fairy had figured out what they were good for. The thought was not comforting.

A: And the fact that these beings did not accord with what you knew of reality had never suggested to you that perhaps they were not real? You understood chickens and goats, but not that?

S: What contradictions the young mind is capable of embodying, no? Yes, I was able to comprehend the basic principles of economics. To understand when they were being violated. But no, I could not come up with the idea that the violator might not exist. Because everyone I knew behaved as if these three beings did exist. They spoke of them as real beings. Like they spoke of Aunt Rosemary, who lived in Florida. I had never seen Santa Claus. But I had never seen Aunt Rosemary either. I could not imagine a lie perpetrated on that scale. A blind spot of mine. Maybe it had to do with my childhood contempt for those around me. Perhaps I did not credit them with sufficient intelligence for conspiracy. Or maybe it had to do with my supposed autistic tendencies: the autistic inability to "put oneself in another's shoes." That's another theory. You know how some autistics cannot understand the concept of lying.

But even after that banana split with my mother I never thought to put God in the same category as Santa Claus and the

Easter Bunny. Not until Selena Elizabeth Morton grouped them so casually out on the soccer field. But this time I was not relieved. I was terrified.

A: Wait, wait. You're telling me that, even after you came to understand about imaginary beings—fairy tales—that you failed to make the generalization needed to at least suggest that another being you had no physical evidence of might not be real either? That doesn't sound like you.

S: But it does. That's my point. It just doesn't sound like your experience of me. By the time you met me harsh experience had hammered out this and some other defects of my intellect and character. Part of the effect that Selena's statement had on me was the shot of humility it gave me in the arm. I became aware of my blind spot. It was bad enough never to have considered that Santa Claus might not be real. Now I saw how after being told straight out about Santa Claus and friends I had failed for three years of Sundays to generalize from Santa Claus to God. I was embarrassed. Such a lapse was indicative of stupidity. I could not imagine anything worse than being stupid. Except perhaps realizing that you were stupid.

Considering the question that night in bed and with a cooler head, I realized that Selena had no evidence. Mary Browning had no special authority I was aware of. Not to pronounce on the existence of God. My mother knew Santa Claus did not exist because she and my father put the presents under the tree themselves. So how could Mary Browning know that God didn't exist? He was supposed to create the universe and keep it all together. If He wasn't doing that, who was? Not Mary Browning. I was pretty sure. I also doubted my parents were up to the task. On the other hand I was hard pressed to produce any compelling proof that God really did exist. Maybe no one was keeping the universe together. So the question was undecided.

A: That must have reassured you a bit.

S: Far from it. "Undecided" was not a comfort to me. This was doubt. Terrible and insoluble. I had only recently achieved a connection with God. He had given me purpose and drive. An intellect against whom to struggle, and one who would never run out of new problems and twists. Suddenly it turned out He might never have been there at all. I might have been playing at an empty chessboard. Three times the fool. Then again He might have been there the whole time. Everything might be fine. There was no way to tell. What a horrible state of affairs. It would have been better in some sense to know that your opponent had never existed. Then at least you could rationalize the game as solitaire.

At the moment of that realization I felt a swell of pity and fellow-feeling for all humanity. It overwhelmed me. I had trouble breathing. I also felt admiration. Something of a new feeling for me. Perhaps conditioned and prepared by my humbling lapses. Surely most of the adults out there had already known this secret. As they had already known about Santa Claus. There might not be a God. There might not be a God. There might be no author to the universe's riddles. I could imagine nothing more terrible. But these adults went about their day-to-day business behaving as if there were. This was not idiocy. *I* had been the idiot. What strength of character people had! What courage! I fell in love with the human race right then. I wanted to be around them. To be like them. To have that courage wear off on me. Because I could feel I had it in short supply. I considered waking up my parents right then. Just to have their company. I felt that I could not bear this uncertainty by myself. No one possibly could have, I thought. Not alone. So I joined the human race. My mother was pleased.

Now we can fast-forward a bit. There's not much more to tell until high school.

A: Hold on. Surely these cold vignettes can't be all there was to your childhood?

S: No. But I don't intend to waste time telling you stories of dying dogs and first kisses behind the bleachers and rare moments of tenderness from my father. I've told you the essentials you will need to understand what happens later. But beyond that you must begin to get used to the idea that there are qualities about me that you will not like. That perhaps you have even seen throughout our acquaintance but refused to accept. Hidden behind the blinders of friendship. For instance: that concepts were more important to me than what everyone else called the world. From a tender young age. I was a Platonist before I knew who Plato was. Before I knew what play-doh was. Compared to the rest of the world I had an inverted view, when it came to ranking concepts and things, of which was real and which the ghost. The more abstract something was the more real it was. I was quite Greek in that regard. Decay, change, even the possibility of them, were indications of imperfection. Ideas were therefore perfect. They were whole. They did not change. Even the love I came to have for the world did not alter this fundamental prejudice. Largely that love was only a consequence of my learning to draw a straighter line between the concept and the thing. Now may I tell you how this came about?

A: By all means.

S: The history department in my high school was a refuge for eccentrics and weirdos. Dr. Alison was an ex-psychiatrist and still a practicing depressive. He insisted on being called Dr. even by his colleagues. Some of whom had degrees of their own. He started each European History class with "Today's Reason that Life is Worth Living." Wrote a strange fact on the board in yellow chalk. Sharks never run out of teeth. There are no clocks in Las Vegas Casinos. There are 86,400 seconds in a day. There are more connections between your brain cells than atoms in the universe. I objected to this last one. Told him he had to mean "potential" connections. Or were they making connections with something other than atoms these days? He brushed me off. I don't think we were the ones he was trying to cheer up anyway.

Mrs. Blake taught ancient cultures. She had read *Chariots of the Gods* and believed a fair amount of it. Sometimes she dropped references in her lectures. Who really built the pyramids? How can an iron pillar refuse to rust? My sophomore year some parents brought the matter to the school board. She was told to keep the ET's out of it. Class was less interesting after that.

Even in such company Mr. Ireland was a misfit. A mascot. Glasses like a French intellectual's. Overpowering black frames. Lenses like fishbowls. His face was too small to pull any of it off. His nose twitched constantly. As if he snorted black pepper recreationally. A sparse black beard. Neatly kept but probably a mistake. He stuttered and sputtered and kicked whenever he started to speak. Then a stream of talk to shame a politician. He would give Mildred Rosebush a run for her money. Periods like blinks. Commas like winks. He could work into any conversation how many times he had been arrested at Marxist demonstrations (twice). And beaten (once). He had the scars to prove it. So he said. It was hard to imagine him in physical situations. He was so small. But aggressive somehow when he moved. He was allergic to chalk, he had to use an easel with paper and permanent markers instead. Kids sat near him in the vain hopes of getting high on the fumes. He was famous for once having called the principal an idiot at an all-school assembly. And having kept his job. He taught American history. More importantly he also taught the school's only philosophy class. Introduction to Philosophy.

My academic counselor was named Chuck Yeager. Really. He explained to me that "Introduction to Philosophy" was intended for seniors. To prepare them for college. Mostly for pre-law. A few "exceptional" juniors were allowed to take the class after passing an "interview" with Mr. Ireland. There was no possibility of my getting into the class. Not the second semester of my freshman year. It wasn't on the table. Not in the cards. How about wood shop for an elective? What about chorus? "Introduction to Philosophy" would still be there when I was a senior. Mr. Ireland wasn't going anywhere. "Practically an institution," said Chuck Yeager and chuckled. Probably thinking about when Mr. Ireland had insulted the principal. So what other elective would I like to try? What else interested me? After our third such fruitless appointment Chuck Yeager agreed to ask Mr. Ireland if he would talk with me.

The appointed afternoon I knocked on the door of Mr. Ireland's classroom. "Come!" he shouted. Like a submarine captain. He stood up from his desk and moved towards me. Comical but almost threatening. Weaving like a pugilist. Ducking and feinting.

"S-s-s-sooo, I guess you made it clear to our super-sonic counsellor that you wouldn't give up without a fight, eh kid? Good for you. I know a thing or two about taking lumps for what you believe in. Not that you're getting into my class, but good for you. That's the only way the world ever respects you. You may not know that I was arrested twice in Marxist demonstrations? That's right. One time they beat me. But I was already used to that kind of thing. I grew up in a tough neighborhood you know, in Chicago. My dad was a big man. Biiiig. Nobody messed with him. He used to call me "runt." One day he sat me down after some bigger kids had stolen my second pair of glasses and said to me 'Runt, they'll never leave you alone until you lick one of them. Pick the smallest one of them and learn him some manners. Give him a good licking.' 'But Dad, there's not one of them I can lick!' 'Then forget about them. Pick someone you can lick and lick him instead. It don't matter who. Just make sure it's a public licking.'

"There *was* one kid I figured I could lick. Fat Marvin. He was a sweetie. Huge, but wouldn't hurt a fly. Bigger than anybody, but cried when bullies took his ice cream. A real sweetie. I found him on the playground the next day and started in on him just like that, pow! without any warning. I pulled his shirt up over his head and kicked him in the seat of his pants while he bawled, then as he ran away I shouted 'You want some more, Fat Marvin?' The entire schoolyard cheered me on. No one ever bothered me again, and I bought Fat Marvin an ice cream a day for a month. We became friends. I was the best man at his wedding. His wife was bigger than he was. A sweet gal though, and one heck of a cook. You see kid, *everyone* respects you more when you stand up for yourself. That doesn't mean you're getting into my class. But I guess, since you're here, let's see what you've got."

He didn't ask why I wanted to take the class so much. Nothing like that. Nothing personal at all. His approach appealed to me immensely. Right into philosophy. Plied me with tortured arguments. Dared me to refute him. Smiled wryly, scolded. Gave a grunt of satisfaction when I invoked the law of the excluded middle. I loved him immediately. I sensed that here was someone who respected the abstract as I did. Who believed it was more primal than the gross examples we saw around us. More powerful. More important. Had he denied me entry to his class I would have sat outside the door. A non-violent protest. Every day until he let me in. But such measures proved unnecessary. Two hours later he told me he would see me next semester and kicked me out of his classroom.

Chuck Yeager wasn't thrilled. Called my mother in fact. No doubt I was "intellectually and academically prepared" for the class. But what about socially? What if the older kids saw me as an "interloper?" I told my mother I would skip school every day for a semester unless she let me take Mr. Ireland's class. She believed me.

But Chuck Yeager shouldn't have worried. My classmates loved me. I argued with Mr. Ireland the whole class. Every class. Leaving the others free to do whatever they wanted. One day I was sick and missed school. One of the seniors called my house that night. Flirted with my mother on the phone for a minute. She giggled and said what nice friends I was making as she handed me the receiver.

"Yo, bro, it's Joel from Intro. Phil., how you feeling? You think you'll be back tomorrow? Yeah? Quick healer? You pretty sure? Because I need to know if I need to do the reading tonight, man. Class was *rough* today, bro. Ireland was *on* me."

Best class I ever took, Andy. Up through and including MIT. Mr. Ireland was smart, quick, ornery. He had read everything. We agreed on nothing. He pushed his Marxist materialist agenda at every chance. The contradiction infuriated me. Fascinated me. Here was a man I could not figure out. Here was a man who understood argument, concepts, abstraction. Who seemed to love them as I did. But he employed them all to prove that only *things* mattered. He laughed at me openly if I so much as said the word "soul" or "God." He might only chuckle if I said "idea." But he was also the one who introduced me to Featherstone.

Not that Featherstone was on his syllabus. But Anselm was. Mainly so that Mr. Ireland could mock him. "Here's a man who thinks he has proved that God exists. Let's see what the centuries have had to say. Oops, looks like maybe he wasn't as smart as he thought he was." I read the refutations. I understood them. But I didn't really care about them. They were dim spots on the most luminous object my mind had ever seen. Sunspots. An "ontological proof" of God's existence? It had never occurred to me you could even attempt anything like that. The idea that you could start from the *concept* of God's existence and reason to the reality. The idea that the structure of ideas determined the structure of the "real world." From the concept to the thing. It confirmed my suspicions, my prejudices, my gut feelings about the world. As such it was thrilling. Intoxicating. I could not understand why others were not as thrilled as I was. They did not even seem to notice. I pestered Mr. Ireland about the ontological method all class. Prevented him from moving on to Aquinas and Bacon. He finally shut me up with a promise to continue our discussion after school. Two afternoons running I harassed him more after school. Trying to refute the refutations. In vain of course. On the third day I could not even wait until after school. I found Mr. Ireland in his room at lunch. I was ready to launch into it again. But Mr. Ireland held up his hand before I could speak. He was holding a book.

"F-f-f-forget about Anselm, kid. He's old hat, washed up, refuted, and good riddance. If you're hot on proofs of God's existence then this is what you need to be reading. It's a load of crap as well—but let's give the devil his due, this is *verrrry* high quality crap. It's such high quality crap that no one has yet managed to prove that it's crap. But someone will. They have to, because it's a load of crap, and don't tell me that's a tautology or I won't give you the book. I just hope I'm still alive to see it. Actually, kid," his face started twitching furiously, "m-m-m-maybe you'll be the one to do it! You've got the chops. Twenty years from now? You'll be just the guy to cut through this crap! Wouldn't that be a hoot and a half? You could thank me in the preface of your book. Promise me that before I give this to you— if you find the flaw in this guy's argument, you'll thank me in your preface. I'll sweeten the deal for you: if you find the flaw *this semester*, I'll give you an automatic A. You don't have to write the final paper, or take the final exam, or anything. You don't even have to come to class if you don't want. Deal?"

I found the offer vaguely insulting. If he had offered me a free A with no strings attached I would not have taken it. But I wanted the book. And he seemed dead set on the deal. He even made me shake hands on it. And then he handed me *The Divine Logic* by Kingsley Featherstone. Brown cover coming off in front. Almost every page with marginal notes in Mr. Ireland's handwriting. He'd been at the book with a vengeance. He looked almost relieved to be giving it to me. Passing the hot potato perhaps.

I was not going to wait until I got home to read this book. I skipped my afternoon classes and hid in the auditorium. I missed the late bus home. Missed the late late bus home. It was almost eight at night when the principal found me. She was furious. Hadn't I heard the announcements on the PA? Did I have any idea what I had put my parents through? I burst into tears which vanished just as quickly. This seemed to satisfy her. For a freshman male of my height to cry must indicate a deep repentance. When my frantic mother came to pick me up in the office the principal came to my defense. Told her to take it easy on me. I had already "learned my lesson." Clearly meaning the tears. But those tears hadn't been tears of shame. They were tears of indignation. Like the tears of a young boy ripped from a movie theater while the movie is still in progress. Into the harsh afternoon. It was more than I could stand to have been ripped from this book. This miracle of a book. This book that had achieved what I would have thought impossible. Selena Elizabeth Morton had moved to Houston earlier that year. I wanted to look her up. Call her. Fly out and see her. She was wrong, and I could finally prove it to her. And Mary Browning too.

A: So you understood the proof right away? And you accepted it? It comforted you?

S: Of course I did. The proof was perfect. God had been restored to me. There was no longer any cause for doubt. Faith was unnecessary. The relief was indescribable. Like realizing your mother had not really left you as she stepped out from behind the curtains. She had just been hiding. Playing. My anxiety was gone. I could not understand how I had never heard of this book before. How was it not issued like an instruction manual to each of the world's citizens? A fundamental reassurance? How was it the Bible and not this book the Gideons left in hotel rooms? I wanted to tell everyone the news. People of Earth, do not fear: God is not risen, He is proven. I tried a few times. I drew the perspectival logic out for friends. They hardly looked up from their first person shooters. The next Sunday after church I asked my delighted mother if we could stay so I could talk to the priest. I asked him what he thought of Featherstone. He could not have cared less. I even tried with my father. I had managed to convince myself his gruff exterior was the result of fear and insecurity. Worry that he might be living in a Godless universe. He bellowed so loudly at me to get out of the living room that I was worried he would do violence to the book itself. Nothing had ever shaken my faith in humanity like the general indifference I encountered in this mission.

Over the next weeks I spent every free minute with Featherstone. I would finish the book and turn back to the first page. Start again. I practically committed the book to memory. I kept reading anyway. Nothing pleased me more than to rehearse those arguments. Mr. Ireland's marginalia were like dashes of spice. Bonuses. "This can't be true." "Surely this is hogwash...but..." "Haven't I read a refutation for this somewhere???"

You know the proof as well as I do, Andy. Or almost as well. We'll get to that in a moment. You remember how it felt to read it the first time? First the chapters explaining perspectival logic.

The brilliant techniques and mechanism. The feeling you are taking side doors and secret passages through the House of Truth. Slipping into locked rooms. Stealing artifacts that didn't even officially exist. Getting out by the fire escape just before the Contradictions catch up with you. Their fingers closing just behind your back. Your prize intact. But no mention of God. No hint even. Then comes chapter 14. Starts off quietly. Seems to pick up right where 13 ended. Almost a recapitulation. The next movement of a symphony hearkening back. Not moving on. Reluctant woodwinds. No crashing cymbals. No distant timpani to suggest approaching footsteps. Nothing that obvious. Only these new concepts: "contingent," "perfect," "absolute." You hear something missing beneath them. The missing root of a chord. The concepts unfold like a highway map. More and more territory revealed, addressed, affected. But still no mention. And then Featherstone lets drop casually that we are describing "a being, not a state of being." He doesn't even capitalize "being," still so coy. By now it's like the moment when you see someone you know you know but have forgotten. Familiar and strange. "I know him, who the hell is he?" The argument is wrapping up, and still no crashing cymbals. Still the map is creased somewhere. Such patience. Such restraint. He waits until the very end of the chapter. The last two sentences. Then he drops it like a change of key. "An interesting corollary of what we have just shown is that there exists a being who cannot *not* exist, and is perfect in all respects. Or, as one might put it differently: there is a God."

The later chapters are wonders in their own way. Chapter 17: discovering that God changes. That in fact He is always *becoming*. Chapter 19: that He learns our decisions along with us. All wonderful, astounding. But chapter 14 is the gem. The ultimate. The experience.

A: What about the alternative to God's existence? The possibility of total meaninglessness? I would think that would have fed your doubts powerfully.

S: The alternative conclusion to the proof never bothered me. Not in the slightest. The "escape hatch." That there is no meaning at all. Not that I could demonstrate it to be false. But it was senseless to worry about. How could you ever prove it to be true? You would be proving that it is impossible to prove something in the first place. The serpent swallowing its tail. Even the critics of the proof have been reluctant to take this escape. Generally. They want to reserve their right to mean something. They are not willing to give that up. They just want to mean something *else*. You know some of these critics claim that the proof is "technically correct" but only proves something "worthless?" Of course you do. Various religious figures, upset that Featherstone did not prove the God of the Torah. Or the New Testament. Or the Koran. My respect for organized religion only dropped to new lows after that. Atheists claiming Featherstone did not prove "God" at all, only "a necessary and perfect being." Could be an alien from the planet Flaga. A young girl born in Nepal. The puking drunk on the subway. How are we to know who is "perfect" and "necessary?" I never understood these people. Here, the greatest gift yet given to mankind. To know that there is actually a *being* out there. A being tied inextricably to the very concept of perfection. An author for the universe's riddles. A witness for the universe's events. Great and small. Supernovae and birthdays. Quantum happenings. And these people want to find a way to give it back. Exchange this gift of a perfect being for another one. In a different color. Goes better with the living room they already have. Accords better with the books they have already written. Or they just want to give it back entirely. Rather not, thanks. Just an empty box for me. Preferred the empty universe the way it was before. It seems insane. Seemed insane to me then, too. Especially after I found there *was* a way to give Featherstone's gift back. The terrible gift receipt. I wished so hard I could unfind it.

A: Wait...unfind it? What exactly are you saying?

S: What you think I'm saying. Ah, Andy. You of all people might appreciate this. You as an expert on Featherstone.

I had been reading the book for two months. Day after day. Rehearsing. Refining my understanding. It was a Thursday night. I was reading with a flashlight in my room. My father snoring next door. So loud the empty glass on my night-stand rattled. And I noticed something. Something strange. It couldn't possibly be right. Quietly I got up. Took a spiral notebook from my desk. A mechanical pencil. The click to advance the lead seemed impossibly loud. I didn't want to wake my parents. I diagrammed my idea with Featherstone's own notation. His own methods. Perspectival logic. Tracked down the contradictions. Closed them off. But what remained made no sense. I must have made a mistake somewhere. I flipped to a fresh page in the notebook. Tried again, slower. Again, faster. Differently. Again. It didn't matter how many times I tried. I got the same result. Over and over. By the time the sun came up I was heartbroken. But I had accepted it: I had an automatic A in Mr. Ireland's class. I had found a flaw in Featherstone's proof.

CHAPTER ELEVEN
README.TXT (Continued)

At this point I had no choice but to stop reading and use the bathroom. I had been putting it off for many screenfuls of text, and after I read this last sentence my hands had begun to tremble and I felt I might really lose control of my bladder. Caught agonizingly between the need for speed and the desire to remain quiet so as not to wake up Cheryl, I picked my way down the stairs to the guest apartment and groped through the dark to the bathroom. Then, once relieved, I returned stealthily upstairs, desperate to continue reading.

But a sudden inhibition prevented me. I remembered Cheryl's admonition that I was not going to like what I found in this document, and I sensed that I might have reached the turning point, the point past which her prediction would be proven true. There was something horrifying, almost grotesque, in Sothum's assertion that he had refuted Featherstone's proof. I was burningly curious to see if he had really done it, but also uneasy at what it might mean if he had. Featherstone's proof was supposed to be unassailable. It was the closest thing there was to a sure bet in philosophy that this proof would not be refuted in our lifetimes at least. If what I had just read was true then I was about to experience a philosophical revelation, a revolution in our field. Something to cast entire disciplines in a new light, something that could demolish whole careers—

perhaps even my own. My doppelgänger in the dialogue seemed to be suffering some of the same doubts.

A: Back up. You mean to say that in your freshman year of high school you found a flaw in Kingsley Featherstone's proof of God's existence? The same proof that has maddened and defeated the most brilliant atheists and agnostics for thirty plus years? You must realize how unlikely this sounds.

S: I'll assume it's not my abilities you're calling into doubt with that question. But yes. Everyone else had missed it and I had found it. I never claimed my A of course. I never even told Mr. Ireland what I had found. Not even a hint. The next week I returned the book to him. He asked me about it. Half-joking. "Did you find anything?" Yes, I told him. I found out I don't know enough about logic. He laughed.

A: Of course I don't doubt your abilities, Sothum—but that proof is one of the most attacked pieces of logic in the history of philosophy. There are other proofs that prove nothing more than its correctness.

S: It was a strange sort of flaw I had found. To be clear. Not a flaw within the proof itself. Nothing wrong with its preconditions or the links of reasoning it forged from them. They were all perfect. It was where that chain stretched afterwards. After the proof as presented in the book had ended. What else you could prove from Featherstone's proof. An absurd implication.

I've left a copy of the perspectival logic for you on this laptop if you want to go read the details now. It's in the "Featherstone" folder. I don't have the time to walk you through the long version. But I'll wait until you get back. Or for now you can accept the short version on faith: according to Featherstone's proof the future implies the past.

A: That sounds absurd.

S: Because it *is* absurd. Backwards. Obviously wrong. It violates common sense. More importantly it violates the second law of thermodynamics. Entropy tends to increase in a system. Disorder grows with the passage of time. For example: if you were to delete this document from the laptop it would be gone. You can't run the clock backwards. You can't undelete it. There would be nothing in the future, where this document does not exist, to imply the contents of the document in the past. To reconstruct it as it had been. But this is precisely what Featherstone's proof of God's existence implied. That you *could* reconstruct the document after it had been deleted. And this absurd implication brought the proof crashing down around our ears. If the proof implied an absurdity then the proof itself must be absurd. Despite any and all appearances to the contrary.

A: Sothum, if this is correct it is astonishing! Why did you never tell me this? This is a breakthrough in the field. This is the kind of thing that makes and breaks whole careers—whole departments!

S: I never told anyone. You don't understand, Andy. I wish you did. I wish someone did. This wasn't about papers and departments and books no one reads. Nothing about this was academic. This was your recently returned father leaving you in the supermarket on your birthday. Never coming back. This was waking up alone without a note after a night of reconciliation. Perfume still on the pillow. This was a private hurt. The world had already shown exactly how much they cared. They wanted first person shooters and sitcoms? They could have them. I wanted God. That's what I wanted. I had only just regained Him. I had only just found some purchase on the universe again. And now I was slipping, adrift, falling once more. He was gone. Snatched away. A cruel joke the whole time, or an illusion.

Or that was how I saw things to begin with. I was heartbroken. Devastated. For the first time in my life I considered suicide. My mother noticed something was wrong. This time she insisted I see someone. Over my father's objections and my own. But I was not so impaired as to be defeated by a shrink. He told my mother I was intelligent, serious, well-adjusted. I had said all the right things to him. I had seen all the right things in the inkblots, had heard all the right things in the stories he asked me to interpret. Meanwhile I was internally debating methods and time frames.

But I never quite had the courage to do the deed. And then over a period of months I began to develop a different point of view. A different understanding of what had happened to me. To see things correctly. To understand. Not only should I not have been devastated. I had missed the point entirely. I should have been happy. Overjoyed. And eventually I was. My mother remarked with relief on the new "spring in my step." Of course I had a spring in my step. I was no longer just a boy with a puzzle habit. A riddle hobby. I had a destiny now. I had a purpose.

A: You've lost me again.

S: Here was God's real riddle, you see. Intended just for me. Not the habits of the honey bee. Not the secrets of cloud formations. Not even the mysteries of the human soul. But precisely this: Am I out there? Are you sure? Can you prove it? Yes, yes. And no. Not yet. But I was going to prove it. I would succeed where even Featherstone had failed. I was going to rehabilitate the proof. Recast it. Remove the offensive implication. It was so clear. That was the purpose of my life. The private meaning. And I decided it would *remain* private until I was done. At least that long. If not longer. I would risk no more glazed looks from friends. No more slights from priests and parents. I would not allow them another chance to cheapen and mock. I would do this work in secret.

I got started right away. I asked Mr. Ireland to give me a list of everything I would need to read if I wanted to know "as much about logic as Featherstone." He whistled. "That's a tall order. And a long list." I told him I had time. He laughed. He thought I was making a joke. "Let me call some friends from graduate school and see what they suggest."

He came back with the list a few days later. Nine sheets, typewritten. Front and back.

"I told you it would be long, kid."

He sounded apologetic. I told him I had hoped it would be longer. I looked through the pages. Books I'd never heard of. Philosophers I'd never heard of. One line at the end caught my eye. Not typewritten, pen. In blue ink. Shorter than the other lines. Math?

"You're damn right, math. I put that on there for you myself, that's my contribution. Do you have any idea how much math Featherstone knows? Gee whinny Christmas! Just the set theory alone. Also I figured if you learned enough math you could do your own taxes. That's the easiest and quickest way to get you over to my side of the political fence. Once you see how much you already pay and how little you get in return, and think about how much you could get with just a little more, you'll be a Marxist in no time."

He tried to grin wickedly. Thwarted by a bout of twitching.

I got an A in Intro to Philosophy. Even though I did not tell Mr. Ireland about the flaw. "An A with extreme prejudice," said Mr. Ireland. At the time I did not get the reference. I wrote my final paper on the internal inconsistencies of Marx. Mr. Ireland covered it with red ink. He loved it though. That A was the only grade that meant anything to me.

Unfortunately others around me did not share my low opinion of the rest of my classes. Besides philosophy and math my grades had dropped off sharply. Since Mr. Ireland had given me the reading list. I was spending all my time preparing myself. Learning. Making myself strong enough to wrestle logically with

God. What did I care about English homework and history papers? Letters were sent home. First my mother talked to me. Was something wrong? Problems with a girl? She always saw me reading. How could I be doing poorly at school? Was I having trouble "processing?" This was code. She had been reading about learning disabilities in intelligent children. I told her everything was fine. I would try harder. I would do better. But I didn't. I was working on the greatest riddle ever given to the world. Hard to justify much time spent away from it. Why read about the tobacco trade? Who cared about the sodium potassium pump? Don't get me wrong. I was glad that the pump worked its magic in my cells. Glad that it kept me alive and thinking. I wanted to put that life to better use than studying the sodium potassium pump itself. If the pump were capable of agreement it would have agreed. If pumps could be grateful it would have been grateful. To have been employed to this end. I was sure.

More letters home. This time my father talked to me. He took me on a ride in his van. He didn't wear a seat belt. Said I didn't have to wear mine either. He was more direct than my mother. He didn't give a shit. Pass or fail, up to me. But he wasn't paying for college. I could go on scholarships if I could get them. Or I could become a plumber. He would teach me and charge me rent in the meantime. I didn't even have to finish high school if I didn't want to. We could start tomorrow.

On the way home he missed a stoplight. Slammed on the brakes. Tubes and fittings and wrenches everywhere. My head hit the dashboard so hard I felt nauseous on the way back up. Blood streaming from my forehead. We told my mother I had slipped on ice waiting for my father outside the liquor store. "You want me to bring him into the liquor store next time?" said my father.

My grades went up again. Not all the way. But up. I studied on the bus. Wrote papers the night before instead of not at all.

Spent lunch doing the absolute minimum required to finish my homework. Far from the straight As of middle school. But good enough. To stop the letters home. To ease the tension at the dinner table. The gash on my forehead healed, became a white scar.

The dashboard had knocked something else into my skull. My father's mention of "rent." Money. The fundamental equation of the real world: money equals freedom. Money bought four years of college. Money bought books. Money bought space for quiet reflection. As God was the secret of the universe money was the secret of human opportunity. The essence. The distillation. Either you had enough, or not enough, or it had no hold on you. You were a saint. I would never be free of its hold. I knew that. I wasn't a saint and I wouldn't be. The life of St. Francis? Made for great reading. Lovely paintings. But it wasn't for me. Not for me my parents' life either. They weren't free. They didn't have enough. Not nearly enough. At the dinner table one night my mother asked me what I wanted to be. Rich. But rich from what? From having money. Nice work if you can get it, said my father. He took his plate to watch the game.

Chuck Yeager the academic advisor asked me the same question two years later at one of our sessions. The end of high school was approaching. Big choices coming up. What did I want to be? I gave him the same answer I gave my mother. He means more, what do I love. If I do what I love, the money will follow. No, I told him. The money must lead. The money was not an end for me, or a side effect, but the means to an end. He sighed. He had to write something in the little box. Put whatever earns the most, I said. Put "heir." I'll put finance as the first choice, he said, and computers as second. I never got a chance to thank Chuck Yeager.

A: So this was the beginning of your theories on money— money as power as the cardinality of free will.

S: Yes. Though it took me years to formulate it better. But I sensed how much I needed money personally. I was never cut out to be a starving philosopher. I think better in comfort. I always have. I believe it is the same for everyone. Really. In a state of perfect comfort you are perfectly productive. Your potential is entirely unlocked.

Even with my inconsistent grades I received a full scholarship in Boston. On the strength of my essay and SATs. So my high school graduation could be a joyous occasion. Free of anxiety. I collected my diploma like everyone else, walked across the stage like everyone else. I sat through the address, delivered by a local author. He arrived on a bicycle. Notes scribbled on a napkin. Talked about finding your purpose in life. First he said "higher purpose." Then he backtracked. Apologized for using "that word." "Higher." He really meant something not attached to money. He hadn't meant to be heightist about it. Got a round of applause for that. Another for reminding us that commencement meant not "end" but "beginning." An idiot in other words. Then mortarboards tossed in the air, big cheers, all done. Afterwards while I tried to find my parents in the crowd I heard someone call my name. Somewhere behind me. It was Mr. Ireland. Here you go, kid. Thrust something into my hands. A book. Unwrapped. His old copy of *The Divine Logic*, long returned. I thanked him. I might have said more, but I heard my mother calling me. Mr. Ireland heard it too. I don't think he enjoyed meeting parents. He twitched his face furiously at me once and left.

Before bed that night I took the book out. I was uncomfortably full of my mother's cooking. Exhausted from the attention at the party she threw. I tried to stop her. "Your only son only graduates from high school once." "If that," said my father, but almost smiling.

I opened the book. Strange to hold this copy again after all that had happened since. Different than the cheap paperback copy I had bought later. This one gave off an aura. It was a talisman. A grimoire with notes from an earlier wizard on each page. On the front-piece he had written something. Under the faded "Leo Ireland, Cambridge University." In black ink: "The philosophers have only interpreted the world in various ways; the point, however, is to change it. —Karl Marx". Below that, in blue ink and last-minute letters: "Kid: Call me if you ever find the flaw in this or get arrested."

A: Did you keep in touch with him?

S: I didn't. I'm not sure if he's still alive. I was tempted to look him up recently. Now that I'm putting my affairs in order. But in the end I never quite did it. Half terrified that I would find out he had died. Half terrified that I would find out he was still alive.

A: And you were afraid that you would be unable to resist telling him about the proof.

S: Maybe. But more than that I didn't want to see him diminished. Slowed down. Shaking. Perhaps one side of his mouth dragging from a stroke. You never know. I couldn't face that with a figure who loomed so large in my memory. An irascible and irreducible energy. The man who introduced me to Featherstone. The twitching little Marxist. Who somehow set me on the path. Pointed me towards the great project of my life. I suppose I was afraid he would reflect the disrepair into which my life and its project has fallen.

A: Because of the proof? Did it work? Did you manage to rehabilitate it?

S: Mankind has produced a handful of perfect things, Andy. The Parthenon. A few sonnets in Italian and English. Parts of Mozart. "Perfect" meaning they cannot be altered without injury. Add something: worse. Take something away: worse. Change one element: you'd better change it back. Or else you have to keep altering. Alter more and more. Unmake the perfect object. Change by change. Build something new. And by the time you have gotten back to the original level of quality what you have made does not resemble the original. A new sonnet. A distinct symphony. A different building. No one would ever confuse the two. The second is not an *edit* of the first.

I was dealing with one such perfect object. Featherstone's proof. The realization did not come all at once. It was the result of repeated and classifiable failures. Every tweak caused springs to leap out. Moving one brick made the structure collapse. Fiddling with a single premise negated the entire argument. Finally I had to face the conclusion. I would never be able to edit out the offensive implication. It could not be separated from the proof because it was part of the proof. Woven through its DNA. You might as well try to edit the circle. Please keep it just as round though.

I spent many nights in my freshman dorm room facing this dilemma. Lucky I had no roommate because I almost never slept. Drugs helped with that. Made the details so intense. The crackle of that blue plastic mattress as I shifted in bed. The pool of light glaring in the curved windows. The sounds below of drunken classmates coming home. Having taken on Boston and lost. Flirting, fighting. Howling at the moon. I knew these people. These were my childhood friends with their first person shooters. These people were my father with his football games. Chuck Yeager with his forms and checkboxes. The priest with his tea and Bible and no interest in God. These were the people who somehow did not care whether God existed or did not. Could not care less whether you could prove it or could not. They were the people who could not understand how I could care about nothing else so deeply. Though I did not want to join them I was almost jealous of them. Their lives were so simple. Their paths so marked. Meanwhile I was stuck.

I could find no way forward. I couldn't edit the proof. I couldn't tweak the implication out of it. So what? Create a whole new proof? Try a new approach? I made a stab, but half-hearted. From the start. Featherstone's proof *was* the proof. *The* proof. I knew it in my bones. The translation of the concept to the being. The idea to the thing. Whatever else I tried to create would slowly morph, transform, improve itself. Until it was just Featherstone's proof in different handwriting. I needed a new idea. A nudge. Something from outside myself. You gave me that nudge, Andy. I even thanked you for it. In my book.

A: What are you talking about? I can't remember a time you ever took my advice about anything—and you certainly never asked me about Featherstone's proof.

S: It was the night of your first paper for the Three Wise Fools. "Mankind, the poor missile." Flung by origin, drawn by destiny, guided by his will. Buddy raked you over the coals. I defended you. At the time out of kindness. To make sure you came back again. I did not see right away the genius of your approach. But something tickled in my brain. Kept me coming back to the idea. Over the coming days.

Then one night: what if Andy's got it right? Maybe not "right." But what if he's "on to something?" A naive approach. These three forces seem to exist. Seem to be at odds. So maybe they are. Taking things at face value. Don't try to shoehorn them. Don't bend them to what "must" be true. Why didn't I try the same thing with Featherstone's proof? Turn the problem on its head. Take it as it is. A crackle of electricity, of mental excitement. Don't "rehabilitate" the proof. The proof is already perfect. You know that. You've known it all along. So prove the "absurd" implication. Show that it isn't absurd at all. And just like that I had it. All that I had to do to save the proof was prove that the future implied the past!

A: "All" you had to do?

S: Your skepticism is not unfounded. Over the next few days the energy faded. The purpose burned lower. I was going to prove something absurd? All right. How? Maybe my majestic decision had been all bluster. All gesture. Like a stranded mountaineer. Who decides—*decides*—he will not die in this godforsaken place. Stamps his feet in protest. Shouts words to that effect at the empty sky. The cold mountains. At God Himself. A good scene for a movie. Because in a movie you cut to montage. Our hero climbing. Trekking through a snowstorm, grunting. Making progress. A swelling soundtrack. But in real life you don't cut to montage. You finish your display. Run out of steam. The echoes of your protest die. And you are right back where you were. Just as remote. Just as lost. Only a couple fewer calories to your name. You still have to decide what's next. To take a step in one direction or the other.

But I'll spare you the reality. Let's stick to the montage. Cut to Stanley reading mathematics. Learning to program late at night. To model and run large simulations. The green glow of the monitor. Popping pills to keep going longer. Waking up with his head on the keyboard. Shaking the sleep away. Starting to type again. Throwing a book against the wall in frustration. Picking it up again. So many blind alleys. Crashed simulations. And so many times I thought I had it. Only to notice the missing brick. Everything crashing down again. And at the end of the montage college was over. Overnight it seemed. My "undergraduate career" done. The proof still unproven. All I had were some vague ideas. Hopes for bigger simulations. More detailed representations of the passage of time. I did not have high expectations for them. But they were all I had to pursue. And they were going to require time. And expertise. And money.

A: So that's why you really went to MIT then? That whole line about money and free will you fed me was just a line after all.

S: Not entirely. I believe everything I said to you that night. Everything I wrote in *Degrees of Freedom*. But my argument was about the general exercise of free will. I had some more specific applications in mind. That's the only difference.

But back to our movie. MIT. It's fall. Stanley is running to class. As much as a man of his height can really run. He takes the stairs in twos. He's late anyway. Tries to sneak in the back of the lecture hall. Up at the top of the stadium seating. Professor notices though. Makes some sarcastic remark. How kind of you to join us. Something like that. The class turns to look, to laugh. Stanley mumbles something in apology. The class turns back. Stanley starts to unpack his things. But then he notices. One member of the class hasn't turned back. Is smiling at him. Familiar somehow. Then he places it. He knew her. In his childhood. He used to love her in fact. How about that. But he was so young back then. It could never have worked out. Still he had always wondered. What if things had been different? If he had been more mature? And now here she is. Coincidence? Coincidence is just an alias for Fate. Kismet. The same force at work. He makes an expression at her. You? he asks silently. Me, she answers with only expressions. And turns back to the lecture.

But both know they will find each other in the hallway after class. Catch up. Make plans to meet again. Sit next to each other in the following week's lecture. One thing to another. Way leads on to way. And soon they are spending every waking minute together. Some of the other moments too. Stanley begins to forget about his obsession with Featherstone's proof. This foolish proof. This all-absorbing riddle. It's not completely gone. Just on the back burner. That's all. And just for now. He tells himself.

But there it stays. And the back burner keeps getting turned lower and lower. So much of his time and attention is going into this new relationship. He likes the way it makes him feel. It's clear and easy. Well. Clear and easy compared to the madness of the proof. There's plenty of time for that. He'll get back to his obsession when he gets to it. That's pretty much what happened to me at MIT.

A: I'm speechless. You never told me about any of this. Who was she? Did I ever meet this woman?

S: Not a woman you've ever met.

A: Not the girl with the daisy?

S: No, it wasn't Selena Elizabeth Morton. Wouldn't that have been something. A hoot and a half as Mr. Ireland might say. And it wasn't a woman you'd ever met because it wasn't a woman at all.

A: Umm...

S: Not even a human being. It was a discipline. A field of study. I fell back in love with cryptography. Codes. Ciphers. Head over heels. On a whole new scale. Not the frequency charts and pencil and paper of my childhood any more. Elliptical curves and S-boxes. Grids of computers at my command, ready to spring into action at a keystroke. Panting to crunch and analyze.

At first I told myself it was just a way to learn more math. All the better to attack the proof. To create more sophisticated simulations. Then I told myself it was just a brief holiday. A respite. After which I would return fresher to my real work. Then I stopped bothering to make excuses at all. Plunged in whole hog.

A: So after all that, you left the proof behind—this proof that was supposed to be the secret meaning of your life? It seems to me that you had managed quite well working simultaneously on multiple fronts up until now. At least in college your extra work on the proof had not interfered with the many other philosophical tangents you pursued. Newcomb's paradox, your ideas in *Degrees of Freedom*. Your studying cryptography I understand. Your giving up working on the proof to do it I don't understand.

S: Andy, I...was afraid. It's hard to admit even now. I finally had to face the possibility that perhaps I was not up to this challenge. I could not see a way forward. Perhaps I never would. Perhaps I would always be better at taking things apart than putting them together. Maybe I should embrace this limitation. Try to accept this about myself. But this proof, and fixing it, had been the center of my life. For a long time. A long time for a young man. I did not know how to let it go without introducing some new obsession in its place. Cryptography fit the bill. It was difficult. One puzzle after the other. It appealed to me. To my love for the envelope as much as the message.

A: And you still didn't tell me or anyone else about the problem you had discovered in Featherstone's proof. You sat on it. You do realize that this is a form of intellectual miserliness? You could have told me, at least. I wouldn't have ignored you like your childhood friends and your father and your priest. I would have cared a great deal.

S: I know you would have, Andy. But you would have cared about the wrong thing. Or in the wrong way. A professional way. This was not a professional matter to me.

A: Maybe it should have been. Maybe things would have been different if you'd come back to philosophy, where you belonged.

S: I could always feel you trying to pull me back there. To the profession of philosophy. Sometimes your emails would cause me a twinge. A pang. Anecdotes of Featherstone. Reminders of the great challenge I had set myself. My ultimate work. My life's great purpose. Now gathering dust in the desk. But twinges pass. Pangs subside. Way leads on to way. Four years went by. And then another graduation loomed. At least I knew it would be my last. I felt more shame than accomplishment. I had done well, but not right. An uncomfortable thought. Hard to face. So easy to dodge. Especially as there were other pressing matters to deal with. Such as: I had to find a job. I was not going to move home after all. That option wasn't on the table. I was close to being the living embodiment of my "flat broke in a field" thought experiment. Alarmingly close.

You know what happened then. Machine Translation Technologies. Called me about my dissertation. Translation as encryption. Did I have any interest in putting the idea into practice? Well, sure. Maybe. They flew me out to California to talk about it. I must've talked all right. They offered me the job. They mentioned some pretty big numbers. Not quite the price tag of freedom. But a good start. Put her there. And suddenly I was employed, and a resident of California.

I almost bought a return ticket. That first week. Machine Translation Technologies was a horror show. A mess. Not the physical premises. The office was classic startup. Nondescript office building. Stuffed with leather couches and beanbag chairs. Ping-pong and foosball. Intellectually they were a mess. Their approach was backwards. 180 degrees wrong. They were treating translation as *decryption*. An odd testament to the brilliance of the workers that anything functioned at all.

A: If it's important that I follow you at this point, you should know that I'm not.

S: Yes. This is going to be important. Let me back up. Let's get some terms. Like the old days, no Andy? Defining first principles. Arguing in the dorm. Or the library.

You remember "plaintext" from the cryptography crash course I gave you once? "Ciphertext?" "Key?"

A: I think so. Plaintext is the original, unencrypted message. Ciphertext is the encrypted message, garbled and unreadable. The key is the "secret password" you use to do the encrypting and decrypting. If you have the ciphertext and the key, you can decrypt it back to plaintext and read it. If you have the ciphertext without the key, you're out of luck.

S: Nice to see our time together wasn't wasted. So let's say you had a passage of French. You wanted it in English. Here's how you do it, Machine Translation Technologies style.

Pretend that some imaginary author somewhere actually wrote the passage not in French but in English. *Originally*. Then it fell into the hands of a Frenchman. A bad Frenchman. Sly and dastardly. Cartoon mustache and all. He doesn't want you to read the original. The plaintext, let's call it. So he translates it. *Encrypts* it into French. Let's call that the ciphertext. Then he eats the document. The original. The precious English plaintext. And he licks his lips and chuckles evilly. It's gone forever now. Sacrificed to entropy. Your mission. Should you choose to accept it. Decrypt the French back into the imagined English "original." The plaintext that never really existed. I admit it's brilliant in some twisted way. But it's perverse. Even for my backwards and inverting tastes.

A: You had a better way, I take it.

S: Yes, then there was my way. Which has the virtue of being a little closer to reality. There is no imaginary plaintext. No hypothetical English original. No sly Frenchman. Just the French passage that we want in English. The French passage is the *real* plaintext. We don't *de*crypt to get it there. We *en*crypt. Into English. There are a few indications that this is the better approach. It fits the facts better. The original is actually in French. And more importantly you can translate one passage of French into many English versions. More or less an infinite number of them.

A: You've lost me again. What does the number of versions have to do with anything?

S: Well, if you have the plaintext "hello," how many ciphertexts can you make from it?

A: If you turn a plaintext into a ciphertext by using a key, then you can turn "hello" into as many different ciphertexts as you have keys.

S: Bravo. Using one key might turn "hello" into "f*g1!" while another might result in "ij.2u." To be simplistic about it. These ciphertexts are different. They were created with different keys. But they correspond to the same plaintext. You see?

A: Yes, I see that, but...

S: All right then. Now to translation. When you translate the line "—Hypocrite lecteur,—mon semblable,—mon frère!" from French into English, how many English versions are possible?

A: I don't know how to count them accurately, but certainly more than one.

S: "More than one" is all that matters. Many. So translation is more like encryption. One plaintext to many ciphertexts. Not like decryption. One ciphertext to one plaintext. My theory made more sense. Keep this in mind, Andy. It will be important. Oh, and one more detail. My approach generated translations rated almost fifteen percent better. By native speakers of the target language. After we worked out the initial bugs of course.

But enough tooting of my own horn. Our time together is alarmingly short. We still have some ground to cover. Let's look at our movie again. Stanley is a success. He has won the girl from his childhood. Things are going well. They spend a lot of time together. Stanley is committed. He's making good money. Breaking ground in an interesting field. The future is bright. But something starts to distract him. Makes him restless. A memory like a distant bell. A whiff of the ocean.

More and more his thoughts turn away from what he is doing at the moment. His job begins to suffer. His relationship with the girl from his childhood. He feels a destiny passing him by.

Perhaps already passed. He hopes not. He prays it's not too late. But all the same he can't quite summon the will. To shake things up. To face the work of breaking up. It's hard to do. And then there's all the work to get back to his old project. Not even to make progress. Just to return to the swing of things. To get back to where he used to be. Not to mention the possibility of failure. It still hangs over this other venture like an ax. Nothing has gotten any easier in his years of ignoring it. No elves have come in the night and proven anything for him. So he can't return to the idea. But he can't give it up either. Over days, weeks, months, the dissatisfaction builds. He is like a boulder on a cliff that cannot quite fall off. But edges closer and closer to the ledge. Waiting for one good shock to send it on its way. Just waiting. And waiting. And that shock would have come. I know it would have. Something would have tipped me back to my proper concerns. To the project that was supposed to give my life meaning. My life's work. It would have happened. I know it would have. There is no doubt in my mind that it would have. If disaster had not struck.

A: What disaster? You mean the reception of *Degrees of Freedom*? Congressman Harms?

S: What? No. That was annoying. Mildly disheartening. Not a disaster.

A: I thought that nearly destroyed you.

S: A coincidence of timing. Nothing more. I am talking about a real disaster. Right around the same time though. One morning I arrived at the office. Late morning, as usual. Say 11. There was a yellow sticky note on my monitor. "See me as soon as you get in." Signed R.R. R.R. being Reginald Reginald. The redoubtable CEO of Machine Translation Technologies. I wondered if I had landed in hot water somehow. He had underlined "as soon." And you know I have a talent for making people angry. Sometimes even without meaning to. But when I saw him my unease vanished. He was thrilled to see me. Bursting at the seams. He pulled me into his office, closed the door. Sat me down.

"Futureman, I just had the idea to end all ideas. Man, this is going to put us on the map. No, you know what? *Fuck* 'on the map,' we're going to be a glowing *star* on the map, a fucking *Chernobyl* on the map.

"So last week for our anniversary I got my wife one of those GPS units for the car, top of the line and everything, and I give it to her with this note that *I* thought was the last fucking word in romance: 'For the woman I would be lost without.' Or words to that effect. And as soon as she reads it she starts crying. And at first I think she's just overwhelmed by the sentiment or whatever, and so I'm all 'Baby, Baby, it's OK,' and she finally stops crying and looks up at me and she is furious, right? I mean she is *ripped*, and she says to me 'You think I can't find my way around without electronic help? Well there are some other things I'll only be doing with electronic help from now on.' And then she just like *storms* out of the room.

"Now a dozen roses and some obscenely large diamond earrings later I'm, like, the proud owner of a top of the line GPS. So I figure this morning, let's give the old rollerblades a break and see how this thing guides me to the office in the Hummer. Just to test it.

"And I'm sitting in front of the light at Highland and Main, which is the *longest* light in all of God's green creation—or I guess green yellow and red creation—whatever—and I'm fiddling around with all the options on this thing, and I'm like 'Woah, cool, I can change the voice to sound like Bob Dylan, or like Alec Baldwin, or like, your Generic English Chick, and then *pow*, it hits me. I mean, it hits me so fucking *hard* I thought another car had literally plowed into me. So here it is, Futureman: why don't we add *style* to our translator? Like, don't just translate this

French into English, man, translate it into William Fucking Shakespeare, or, like, Holden Fucking Caulfield, right, or translate this Spanish into that Arab fucking poet dude!

"Now I know what you're thinking, because I know you, Futureman. I fucking know you. You're thinking 'As usual R.R.'s off his nut about a mile and a half, this can't be done. It just can't be done.' *But I figured out how to do it.* Listen to this, and I don't know all the terms or whatever, so just, you know, bear with me. All we need to do is to construct these huge, like, probability matrixes, right? And they're full of those *keys* you're always explaining to me—the secret sauce you use to do our translating—but you—and oh, Futureman, do I ever mean *you*— you build up these probability matrixes with like every possible key, and you just massage them so that the probabilities like, magically come out to the style of whoever you're translating into. You know, Shakespeare or whoever, with 'thou' instead of 'you.' But it doesn't all have to be dead people, we could do living people too! Like Vanilla Ice! He's still alive, right? Obviously I don't mean we would translate *exactly* like the person himself would—that would be predicting the future or something, right?—like, knowing what he would do ahead of time—but in his *style*, man. You know? White rap? Turntables and ninjas and shit like that?

"So what do you think? Futureman? Be honest, my brother. I'm a big boy. I can like, handle it."

He watched me. Something like concern on his face. As I stood up and left his office. I didn't say a word. Maybe he thought I was quitting. Maybe he thought I was getting started on his big idea. I didn't care. I couldn't have cared less what he thought. Or the colleagues who watched me walk by in obvious distress. I went to the men's room. Down the hall. Touching the wall the whole way to steady myself. Then I put my fist through the mirror over the left-hand sink.

A: What the hell are you talking about, Sothum? What on earth in that blather could have made you react like that?

S: Has this ever happened to you, Andy? You work on the crossword. The Sunday crossword. Toughest one of the week. Pick it up off and on. All Sunday. And you almost finish it. Just a few words at the end you can't quite get. You know you'll eventually get them though. You're close. Then Monday morning you go to work. Teach all day. Deal with students. Lecture. In the evening you get home. You sit down, you relax. You look around for some light entertainment. Something to distract you. And you see the crossword. Which fits the bill admirably. So you pick it up. But it's already finished. Filled in. In ink. Someone has filled in those last few clues. And now you've seen them. You can't unsee them. That crossword is spoiled for you forever. You will never finish it. You know you would have gotten those final clues. You can't believe you didn't get them already. They're so simple now that you see them. But you can't *prove* you would have gotten them. No way back. Not once you've seen the solution. Like entropy.

Don't even bother to answer, I'm sure this has happened to you. Look who you're married to. It's inevitable. So do you remember how pissed off you were when it happened? How cheated you felt? How wronged? And that was a crossword puzzle. A Sunday afternoon invested. Imagine what I felt. My life's work. The problem I had struggled with for years. Spoiled for me. And by whom! By whom. Yes, it was subtly done. Right up to the end. Such nice touches. Saying "matrixes" instead of "matrices." Properly meaning neither. The whole yuppie backstory. The figures from pop culture. The tang of the present. The verbal tics. So plausible. Even R.R. himself was fooled. He thought it was his own idea. The child of his teeming brain. But *I* was not fooled. He had gone too far. The mention of "knowing the future." That's what had done it. Right at the end. Just in case I had missed it. Just in case I couldn't extrapolate for myself. That was gratuitous. That was sloppy. Reginald Reginald was an ignoramus. He was no more capable of generating this idea than of transmuting lead. Just not up to it. Merely remembering such an idea during his whole commute would have taxed that intellect. No, that had been R.R.'s voice. But the *words* had been put in his mouth. He was the puppet. Nothing more. And I knew who was behind him. Whispering those lines into his ear. Working the limbs into those excitable gestures. I identified the puppet-master right away. And it broke my heart.

A: Sothum, I don't understand what you're saying at all—do you mean you think that R.R. was somehow possessed?

S: I'd had the movie all wrong, you see. Always thought of cryptography as the distraction. The childhood crush. The siren leading me away from the proof, for good or ill. Probably ill. But cryptography wasn't the siren at all. Cryptography was Fat Marvin. And I was Mr. Ireland. Out in the schoolyard of ideas, giving cryptography a good thrashing. A drubbing it wouldn't soon forget. Earning the respect of those other ideas who stood around. Watching, cheering me on. And cryptography had even become a friend afterwards. Just like Fat Marvin to Mr. Ireland. An ally. A better ally than I had even understood. Cryptography had never been the distraction. No. It had been the key. The key that unlocked the proof. The key with which I could prove that the future implied the past. And I had been so close for so long, without knowing it. Inches away! One idea, one thought, one connection from resolving the problem of past and future! From rehabilitating Featherstone's proof.

A: I'm entirely lost, Sothum. What does any of this have to do with R.R.?

S: And then God Almighty Himself, for some reason. For some reason. He had nothing better to do apparently. No galaxies to create at the moment. No planets to set spinning. He spoiled everything. Gave it away. Put words in the mouth of Reginald Reginald. Filled in the missing clues. In ink. Denied me the chance to ever solve the riddle myself. Not *a* riddle. Not like your Sunday crossword. *The* riddle. The one even Featherstone had not finished. The one I had devoted myself to solving. The one that was supposed to give my life its secret meaning.

A: You're beginning to scare me. Are you saying that you believe...

S: I could not understand why He would do such a thing. Wars I understood. Hunger I understood. For free will to be real He had to let things run their course. Consequences had to be genuine. Horrific or not. Don't get involved. Prevent nothing. Stay out of it. Just like Featherstone says. All of that I understood. So why get involved now? Why deny me this? That wasn't profound. It wasn't tragic. It wasn't woven into the fabric of human life as death and grief were. It was a miracle. In one sense. An extremely rare occurrence, God becoming involved. But it was jealous. It was petty. Out of line. Uncalled for. It was a petty miracle. I was left grasping for reasons. Trying to find some way to make it my fault. Was I being punished because I had put the proof on the back burner for a while? Taken some time off? Been slow to return to the problem? "Sorry, your time is up? Let's show you the answer?" What overreaction! What intolerance! And all directed towards me, who had been a champion of His? Who had spent his life toiling on the proof of His existence while others played first person shooters and beer pong? It made no sense. Don't try to make excuses for Him, Andy. No references to hints, please. To inspiration. To "getting me over the hump." I didn't ask for any of those. I didn't need them. If He thought this would not spoil the problem for me He should have known better. Like those idiot authors in the riddle-books of my childhood. The ones who printed the answers upside-down. Right below the questions. What fool can't read upside-down? And let's get another thing clear. I don't want to hear about demiurges or blind gods or devils or demons either. I don't believe in any of it. This was an act of *God*. Pure and simple. God, speaking through Reginald Reginald, resolved the proof. He handed me the answer. God gave away the answer to the riddle of my life. And I had never been so furious or hurt.

CHAPTER TWELVE

README.TXT (Concluded)

A noise startled me—a low wail or a moan from the second floor. It seemed to be coming from Buddy's room, and I wondered if he might be having a nightmare. The sound was extremely unsettling. He sounded more like a sick infant than a grown man. No more than ten seconds after the moaning had begun, Mildred's door opened and she came down the wooden stairs on her scratchy slippers, all the while muttering reassurances to Buddy that he could not possibly have heard.

I could not imagine being interrupted at this point. As silently as possible I blocked the light of the laptop's screen with an afghan and crouched behind the sofa, holding my breath, while she fetched a glass of water from the kitchen and returned to the second floor. The water seemed to calm Buddy, and two or three minutes later, when I heard Mildred's footsteps shuffle back to her own room and the door close softly, I stole back to my seat in blackness and tore back into my reading.

A: Calm down—you need to explain a lot of things to me here. First of all, are you really saying you believe that God was speaking those words to you through Reginald Reginald? Do you know how crazy that sounds?

S: I don't "believe" that God was speaking to me. I know it. I don't care if it sounds crazy. It isn't crazy. You will never convince me to the contrary. Rest assured: I have considered all the other possibilities. None of them hold water. And we don't have time for debate. I am trying to tell you what happened. To answer your questions.

A: Let's say I stipulate—reluctantly—that you're right, and that those were really God's words in R.R.'s voice—or at least I stipulate that you honestly believe this yourself and cannot be convinced otherwise—what does that have to do with Featherstone's proof? I didn't hear anything that R.R. said that would have resolved anything for you.

S: Don't you see it, Andy? The filled-in clues? The inked letters on the grid? It isn't really that hard. Work it out. Work it out with me. If you believe in free will, then you believe you can't predict the future. Not perfectly. Not for sure. That's obvious. Any single free decision might go against your predictions. Remember *Degrees of Freedom*? Free will means an infinite number of choices. Even flat broke in a field. So a single being with free will in the past means an infinite number of potential futures. Immediate futures. One for each free decision. One past, infinite futures. You agree?

A: So far.

S: Then how can you not see the rest? It's the same problem. The same problem I solved at MIT. The same problem paying my bills. The same problem whose solution was humming away on hundreds of Machine Translation Technologies' servers. Just yards away from where I stood bleeding in the men's room. It's just like translation as encryption. One original—infinite translations. One plaintext—infinite ciphertexts. One past—infinite futures.

A: I see the one to many relationship, but I don't see how that gets you anywhere. I might as well say "Polygamist: one husband, many wives." It doesn't shed much light on things.

S: Because you're not thinking about the key. The password, the magic phrase that does the encryption. This is the important part. So get ready. Clear your mind. Ready? The future is the past encrypted with the key of free decision. You got that?

A: "The future is the past encrypted with the key of free decision." I can parrot it. I can see it. But I don't get it.

S: The past is the plaintext. The future, the ciphertext. A free decision is the key. If you see it, you get it. Remember the example of increasing entropy we talked about earlier? How if you deleted this file, it could not be reconstructed by working backwards from the future? How entropy could not be reversed? Think about it that way. It's as if you had encrypted the past and then thrown away the key. Now you can't get back. You can't go from the future where the file doesn't exist to the past where it does. And it's true. If you throw away the key, you can't get back. Not ever. But here's the thing: you can't throw away the key.

A: I'm barely holding on here, Sothum. If the key is the free decision I've made, why can't it be thrown away? Because it's in my memory? So what happens when I die, or lose that memory? It seems to me the key goes with me.

S: Featherstone, chapter 18: God becomes aware of your decisions as you make them, not before. But Featherstone says nothing about after you make them.

A: You're suggesting that God remembers the key?

S: Correct. Obviously. This isn't about *your* memory. It's about *God's* memory. God's memory is outside the physical universe. It is not subject to the laws of entropy. It is a waste-bin that never gets full. And in His memory your decision to delete this file would persist for eternity. Long after you have become dust, your decision will live on.

A: It still doesn't make sense. Even if God remembered my decision to delete this file, it doesn't mean that He remembers the file.

S: Wrong. You are over-simplifying. Your decision to delete *this* file as opposed to another file presupposes the character of the file itself. Remembering the decision to delete this file means remembering the character of the file. And that decision is never thrown away. We just don't have access to it. You and I. We can't see into the past from the future. But He can. He does. He looks back and sees it all—the great recursive encryption of time, played in reverse, back to the very beginning.

A: A lovely image, Sothum, but so what?

S: So what? This resolves the apparent flaw in Featherstone's proof. That's so what. How can the future imply the past? It seems impossible. Because we think of implication as having a temporal direction. I fell off my bike two seconds ago and therefore I am bleeding now. But let go of that. Stick with logical implication. Mathematical implication.

Remember, Andy. One plaintext, many ciphertexts. Varying by key. One past, many futures. Varying by free decision. But from each ciphertext, only one plaintext. From each future, only one past. The ciphertext already contains the key. The future already contains the free decision. Therefore the future implies the past. Logically. Not the other way around.

Voila. Go ahead and check it out. Pull up the essays I wrote on Featherstone's proof. Walk them line by line. I'll wait. You'll see that this resolves the problem. Harms nothing in the proof. Makes its implication palatable. The past is implied by the future. So simple once you've seen it. So simple if you stick to the things you know. Rid yourself of unspoken assumptions. The eternal letdown of the riddle. As bad as the gate my mother put across the stairs. Nothing at all once it was solved.

A: Sothum—I mostly understand the argument—mostly. But I don't see how in a million years you get from R.R. to this. At best—or at worst, if you insist on seeing it that way—that was a hint. Even if God really was speaking to you. There probably aren't ten people alive today who could have made the leap you made there.

S: Ten? There aren't two. Soon there won't be one. I'm not saying it wouldn't have been a hint for *you*. I'm saying it wasn't a hint for me. You think God didn't know that? Adults know perfectly well how to adjust the riddles they give to children. How to pitch them at your level. I learned that a long time ago, remember?

A: Don't you think it's more likely—or at least possible—that you were angry with yourself? Maybe because you'd been so close without realizing it for so long? Or maybe because now the riddle—the thing that had given your life meaning—had been solved? And so what were you going to do next?

S: What next? Exactly. That was the question I asked myself. What does a man do next when he has been cheated of his destiny?

A: That's not how I meant it.

S: Standing in the men's room in the anonymous office complex. Smashed mirror in front of me. Slivers of it glinting in my knuckles. Holding my wrist. Bleeding into the sink. Suddenly without a purpose. A man adrift. Fortune's fool. But not for long. A new purpose crept over my mind. Slowly. But there and then. The rage cooled. Congealed. Froze over. Somewhere in the vicinity of my heart. And became a darker purpose: satisfaction. Or the possibility thereof. I could not hurt God. Not as He had hurt me. But at least I was going to get in touch with God. Face to face. As it were. At least I was going to give Him a piece of my mind.

A: Let's ignore the more insane aspects of that decision for a moment and focus on the theology. You don't think—if you and Featherstone are right about God at all—that He was perfectly aware of what you thought, at the exact moment that you thought it?

S: You're right. Such points are why I love our chats. You have always been willing to come along with me. To see it even when you don't get it. But here the point wasn't exactly His being aware or not. This wasn't a fair fight. I could not strive for an effect on Him. I could only strive for an effect on myself. What I was after was not the conveyance of information to God. It was the *satisfaction* of my telling Him off. Of getting it off my chest. Of addressing Him more like an equal. Of telling Him exactly what I—the Other Capitalized Entity—thought of Him for doing this. How beneath Him it was. How ashamed He ought to be.

A: A tall order, if I'm understanding you right.

S: Sure. But I had some ideas how to go about it. He should really have been more careful in that respect.

I took the rest of the day off from work. Went to the hospital. Got my hand attended to. A jagged track of stitches. I came into the office as normal the next day. I avoided R.R. He avoided me. Never mentioned his grand idea again. Small favors. I got back to my normal work. Behaved as normal. But in reality, nothing was normal. And wouldn't be again. Things had changed. Events had been set in motion. A die had been cast.

A: We have to stop for a second here. I can't wrap my mind around this—I can't reconcile that you and I are talking about the same person. This was really *you* doing and thinking all these insane things? I knew you during this time. I even remember the scarred hand—I saw it at dinner one night after you came back to Boston. You told me you had dropped a monitor on it. You were the same man you had always been—you joked, we laughed. We chatted about movies and politics. That was all an act?

S: You hear people exclaim all the time at the psychology of terrorist sleepers. How can anyone lead a double life like that? Friends. Wife and family, sometimes. All fake. Just props. Stage pieces serving an entirely different set of plans. Dark purposes slumbering. Hibernating. Waiting. Don't their brains split in two? Living a lie like that?

A: Well, don't they?

S: Of course not. It's an idiotic question. It misses the point of the double life entirely. The friends and wife and kids aren't fake. They're real. They're a separate reality. Like origin, destiny, free will. None more real than the other. But antagonistic. Irreconcilable. Those who lead double lives are not so different from any of us. Just a more extreme version of what we all already do. Like keeping bookmarks in two novels at once. The mind even enjoys the variety. You are the man's man at the office. The doting husband and father at home. The sexual deviant in the motel room. The high roller at the craps table. It's refreshing. Like alternately soaking in the hot tub and plunging into the cold ocean. But which is the real life? Well which is more real: the ocean, or the hot tub? Exactly.

A: You can talk about terrorists and psychology all you want, but I still have trouble accepting this. How could I have noticed nothing? Not a single dark look, not a single moment where these other concerns peeked through?

S: Maybe you did notice them. Maybe you wrote them off as just moments. Or thought I was upset about what had happened with *Degrees of Freedom* and the good congressman. You shouldn't blame yourself. If that's what you're getting at. You never really had a chance. Any more than I had a chance to injure God. You were coming at the friendship openly and in good faith. Meanwhile I was already adept at the double life. All those years working in secret on the proof. I slipped easily into this. Ready to tackle something more extreme. By day, a silicon valley technologist. Friend to Buddy, you, others. Serial and casual dater of the gorgeous California women. By night, something else. What's the word for it? Vigilante? Opponent? Rebel? Investor?

A: One of these things is not like the other.

S: But I had to become all of them. You see, I had a plan. But it was an expensive plan. You know how people say "as rich as God?" As in, "That Bill Gates isn't just rich, he's as rich as God." What do you think they mean by that? Really mean? Even if they don't quite understand it themselves? It should be obvious by now. If wealth is the cardinality of human freedom. What they are really saying is: "He is as free as God." Hyperbole of course. They mean something more like "His level of freedom is so far above ours as to appear more like God's at first glance than like ours." Not quite as pithy when expressed like that. But that was exactly what I needed. First and foremost. If I was going to pull this off. Those levels of freedom. Options way beyond the normal. Freedom to attempt things a normal person might consider impossible. Science fiction. Or simply crazy. Those levels of freedom aren't easy to come by. Not easy at all. But luckily God could not erase the clues He had filled in. He could not cheat me of the practical applications of the idea He had crammed down my throat.

The market is an imperfect simulation of reality. You see. Much simplified of course. But a similar equation governs the progress of the market and the passage of time. Most of the mathematical and statistical traders have attacked the market backwards. Just as Machine Translation Technologies attacked translation: as a process of decryption. They try to decrypt today's stock price into tomorrow's. But that's 180 degrees wrong. Just like reality, the market encrypts itself. Instant by instant it encrypts itself. And throws away the key. Or tries to throw it away. Because the aggregate human consciousness around the market behaves more or less like the consciousness of God around reality. It collects the scraps. It retains. It does not allow the key to vanish.

A: Surely you're not saying that human memory is infinite?

S: No, of course not. But it's long. Long compared to the moments of the market. The market imprints its character in that memory. And then you're just solving an equation. The market today. Decrypted by the key imprinted on the collective market players. Equals the market yesterday. You know the market today. You know the market yesterday. You solve for the key. With that key you learn a tremendous amount about the character of the market. And you exploit that knowledge to your advantage.

A: It can't be as simple as you're describing. Are you just trying to hide the techniques from me?

S: Once you have the idea—and the cryptographic math—it's really not so hard. Not as hard as you'd think. The character of the market is an aggregate. An aggregate of all the characters around it. They are all different of course. But precisely because of that they tend to cancel each other out. One low where the other is high. One high where the other is low. What you're left with is a primitive character. Easy to understand. Easy to exploit.

A: Surely it's not that easy, Sothum.

S: It was expensive to get all the data, expensive to crunch it. Other than that it was just a lot of plugging in. Some tedious monitoring. Some manual tweaking. Trust me. I've done it. The hardest part was figuring out how to hide how much I was making. It was all nothing to write home about really.

A: You've lost me in some of the details, but if I understand you right then it's actually quite incredible—both what you've done and how wrong you are about it all. You're saying you made your money in the market using the same insight with which you resolved the problematic implication of Featherstone's proof? This isn't something you should have been angry about—this wasn't something you should have been seeking vengeance for. The idea that this all came from God spoiling something for you is—well, not to put too fine a point on it, it's crazy. *You* did this. You with your intellect and years of work. R.R. had a crazy, idiotic idea. You found the accidental nugget inside it and turned it into something brilliant. You turned this fundamental insight into a financial generator as well as a philosophical triumph. These are *your* achievements, and you should have been proud of them.

S: Should I have been? Babel Investments was an achievement of sorts. I suppose. Specul8, my automated investment system, was an engine of wealth. I should have been proud? But I couldn't be. I couldn't forget how the idea that made it all possible had come to me. Say a man finds a scrap of paper on the street. Maybe the ink has bled a little in the rain. He has to squint to read it. He uses the formula he finds there to play the market. Wins big. Is he proud? Maybe in some small way. Maybe for bothering to squint. Maybe for recognizing the application of the formula to the market. Can't be proud of the formula, though. It's not his. The money is his. Sure. No argument there. But somewhere out there is the man who created the formula. The pride belongs to him. Properly.

A: Well at least you admit the money was yours.

S: And I enjoyed the money. As much as I could. Treated myself to things. At least to the things I wanted. I stopped cooking right away. Never picked up a chef's knife or a spatula again. But I didn't want yachts or mansions. I moved to Beacon Hill. That was fine. Pretty. The gas lamps at night. The park close. But it was all like a chocolate Easter Bunny. You bite down too hard on it and whoops. Nothing in the middle. Hollow. No substance.

And these creature comforts weren't what the money was about for me anyway. They weren't why I needed it. I had some expensive ideas in mind. Things that cost a lot more than a yacht or a mansion. Things that demanded serious funds. Real Money. You need to drop more than a dime to use the Godphone.

A: I'm sorry, the what?

S: Don't laugh. That's what I called it. Only a working title at first. But I never changed it. It stuck. Stupid? Maybe. But I needed to call it something. I wasn't planning on describing it to anyone. And as stupid as the name might sound it's a decent description of what I was trying to build. A divine dial tone. A connection from my mouth to God's ear. How does that gospel song go? "Call Him up and tell Him what you want." Well I couldn't call Him up and tell Him what I wanted. Because precisely what I wanted was to call Him in the first place. To have the opportunity to tell Him exactly what I thought of His behavior.

A: Now we are entering the realm of pure madness. We have to be.

S: Not easy to build such a thing. You can imagine. But the underlying concept was simple. Yes, He had really said too much through R.R. that day. He should have left out that part about the "probability matrixes." He underestimated me. I saw right away how it might be possible to talk to Him. You just had to make yourself like a god.

A: Oh, is that all? You seem to be throwing out a lot of impossible tasks in a short span here.

S: Note: not make yourself God. That's impossible. Probably. Not even make yourself a god. Just make yourself *like* a god. And not forever. Just for a little while. Even a few seconds might do the trick. Just long enough to get your message across. Still sounds pretty hard. But it sounds harder than it is.

A: Sothum...

S: Just follow me on this, Andy. See the idea and then we'll talk about how advisable it was later. If a single free decision of yours is a key that encrypts the past into the future, then what are you? Come on. What are *you*?

A: I don't know. What am I? Right now I am a figment of your imagination that is terrified at the thought of where you are headed.

S: Wrong. You are a "probability matrix." Just like Reginald Reginald talked about. Each free decision you might make is a key. Each key has an associated probability: the likelihood that you will make this free decision at this instant. There is some probability that you will raise your right hand. Some probability that you will raise your left foot. And so on. So I can model your character at this instant in time just so: as a "probability matrix." I can't predict exactly what you'll do as a result of this matrix. That would violate free will. At any given instant you might shock me. You might dance a very unlikely jig. You might recite "Friends, Romans, Countrymen." But I can model the probability that you might do so. Define you as a type. Just like the genie I created back in college. Stop trying to object. Listen to what I'm saying. Don't wait to speak. Listen.

So now I can model your character. If Featherstone is right then God has a character as well. A character in time like the rest of us. So theoretically I can model His character too.

A: But you have no idea what His character looks like.

S: Thank you for contributing something of value instead of mere objections. You've put your finger on the problem. I have no idea what the character of God looks like. But maybe I can come up with some idea of His character. Some approximation. You remember chapter 20 in *The Divine Logic*? A perfect being, by virtue of his perfection, does not *prevent* other beings. Either from existing or acting fully within their capabilities. In general. God is as perfect as *it is possible to be*. While still having a character. So nearly always He does nothing to prevent the will of others. The exceptions, when God acts and imposes His own will, being so rare we call them "miracles." Miracles are not a sign of perfection, Andy! Quite the contrary. They are the rare imperfections in His nature. The brilliant flaws in the dark bedrock. The times when he simply cannot hold Himself back.

A: So?

S: So this gives us tremendous information about what God's character—his "probability matrix"—must look like. At any given moment. It looks like a "probability matrix" full of zeroes. At any given instant, the most likely action God will take is to do *nothing at all*.

A: But you just said yourself that miracles are possible—rare, but possible. According to you, in fact, you witnessed one, when the voice of Reginald Reginald—supposedly—spoke the words of God. I can't believe that you are drawing me into debating this.

S: You're right, the zeroes are approximations. But the Godphone was not a philosophical or mathematical enterprise. It was an exercise in engineering. Approximate was all it had to be. It just had to be *close enough*. Because I was not trying to model the character of God exactly: I was only trying to alter my own character to be as godlike as possible. To zero out my own probability matrix. Or as close as I could come. To become like a god. Briefly. Close enough at least to communicate with God. To ring His line. To compel Him to hear me.

A: What do you mean, zeroing out your own probability matrix? Are you talking about suicide? Flatlining temporarily? You're not making sense.

S: I don't mean suicide at all. I'm talking about snuffing out your character, not your physical being. It makes historical sense, no? Saints flagellating, monks repeating rosaries, Zen masters seeking the blankness of enlightenment. All try for some obliteration of the self. Snuffing out the will. Just what we've been talking about. Bringing the probability of each free decision close to zero. Only they did it through meditation. Self-denial.

Mortification of the flesh. I had something more radical in mind. You know me, Andy. I've never gone homeopathic when there's a chemical option available.

So think like a Westerner. Think like an engineer. Think "close enough." How can we get at your character mathematically? How about brain waves? Fine, so they're not your entire character. But they change when you meditate. They must be reflecting something. Maybe there's a formula relating the shape of your brain waves to your "probability matrix?" I can hear you chuckle, Andy. "Lots of luck finding that," you want to say. "Good hunting. Don't hold your breath. Soon enough you'll agree with me that all this is insane." And I agree with you. In that the formula would be pretty tough to find. But the beauty was: I didn't need to find it. I only needed to figure out enough to construct the opposite. The inverse. Low where you were high. High where you were low. To build your anti-self. To cancel out your character. Like the market does. To beam that character back into your brain. Then I could cancel out your will moment by moment. Boosting you forcibly to higher levels of perfection. Making you more and more godlike. At some point in this loop the Godphone should start ringing. And maybe Someone would pick up.

A: There's no way that what you're describing could ever work. Even without understanding it I can tell you that. This is brain cancer speaking, pure and simple.

S: In fact this was all well pre-cancer, as you'll see. But in deference to your skepticism I'll spare you the gory details. Or even the slick montage. I'll cut right to the chase: I built it. I tested it on myself.

A: You can't have. You're describing something impossible.

S: Right. Impossible. Just like Newcomb's genie was impossible. Just like it was impossible to find a flaw in Featherstone's proof. Just like it was impossible to fix the proof

224

by showing that the future implied the past. That kind of impossible. The kind of impossible that I *did*.

The nerves at that moment, Andy. You can't imagine. The apprehension like nothing in my life. As I switched it on. Heard a gentle hum. Components warming up.

A: And you're really going to tell me you saw God? Or heard Him—spoke to Him?

S: No. I didn't. I blacked out. Then I came to an hour later. Still expectant. Still waiting for the experience to begin. When I realized it was already over. I remembered nothing. Not at first. Then came flashes. Flashbacks. An image here. An odor there. A concept. It all came flooding back that night in much more complete form. In my dream. I woke up desperate. Trying to write down as much as I could before the feeling faded. It's pointless trying to describe the feeling. But I imagine Dave at the end of *2001* felt something similar. As he became the Space Baby. The colors and the growing old and young and all that.

A: That's more like it. So in other words it didn't work. In other words you fried your brain and experienced some kind of hallucination.

S: Not exactly what I'd hoped for, true. But not nothing either. Definitely an effect. Definitely an experience. A start. Encouraging from that point of view.

A: Don't tell me you took this as encouragement! You were frying your brain, and that's all! Of course you had physical side effects. Please tell me you realized that, and that you terminated the experiments immediately. Please.

S: I began tweaking. Rebuilding. Experimenting. Godphone Mark 2. Mark 3. There were changes in the experience. Improvements. I still couldn't remember anything immediately after. But the flashbacks became more intense. The dreams more vivid. I've left some attempted descriptions of them for you elsewhere on this laptop. If you're interested. But the experience wasn't the purpose of the Godphone. And the purpose was still unfulfilled. Still no ringing. Sill no one picking up the line. That was frustrating.

And another thing. An unforeseen problem. Whatever else I had or had not managed to construct, I had invented a new drug. A potent one. The experience itself was intoxicating. Addictive. I noticed in the lag between Mark 7 and Mark 8. Just a couple weeks. But I found myself driving over to the machine at odd hours. For no good reason. Like you might wander to the coffee pot in the morning. Even though you're "off coffee" for the moment. I started to get headaches. Nightmares. Sweats. All of these cleared up the next time I used the Godphone. I mean instantly and completely. The implication was clear. Soon I couldn't go two weeks. Then not even one.

A: How could you not have stopped then? How could you not have understood what you were heading for? I should have known. You were going mad, living all alone and spending time with nothing but your strange ideas. I saw you what—maybe once or twice a month? You probably saw Buddy less than that even. You didn't see anyone regularly—you had no co-workers, no regular girlfriend—you had no one to steady you. I wish I could have clued in somehow—I wish I could have read the signs and stepped in. I could have intervened. I could have made you understand! I could have saved you.

S: But I *did* understand. My eyes were open, Andy. I knew that I was wrecking my health. Destroying my body. Killing myself. I didn't really care at that point. What did I have that was worth living a few extra decades for? My life had only one purpose left. I just hoped I was killing myself slowly enough. Or making progress fast enough. But something else too. Kept me in this course. Almost enjoying the slow destruction. The death by degrees. I have never been able to get you to commit one way or the other. On the question of God. Let me ask you now. Does He exist? Were you convinced by Featherstone's proof?

A: That's really what you want to talk about now? You want to ask me if I believe the proof?

S: You see. Just like now, you've always found a way to dodge the question that the proof raises. Even when we were discussing the proof itself. As if you could treat "the proof" and "what the proof proves" as separate quantities. Inviting one into your house for dinner and asking the other to wait in the foyer. Not in the street. Just not fully inside either. I wonder if at least you believe in "the gods." And will let on that you do. Even though they are "just" representations of forces at work inside us. I wonder in particular whether you believe in Nemesis.

A: This is what you're asking me now? Really? All right, then, Sothum. The answer is no. I don't believe in Nemesis.

S: She is the most misunderstood of the gods. For my money. Always depicted cruelly. She punishes. She cuts down to size. A hunter. Always on the lookout for hubris in any form. Exacting the toll. But she's gotten a bad rap. The press has distorted her. She is a goddess of love. In reality. Pure love.

Looking back you can feel her watching over you. Like a departed parent. She is always watching you. Getting to know you. For years. From the day of your birth. Far more attentive than Santa Claus. Far less judgmental. Never interfering. Not even pushing you in small ways. Entirely hands off. Just watching. Learning. Understanding you. Everything about you. Especially your flaws. She watches them develop. The sins of pride that are quintessentially "you." She does not punish you for them. That is a myth. A slander. She would never dream. In fact she loves you for your flaws. Not in spite of them. And you feel the pleasure of this love. You bask in it every step of the way. On your path to self-destruction. Sometimes it flares up almost painfully intense. A single decision. A die cast. Nemesis claps her hands and gives a little gasp. Like a mother whose son has just won something on television. And this love pulls you. Draws you forward. Leads you on. To the moment. To the instant when your flaws have grown too large. You can't sustain them any more. The process has begun. The final spiral of your destruction. Irreversible from that point on.

A subtle moment when it happens. It passes unrecognized for many. But if you think back you can usually locate it. Because you can feel the effect. Not on you. On her. On Nemesis. A culmination. Her heart swells. Splits in two. Pride and pity. The moment when a mother realizes her boy is all grown up. So proud. But all the same wanting to turn back the clock. To witness it all again. This time with even more attention. I know the second that the cancer started. The precise instant that the first cell refused to die. Broke from the pack. Instigated the riotous division. I know because I have never felt so loved as in that moment. Do you believe that at least?

I won't make you answer, Andy. I know what you are thinking. I'll say it for you. So, you say. Sothum. Perhaps you are insane, with your talk of Godphones and Nemesis. Perhaps you are not. Be that as it may. As pitiable and horrific as it is, you have every right to destroy your own life. To work out your misguided grudge against your supposed God in any way you desire. To externalize your death wish and make a mother goddess out of her. Go ahead. Melt your own brain. Stick your head in the microwave if you get a kick out of it. On high. But... Come on, I know what you want to ask. Ask it. But...

A: But what business did you have letting Buddy get involved?

S: There. We have arrived. The real question has been asked. The confession and the apology have become one. Sothum, you ask, how could you have brought Buddy into your own private madness? Knowing what you already knew about its dangers, how on Earth could you have let a man you called your friend use the Godphone? Not an easy question to answer, Andy.

A: Answer it.

S: I keep trying not to ask for your sympathy. Not to invite you into my shoes. But maybe that's what it's come to. You know in every undercover cop movie we arrive at "the moment." The dual lines of our hero's life have become so strong they must merge into one. Or the moment when an addict can no longer hide his addiction. Or when a criminal confesses. Simply because he is so lonely. Doesn't want two lives anymore. Wants one. There was something of all this in it. And a strain of sympathy too. Believe it or not. Because Buddy certainly didn't believe in Nemesis. Didn't understand her as I do. Couldn't feel the love she had for him. Its anodyne effect. How her heart burst smilingly when he published that second book.

He was staying with me after that. "Lying low." You know Buddy. You can imagine what "lying low" meant. Reading every review he could get his hands on. Flying into a rage. The only cure: more reviews. Sending me out to buy them. "In case he was recognized." Mobbed. When I refused he would disguise himself. Sunglasses, baseball cap, hooded jacket. Like an actor going to a baseball game. He fumed. Bitched. Constant phone calls to his publicist. His agent. How could this all have happened? How could they have allowed it? I recommended the philosophic view. The long view. The next novel as the best revenge. None of that. Oh no. No one understood. No one could possibly understand. And in particular I probably understood least of anyone alive. I who had never been touched by failure. Never felt its stain. Whose own book did not even deserve its success. I was probably the worst equipped human being on the face of the planet to understand what Buddy was going through. When you got right down to it. So thank you very much for my advice. But no thank you.

Of course he annoyed me as well. Here I can be sure of your understanding. His whole act. All that "he jests at scars" crap. What did he know about failure? About regret? He had written a lazy book. And the public was eating it up. Making him richer for his troubles. Meanwhile the critics simply did what they have always done. What they will always do. But to hear him talk you would think of all human creatures he had suffered the most. He had not the slightest inkling of what I had suffered. So I told him.

A: Because he was pissing you off? That's why you finally let someone into your double life after all this time? Because Buddy was whining and it pissed you off?

S: Not just because he pissed me off. In some way that would have been nobler than the truth. The truth is. I was lonely too. Finally. Tired of living two lives. Low. I had solved the riddle of my life decades too early. Work on the Godphone had stalled. I had only that one purpose left. Telling God off. And that pursuit did not quite sustain me. Not like the earlier quests. To be expected, I guess. A grudge. An addiction. These are not the highest things in human life. Perhaps they drive you onwards. Get you out of bed in the morning. The late morning. But they can't fulfill you. I wanted someone as well. To talk to. To understand. And I knew Buddy would be capable of understanding. Intellectually at least. The concepts involved. That twisted path that I had taken to arrive here. So yes, I told him to shut him up. And also because I wanted company in my madness. Oh, and because of one more thing. Because I wanted to say to him: remember our long-standing disagreement about God? Whether He exists or not? Well I was right. You were wrong.

A: And he believed you?

S: I'm not sure he believed exactly. But it troubled him. The power of the revised proof. The corroborative evidence of the money I had made using the same ideas. He found that more persuasive. We talked far into the night. He didn't take it well. Not in the way I expected even. Felt "personally betrayed." Because I'd never told him any of this before. All those years as friends. As "friends." All those discussions. He had told me about every article he had worked on. Every short story. Every up and down in his life. How could I have kept him in the dark about this? The "project of my life?" I couldn't find a way to make him understand. I'm telling you now. That's what I kept saying. I'm telling you now.

A: He should have felt lucky. At least you told him while you were alive. Not like me.

S: After the huff came the questions. He wanted to know everything. Why this? How that? He didn't care if he wouldn't understand the math. Wanted to see it all done out. How had I built the Godphone? Where was it? When could he see it? When could he try it? He wanted the experience himself. He wanted to see what these ideas felt like as they became the thing. How it felt to have your will canceled out like that.

A: And you let him.

S: I told him no. I told him never. Of course that's what I said. The first time he asked. The second. The third. Never. Never. Never. He wouldn't stop though. Began and ended every conversation by asking. Like Cato the Elder. *Carthago delenda est.* He would not be denied.

A: All you had to do was keep denying him, it seems to me. To match his insistence in the negative.

S: Say what you want, your honor. You certainly have the right. But grant me this at least: I had taken his mind off his troubles. He did not speak about his novels and their reception any more. He wanted nothing in the world so much as to use the Godphone. At least let him see it, he said. So one night I drove him out to see it. Still wouldn't let him use it. Or even touch it.

Then another night I let him watch me use it. Then I let him operate it. On me, only on me. And look, I was OK. I was fine. Always his point. So slowly he ground me down. Never became maybe later. Became maybe soon. And *once*. Only once. Became tonight. Tonight only.

A: And you want me to believe that this was all out of the goodness of your heart—because he wanted so much to use it, and you couldn't deny him.

S: Well. I was curious myself too. As the maker. The engineer. Theoretically the Godphone should have worked the same on anyone. Any character. Any "probability matrix." There was nothing in the algorithm specific to me. But no one else had actually used it. And it might be interesting. To see how it worked. What he experienced. To compare notes. He wouldn't become addicted. Not from only one time. He couldn't possibly. And Buddy was an adult after all. Knew the risks. Still wanted to take them. That's what I told myself. That this was his choice. His free decision to make. His future to choose. Not mine.

So we drove out one night. Nerves kept us quiet on the way over. I helped him climb in. Fasten all the fixtures. The circlet hardly fit around his head. Bit into the flesh of his forehead. I asked him was he sure. Yes. Really sure? Yes, don't ask again. Lie very still then. Try not to move. Just relax. And don't worry. I was only going to give him the briefest dose.

I sensed right away something was wrong. He was so still. Eyes open. Tracking nothing. Buddy. Buddy! Can you hear me? But he sat up when I helped him. On his own power. No dragging or lifting needed. Just not of his own volition. No intention there. Like an automatic door opening when you pushed it. Can you hear me? Are you all right? What happened? Did you hear something? See something? Shouting. Shaking. And then. Finally. He looked at me. Once. Briefly. *Saw* me. Said one word. Just one. "Sorry." And then he looked away. Never looked back.

A: And you didn't take him to the hospital? You didn't reveal what had happened and get him immediate medical care?

S: Go ahead, Andy. Hate me. If you want. You can't blame me more than I did myself. Those first hours. You can't imagine the loneliness of the situation. Those first days. I thought only of helping him. Well. Not only. I admit. I was self-preserving as well. As careful as I could be. I did get him to a doctor right away. But a discreet doctor. Very expensive discretion. You can't do the kinds of tests we needed off the map. Not entirely. So everything under my name. Not just the billing. The treatment. MRI for Stanley Riordan. Blood tests for Stanley Riordan. Etc.

A: Which is why Mildred knows him as such. I see.

S: Batteries of scans. Tubes and tubes of fluids. Nothing was wrong with him. Nothing they could find. Nothing physical. Numerous variations on: "In my medical opinion your friend is able to speak. He does not want to speak. Perhaps a psychiatrist might be able to do more good."

A: But you never told them about the Godphone, did you? Maybe they could have done more with that information.

S: I told them his brain had endured an "electro-magnetic event." What more would they have done with the schematics? They were unanimous in recommending psychiatrists. And the psychiatrists? More sessions always indicated. "I feel we are starting to get through. Same time next week?" Only one of them was worth a damn. "Surround him with familiar things. Objects and activities he loved. He'll come back for the objects." Of course! So simple. Buddy had always loved objects.

That night I sat him down. Gave him his leather notebook. A pen. He started immediately. Writing. Not hurried. Evenly. Never pausing. Well-formed letters. Sane-looking. We've done it,

I thought. Broken through! We're in touch. Communicating. Then I read what he had written.

"The water-wheel clacks away, on and on, dull and monotonous. The woman watches. She has brought a bucket of lightning from the well of clouds. She tells me to rest from my labors, to take a draught of lightning, as this will refresh me body and soul. 'I am not a cloud,' I tell her. I begin to rain."

It was all like that. You've seen it. Absurd. Imagistic nonsense. I tried at first to crack the code. To interpret it. Showed everything to the experts. There must be a message. I'm in here. Help me. Here's how. But we didn't find anything. Just the random firing of neurons. I was forced to conclude. Stir of echoes in a vast but hollow mind. But he seemed to enjoy it.

A: Or maybe he didn't care either way—maybe it was just easier for you to see him writing than to see him doing nothing.

S: Perhaps, your honor. In any event. I kept him supplied. He would only write in those notebooks. That brand. That model. That color cover. Ignored everything else you put in front of him.

A: And then you got rid of him. You didn't even tell his mother what had happened. You just dumped him on Mildred Rosebush. Under your assumed name.

S: I had to make some tough decisions, Andy. He ate when you gave him food. Used the bathroom when you positioned him. Walked when you led him. But nothing on his own. Except breathing. And writing, if he had a notebook. He was going to require full-time care. Would have starved if left alone.

A: That sounds like your penance to me.

S: Probably should have been. But I confess: I didn't have the nerves. I wasn't strong enough. The blank eyes. The details of hygiene. And the guilt. The guilt was crushing. It prevented me from doing anything else with myself. Productive or otherwise. I just couldn't be around him that long. Think what you will.

Then for some reason I remembered Eldred. For some reason. A family vacation there, years ago. Remote. Good for the spirit. Crisp air. So I bought this house. Lots of light and air. Cheery during the day. I found a caretaker. She treats him well. You cannot deny that. Never shuts up. But I don't think he notices.

A: I wish he would.

S: I do too.

A: And even after all this, you didn't bring me in. You didn't confess. I would have helped you, you know. I would have pushed you in the right directions.

S: The step from double life to triple life was hard. Harder than I thought even. Guilt was a constant. Watching the world notice he was gone. Thinking about his mother. Hearing you chat about him. Theorize. Worry and gloat a little. Sometimes I wanted to tell you just to shut you up. The urge to come clean was so strong. But never stronger than the fear of coming clean.

Also hard: what about the Godphone? Within a few days I was using it again. Of course I was afraid. That first time back. But I had to. Couldn't function without it any more. Couldn't have possibly attended to Buddy in the throes of withdrawal. Then later, with more time. More calm. What was I going to do with it? I considered destroying it. Of course. Burn it. And the blueprints too. Rehabilitate myself. But I didn't. I couldn't. What else did I have? My insane pursuit had already cost so much. So much sunk into it. What else was I going to do with myself? Day by day. Hour by hour. Also. From one point of view I owed it to Buddy to continue. He now had a complaint to add to mine. A second suit. He was invested. And God had even more to answer for now. So I started again. Tweaking. Changing. Testing. The same old cycles. The same vivid dreams. Everything the same. Only I never put on the circlet without a moment of fear and pity. Remembering Buddy.

Then. Then! Our dinner at Huanchen America's. The Buddy sightings in Atlanta. Something clicked. Not a tinkling bell. The sonic beating of a gong. A gut shot. One of Buddy's scribbles. From his first notebook. You've seen it. I left it in the box for you. I saw you notice my reaction. I knew the game was up. Right there and then. I knew that my third life had bled through. I knew that would be our last friendly dinner. A relief in some way. Sorry to sound so cold. But time is very short now. No time for lying or sugar-coating. I did miss you. Do miss you. But it was one less life to lead. One less act to carry on. To worry over. One less situation in which to pretend that I was not alone.

A: Sothum, you were never alone unless you chose to be.

S: But Buddy's scribble. The uncanny resemblance to the sighting. I went back. Read everything of Buddy's again. Paid more attention. And I found something. I found a lot. Nothing obvious. Nothing plaintext. Everything twisted, transformed, encrypted. Filtered through some individual iconography. Imagistic symbols. But it was there. Events in Buddy's life. My life. World events even. All written down *before they happened*. It made me wonder: was *any* of it meaningless? Or was every chunk an event? Real or potential? Something that had happened or could have, somewhere, in someone's life? If only you knew how to interpret it? Also—and more importantly: how was he doing this?

The more I considered it, the more I realized. I'd assumed something had gone wrong. When Buddy used the Godphone. What if I was mistaken? What if something had actually gone right? Or right, then wrong? Maybe it had actually *worked*! Overlaid the inverse onto Buddy's character—reduced his will to zero. Made him godlike for an instant. But somehow the result had not been temporary. It had not worn off as expected. It had taken hold and become permanent. Now he was docile. More perfect. Preventing nothing—or as little as possible. Now he was aware of the equation—the world's constant encryption. Past into future. He could sense it. Sort of. He could solve for our characters. Our keys. Our "probability matrixes." And then he could translate it into images. Probabilistic visions. What might happen, given his understanding. I had been feeling sorry for Buddy. Guilty. Maybe I should have been feeling left behind. Jealous. Maybe I should not have been so worried about the disaster that had befallen him. Maybe I should have been trying to achieve a recurrence of his success.

A: I am screaming at a movie or a novel—a descent into madness that I cannot stop. Please, Sothum, listen to me. Snap out of it. Stop while you can.

S: Now with a vengeance. Sprinting. Full-bore into the open arms of Nemesis. Higher energies. Riskier changes. Longer sessions. Trying to recreate what had happened to Buddy. To capture that lightning in a bottle once more. Sometimes I thought I was so close. I would lie there. A breath away. Feeling on the edge of something. Something blank and deep. But you know what happened. Or more to the point what didn't. I never managed to duplicate Buddy's success. I failed. Again. And again. Only managed to give myself stranger visions. More astounding dreams. Oh: and cancer of the brain.

So, Andy. So. That brings us up to date. Au courant. Just about. Which is good. Because it's getting hard. To type, to think. To remember. To imagine what you would say to me. If we were really talking. Just about au courant. Only a few more details. Loose ends to tie up.

First of all. Just in case. Regarding the accuracy of these events. The crazy factor of this apology. I've done my best. Wrote what I remembered. As I remembered it. There are bound to be some mistakes. Some events out of place. Holes and so on. In my state. What's the phrase? On the acknowledgements page of every book? "The errors that remain are all my own." But this is what happened. More or less. In its essentials. Still of sound mind and body. Or sound enough for government work. For a little while longer.

Second. A little direction. A codicil to the will. I was going to have you destroy this laptop. Force you, in fact. A highly customized model. "This laptop will self-destruct in 5, 4, 3..." That kind of thing. Don't worry. Don't go looking for the abort button. I just didn't want any of it getting out. Not even the essays. The stuff about Featherstone's proof. I was pretty raw. Still angry at God. Furious. Just wanted it all to vanish with me. Once you'd read it. The whole ugly drama. You can imagine. But a happy coda. Delighted to report. I figured something out. Realized something. Just the other day. At this late stage. The 11th hour. Remember what Buddy said? His last word? To date, at least? Sorry. Not help me. Not goodbye. Sorry. How could it have taken me this long to figure it out? To realize who was speaking? The last time I had heard that voice I knew it quick enough. The Godphone had worked. You see. Buddy got through. Someone picked up. That "sorry" wasn't Buddy's. Of course not. What did he have to be sorry for? He was just passing it along. Playing operator. A message. From Someone Else. Which is good. Which makes it all worth it. Settles all accounts. As far as I'm concerned. I got what I was looking for. And I leave reconciled. Perhaps to you that sounds like the craziest assertion yet. Here I'm going to invoke authorial privilege. I'm going to make you keep it to yourself. This is how I'm going to take things. This is how I choose to go. And this casts a different light on some other matters. The contents of the laptop for example. I'm undecided now. As to their fate. So: it's up to you. Do what you want with them. Destroy them. Publish them. In whole or in part. I trust your judgement. Just remember if you do publish them that my obligation transfers: you have to mention Mr. Ireland in the preface.

Finally. A tough subject. You and me. Friends. I've been a bit of a bastard. In this apology. I know that. But remember what I said about double lives. Undercover lives. They're both true. Both real. You and I were friends. You were a better one than I was. I've left all that out of this. I had to. The interests of time. Life is like light, Andy. Duoform. Particle and wave. Moment and story. I've cut a lot of moments. Stripped a lot of points. Outliers. Those that didn't conform to the story I needed to tell you. It doesn't mean they weren't real. Part of other stories. Or that I don't remember them. Fondly. With regret. I've been a bit of a bastard in real life too. To you. Kept you out of things. Set up this treasure hunt for you. Shocked you with Buddy. I'm sure. Well I'm afraid I'm not quite done. Being a bastard. I know I said I'd tell you about the envelope. What's in it. That was our deal. You take my confession and I tell you what you want to know. Well I'm breaking the deal. I'm welshing. I'm not going to tell you. That's not the choice I'm trying to put to you. Don't worry though. You'll do fine. I know it. Good luck. Goodbye. Sorry.

CHAPTER THIRTEEN
The Arc

In one small sense Sothum's apology came as a relief. For years I had been suppressing a certain question about his life, refusing to give words or even conscious thought to it, experiencing it as a vague anxiety I imagined to be very much akin to parental love. The question had only become sharper since his death. After reading Sothum's apology and learning that my particular anxiety had been groundless, I found that I could put words to this worry I had carried so long. They went like this.

Coming from ordinary if not exactly humble beginnings, Sothum had put a list of indisputable accomplishments on the public record. Purely on the grounds of academic merit he had secured a full undergraduate scholarship at a fine university, becoming the first in his family to attend college at all. He had continued on to earn a graduate degree with honors at the most prestigious technical institute in the world. He could boast on his CV of having made important discoveries, perhaps amounting to a revolution of fundamental approach, in the field of machine translation. In the meantime he had written a book that attained, whether by accident or not, some measure of notoriety. And to top it all off, he had left the industry in which he had become an influential figure and subsequently made a pile of money under his own shingle as an investor. All these trophies certainly put him far ahead of what your average human being managed to achieve with his years on Earth—and remember,

Sothum had died young to boot. Certainly these accomplishments represented a level of intellectual excellence that I have never attained, and never expect to, so I hope it will be taken in the appropriately humble tone when I say that the question, the worry I never dared give voice to, was "Is that all?"

It was not a question intended to mock or belittle. It was not born of jealousy or the desire to take a greater mind down a peg or two. It was the question of a friend whose feelings for Sothum, and whose expectations for his brilliance, bore more resemblance to a parent's unreasoning pride than to a colleague's professional estimation. But not less accurate for that. I had witnessed the powers at this man's disposal—in conversation after conversation over a long friendship, in page after page of a long correspondence. Was this to be how he disposed of these powers? All he had made of them? A single book, owing its dubious fame to a politician's stupidity and the shortness of the public's attention span? Where was the arc? The blaze of gemlike flame stretching across the sky, drawing cries of wonder and admiration from all of us spectators below, and finally culminating in *something*—a book, an idea, even a mathematical theorem? Something to bear the author's name forward like a standard, to represent it to the coming generations and say "Here is the timeless accomplishment of one man, one who lived and aged and died like all of you, here is the line he added to the Great Dialogue of History, and let those among you who dare attempt as much."

Sothum was right about me, in that I had never been much impressed considering what Featherstone's proof had proven. God existed? All right. That was interesting enough. I supposed I was happier with God existing than without, in an abstract sense that did not affect me or my day-to-day life much. But what staggered me, thrilled me, entranced me, was the fact that a human mind had somehow managed to *prove* that God existed.

The proving itself was the value of the accomplishment. I would have been just as impressed if Featherstone had proven definitively that God was an impossible invention, an absurdity, a contradiction in terms. The lofty subject matter of the proof lent a certain gravity to the achievement—it would have been hard to be impressed equally by a proof of the existence of broccoli—but that was all.

I had always expected and hoped Sothum would produce something on the same plane as Featherstone. He had that quality of mind, and those who knew him had every right to expect that level of achievement from him. In some manner of speaking the cosmos itself had that right. Those questions at least the apology had put to rest. So neatly described there in high relief Sothum had traced his progress—the blazing arc that I had always feared was missing from his days, but which had always been there, hidden from general view.

But as far as consolation went that seemed to be all that I could take from Sothum's terrible dialogue. Paging through screenful after screenful all through that night as I read it and re-read it—admittedly engrossed, enraptured by the strange and inexorable progress of the arc—I had to remind myself that this was Sothum I was reading about. That these were his thoughts I was consuming. That this Faustian creature with his monomaniacal pursuit and cold schemes had also been my dear friend. That he had been warm, human, hilarious. That when he had wanted to convince you of something, perhaps some point about a character in a movie you had both seen, he might grab your lapels and rock you gently on your heels like a southern Democrat. How he was flesh and blood, a giant of a man with beautiful eyes and odd joints. I had to remind myself constantly of these things because the arc had gone from invisible to blindingly bright, almost eclipsing everything else about Sothum's life. It was horrifying.

Sothum had given me some kind of voice in the dialogue. He had anticipated many of my questions, objections, reactions. In some sense he had made me his accuser. I felt all the more paralyzed by these words that he had put in my mouth—as if by predicting my reactions he had determined them. Somehow I felt that all of my objections had already been answered before I could raise them, that all my points of order had already been dismissed, and that consequently there was nothing left for me to say. But if I had trouble giving voice to any lingering doubts, Cheryl did not share my difficulty.

"So what do you think, *Andy*?" she said the next day, when she had finished reading.

"About what?"

"About what? About the very basic questions that this confession raises."

"You mean this apology?"

"I mean this confession. You knew the man—he was your friend, not some philosopher whose extreme personality you read about in a tell-all biography—so I don't think you get to excuse yourself from asking the basic questions that we ask ourselves when someone dies, especially in light of the record we've just read. Was he a good man? Did he live a good life?"

"I'm not sure I can answer that right now."

"I'm not asking you to answer it. I'm asking you to ask it."

I spent the next two weeks reading through all the other materials that Sothum had left on the laptop: the papers on Featherstone, some of his work on encryption, miscellaneous notes on the experience of using the Godphone. There was never any discussion of staying or going during those weeks. For her part Mildred seemed delighted to have us stay as long as we wanted, up to and including forever. Without even telling me,

Cheryl called the kennel that was housing Chester and Novio to arrange for a longer stay. I heard her make the call from the other room. Cheryl was being kind—to me of course, giving me some time to wrap my head around everything—but also to Buddy.

She had become quite attached to him. She went walking with him every day—and she insisted on my referring to the activity precisely so, as "walking with him," correcting me severely once when I asked if she had "taken Buddy for a walk." She would sit with him at the kitchen table while he wrote in his notebooks, sometimes reading a book herself and sometimes only pretending to read, merely watching him instead over the unturning pages.

She even ignited a miniature firestorm once when she took Buddy with her to the Walmart in nearby Monticello to buy some cheap clothes for us—reinforcements for the extremely limited rotation we had packed in our original overnight bags. Mildred, whom Cheryl had not advised beforehand, was furious when they returned, pointing her false fingernail at Cheryl and telling her in an elevated, squeaky voice and no uncertain terms how Norman had insisted that "Stanley's nerves were delicate, not up to...to...to field trips and country excursions!" Her tantrum made for a scene that was both pitiable and funny at once—Cheryl could not restrain laughter at the spectacle—but it was also refreshing to see Mildred address someone so directly, as if she actually cared who she was talking to, and not just excited to be talking to anyone at all. And her voice had the thickness of truth when she declared Buddy to be "my responsibility." When Cheryl and I spoke about the incident privately I took a softer version of the same line, and Cheryl finally agreed to put a moratorium on "field trips and country excursions"—though not without registering her protest that no one in the Monticello Walmart was going to recognize a missing literary figure. She and Buddy continued to take their daily walks.

Meanwhile it was not clear, even to me, what use I was making of the time I was being given. The two weeks I spent browsing the contents of the laptop had not generated any earth-shattering insights or extra information. I had read through Sothum's essays on the Featherstone proof and its potentially troublesome implication, and for what my opinion was worth I had found it watertight. I was much less sure of my qualifications when it came to pronouncing on Sothum's resolution of the same problematic implication. I could not detect any obvious flaws, but Sothum had leaned heavily on cryptographic math and concepts to make his argument that the future implied the past, and in these areas I could not even call myself a neophyte. I had to accept that if these arguments were going to be evaluated properly it would be the work of others, and I was far from being ready to deal with the question of publication—regardless of the fact that Sothum had put the decision in my hands at the end. Aside from the lack of progress on all these fronts, and perhaps more importantly, I did not feel that I was making any progress on the biggest decision that still faced me—and which, though neither Cheryl or I had brought it up in conversation, still hung very clearly between us during the two-week reprieve that she had granted. I mean the question of whether I was going to take the money that Sothum had left me, or the envelope.

It had been a bitter disappointment to arrive at the end of the apology and find that Sothum was going to leave me in the dark on this matter. I did feel, I admit it, a little angry at my friend. Miffed—no, more than miffed. I seriously entertained the notion that Cheryl had been correct, that Sothum was playing with me, having himself a posthumous joke at my expense. But even so I felt farther away than I had ever been from being able to choose, and I sensed the inevitable confrontation with Cheryl drawing closer and closer.

I felt trapped. I was stuck inside Sothum's mind, unable to escape the invisible walls that his apology had constructed between me and the rest of the world. Cheryl must have sensed this detachment, this separation, and in her usual kind and protective fashion she tried to mitigate it—insisting that I get outside on at least a daily basis, and even that I play cards with Mildred in the evenings.

She also gave me a present of sorts—a pocket-sized spiral notebook with a blue cover, in which she requested that I record some of the observations of the natural things I happened to see on my walks. I understood perfectly the spirit that was behind her suggestions, and I took them, but the truth was that the observations helped me very little if at all. Sometimes they only served to draw my attention more sharply to my mental predicament—such as when, jotting down a few notes about the astounding robin's egg perfection of the summer afternoon sky, I could not help but feel something out there, even further out, deeper than the sky or beyond it—a glassy dome, a hushed bowl, as if I were literally trapped inside Sothum's mind, his thoughts pushing always down upon me with their weighted demands.

And furthermore the truth was that in some ways I enjoyed the feeling. I enjoyed feeling something deeper than the sky. I enjoyed staying up late and reading on the laptop in the solarium, feeling like an astronaut beneath the blue smear of light the screen cast in the curved glass ceiling, a cosmic voyager tucked snugly into my tiny capsule, hurtling through an element deadly to me and all my kind, protected only by a few panes of darkened glass.

So when, sometime in the third week of our stay, Cheryl cleared her throat in a meaningful way as we were preparing for bed, I was neither surprised or prepared for the conversation that ensued.

"Have you given any more thought to the question of Sothum's will?"

"Plenty."

"And?"

"Well, I can't really choose, can I? Because I still don't know what's in the envelope. I guess I could *pick*, arbitrarily, but I can't really choose."

"I'm not sure I follow you."

"I've been thinking a lot about this with respect to some of Sothum's ideas of free will. I've been doing some thought experiments."

"'Thought experiments.' I see."

"Do you want to hear or not?"

"I'm sorry. Go ahead."

"Imagine you take a man and you put him in a locked room. You make him stand at the back of the room, and on the opposite wall you've put two buttons. And you tell him he has to push a button to get out of the room. It doesn't matter which of the two he pushes, they will both unlock the door and set him free. And there aren't any extra consequences to the buttons either. It's not like one of them unlocks the door but kills a random person in China as well, or anything like that. They both do the same thing. But—here's where it gets interesting—before you put the man into the room, you've studied him extensively. His physical nature, his history, his preferences, his psychology. Etc. And you have designed the two buttons to be equally appealing to him in and of themselves. For example: maybe you've made one button red and the other yellow, and you know that because of some cultural bias he's inherited as well as his own history with colors, he slightly prefers yellow. So you've balanced that with the shape of the buttons, or their sizes, or their positions on the wall, how high up they are, how far to the left or the right. You've worked all this out so that from where he's standing at the back of the room all his minuscule prejudices and unconscious preferences have cancelled each other out perfectly, a total wash, and each button, *qua* button, is just as attractive to him as the other. And then you tell him he has to push one of the two to get out. What happens?"

"Is that a rhetorical question or do you want me to answer?"

"It's not rhetorical."

"He chooses one of the buttons, pushes it, gets out of the room, and goes on with his life."

"But that's just it—I don't think he *chooses* at all. I don't think he can. I don't mean that he just stands there and short circuits—though that might be a determinist's view of the situation. But remember that part of the apology where Sothum talked about free will? How it can only exist if free decisions have real and genuine consequences? In this situation you've taken that away from the man. There's no consequence to his choice. He can't make a free decision in such a circumstance. A free decision is all about consequences and the understanding thereof. He can only pick one button arbitrarily, randomly. It's not even like he flips a coin—it's like he himself is the coin, and you've flipped him, and how he lands, heads or tails, this button or that button, is a matter of blind chance."

Cheryl sighed.

"Let's say that in the interests of expediency I decline to argue this point with you," she said, "and stipulate that your interpretation of this 'thought experiment' and the conclusions you draw from it are 100 percent correct. What can you possibly be suggesting it has to do with your situation?"

"You really never were much of a philosopher, were you? Never put much stock in reason and logic as the paths to truth."

"Excuse me?"

248

I couldn't answer her. I was still in awe myself of what I had just said.

"You're going to bust out the *philosopher* card?" she continued. "Then I have some sad news for you, my friend, because you are not a philosopher. You have never been one and you never will be."

"I think I could produce a number of people who know a little more about philosophy than you do and who would disagree with that statement."

"I'll bet you I could produce at least as many who knew more geometry than I do and still think that the Earth is flat. I don't care how many expert witnesses in philosophy you drag in, because you're never going to find anyone who's more of an expert on *you* than I am. I know you better than you know yourself. So you want me to tell you who you are? For starters, you aren't a philosopher. Here's *my* thought experiment, if you'll do me the favor of stooping to follow how a mere linguist thinks about things. Philosophy, from the Greek: *philo*, loving; plus *sophia*, wisdom. Philosophy: the love of wisdom. Philosopher: a lover of wisdom. But you don't love wisdom, Andrew. I'm not saying you hate it. Maybe you like it all right, as much as the next guy. But what you really *love* is philosophy. You are not a lover of wisdom, you are a lover of philosophy. A lover of the love of wisdom. And a lover of philosophers. Do you know what that makes you? A professor, Andrew. A professor of philosophy. And that's a noble profession, by the way. There's nothing dirty or shameful about it. I believe you're the only one who has ever thought there was. For my money it's a damn sight more noble than what your friend—who was a real philosopher, by the way—did with his life."

"You don't have much good to say about him, and you never have, but you don't mind taking his money, do you?"

"No. No, I don't. You're right. And maybe that says something unflattering about me. You know what I think? At this point? So be it. I like the idea of what that money can do for us. I like the life we could have. I'm willing to take whatever consequences to my personality might come with it."

"I just don't see what the rush is, is all. We both have jobs— as you yourself pointed out, I'm a *professor* of philosophy, and they pay me for it. They pay you. We have a nice apartment. We're not starving. We don't *need* the money."

"You know what, Andrew? That's the most sensible thing you've said in a long time. We don't need the money. You're right. I'll tell you what. I'll meet you halfway. I'll give up what we don't need if you will. Call the lawyer tomorrow morning and tell him that you choose neither. You decline to take possession of the money and you request that he burn the envelope. And then we're square. We go back to our lives. We pick up Chester and Novio from the kennel. We start getting ready for fall semester. What do you say? Deal?"

She put her hand out for me to shake.

"I'm not asking you to give up the money," I said. "I'm just asking you for some time. Time to do some more research at least. I really could write a book, you know—there's a book's worth of stuff just about Featherstone in that laptop. I would think you could support that, at least. It would certainly further my career as a *professor* of philosophy."

"Bring the laptop with you, then. Steal it. I'll put it in my purse."

She kept her hand out. I was having a hard time coming up with any further objections to taking it—or reasonable ones at least. But I didn't take her hand. And after thirty agonizing seconds Cheryl pulled it back.

I can still see the scene perfectly. The gesture she made. Standing there in her pink Walmart pajamas with their tacky floral print. Suddenly more beautiful than I had ever seen her, and more remote. A tower with its drawbridge up. Drawing back her right hand, and the olive branch with it, lifting it together with the left, palms upturned, until they were even with her head. As if she were releasing like twin doves any further hope of either comprehending or correcting me.

"You know what?" she said. "Knock yourself out."

Three days later she was gone. I still haven't opened the envelope with her note.

That brings us more or less up to date. Pretty much au courant, as Sothum would say. Cheryl left, I stayed.

Though Mildred clearly wonders what happened, she doesn't even mention Cheryl's absence any more. She seems happy enough to have me stay forever if I want to, with Cheryl or without her. My presence takes the sting out of nightfall for her. We share our habits and routines, talismans against the length of each day. Each morning I walk the half hour to the grocery store, making the observations on the way. I shop from the list that Mildred has prepared the night before and walk the half hour back to the house. After breakfast I go walking with Buddy. We walk all the way down to the abandoned and dilapidated house by the pond—the haunted house, as we call it—and then, with a gentle pressure on his arm and back, I turn him around and we walk back home.

Buddy's presence no longer unsettles me as it used to. I have come to enjoy his company. "Who is in there?" I wonder, looking into the blank, peaceful eyes. Who is in there? A man who has, through artificial means, attained the height of human perfection? Or something more, even? It has occurred to me that perhaps the Godphone worked even better than Sothum had intended or realized. That perhaps the reason Buddy can write inspired guesses about the future is not because his own spirit escaped its humanity, but because some shard of divinity remains trapped in him. Some divine essence trapped in time and human form, as helpless as a human mind stuck in a comatose body. The scribbles are like the books tapped out, letter by painful letter, by those patients who have retained only the use of a little finger or a single eyelid. Perhaps this is fanciful and unlikely, but I cannot shake the conviction that there is *someone* in there. Some processes going on. It is just that the processes are too slow for me to notice or understand. My attention is like a hummingbird alighting in an oak tree. "Not much going on around here," my attention says after a few minutes, and takes off. But on a timescale that seems impossible to the hummingbird's blurred wings and frantic heart, the oak tree is alive, changing, growing, acting. I feel this with Buddy even if it is impossible to verify. When our walk has ended I sit with him at the kitchen table, reading and writing while he scribbles or looks through the window.

Each night after dinner Mildred and I play a single round of the game of her choice—usually gin rummy, because it lasts the longest. Then I install myself in the solarium while she watches television. I work there past Buddy's bedtime and hers, when I switch off all the lights in the house and continue working by the light of the laptop alone until I pass out from exhaustion.

In idle moments I speculate: about what is in the envelope that Sothum left me; about what the letter says in the envelope from Cheryl. But I try to fill the hours with other activities. Habit and routine. I try to keep the time for speculation down to an absolute minimum. And this, more or less, is my life.

Or was my life. Until one afternoon I decided. I just decided. It was sudden in one sense—I suppose a decision by its nature is always something sudden—but it was so natural in another, so unremarkable. There were no trumpets or epiphanies. It was less of a decision than it was the realization that the decision had already been made, somewhere beneath the surface, some time ago, and was just now bubbling up—the realization that I *did* understand the choice that Sothum had meant to put to me, and that I had for some time now—and that seeing as I could really only choose one way there was no sense in putting it off any longer. So I did not. I called the Law Offices of X, Y, and Z immediately and asked Mr. X, who seemed mildly shocked to hear from me, to make the arrangements as quickly as he could.

Mildred was very sad when I told her. She pleaded with me to stay a little longer, at least one day more so that she could prepare something special for a goodbye dinner, but I pointed out to her that nothing could have been more appropriate than what she had already planned for that evening and I had already shopped for—which was meatloaf. She did break out a bottle of red wine, which we killed between us—though she considered giving some to Buddy—and I discovered that she was an entirely different person when she was tipsy, and one whose company I enjoyed more. She actually conversed—asking me questions and absorbing a few of the answers. She became genuinely sad recounting some stories from her early youth, things about her family, and when she laughed at some of the funnier points it was not her usual nervous twitter but something a good deal more aware, fuller, richer—more genuine. On the other hand she did require me several times to correct her assertion that the meatloaf was dry—about as many times, I estimate, as she would have if she were sober. After dinner we played four games of gin rummy and then, before she took Buddy up to bed, she gave me a few minutes alone with him in the kitchen "to say goodbye."

I don't know if I expected some sort of miracle out of him— that he might snap out of it for a moment, perhaps delivering a message to me as Sothum had been convinced he had delivered one to him. Nothing of the kind happened. I took his hand, probably hoping to feel some secret pressure, some clandestine squeeze that was supposed to indicate to me that he was still in there somewhere. But all he did was let me take his hand. I spoke out loud to him, I think the first time that I had done that at length. I told him how I hoped that Sothum had been right about what happened to him, and that he was still in there, in some way or another, and most of all that he was happy. I told him that I would try to come back and visit him again some day. I ended by telling him to keep writing, but if he got the joke he didn't seem to think that it was funny.

The next morning Mildred gave me a ride to the bus station in Monticello. She was sober again, and even hung over she had gone straight back to her impossibly solipsistic chattering. But she cried a little when I insisted on hugging her goodbye, and she pretended not to know that I had packed Sothum's laptop—just as I pretended not to know that, immediately upon arriving home, she would dig the envelope Cheryl had left me out of my trash can, open it, and read it.

CHAPTER FOURTEEN
Traveler's Rest

"Slow down," said Cheryl, "I think this is the turn. Yep, that was it."

I backed the car up and we followed the signs through the forested twists and turns leading to the entrance, driving slowly to make sure we didn't miss any more of them. The huge rusted gates hung open, and above them huge letters worked in metal as weathered as the gates themselves spelled out "Traveler's Rest Cemetery."

"Are you sure we'll be able to find the plot in time?" I asked. "This place looks pretty big."

It was pretty big. Straight ahead and to our left white headstones lined a flat expanse and the hills behind, and to the right more headstones stretched out as far as I could see. The ground everywhere was covered with smooth and tidy grass, the green of which I found unnaturally bright, like enamel, and there were occasional trees, squat and less kempt than the lawn, to break the monotony.

"It's in the section called 'Peaceful Point,'" said Cheryl. "Look, you see the box hanging on the gate? I think those are maps. Pull up closer and I'll grab one."

They were maps, and with one in hand we drove slowly down the road that wended left along the graves. Cheryl navigated as I squinted to make out the names and numbers of the areas where they were displayed in worn concrete and marble.

"We should be very close," said Cheryl. "There it is—Peaceful Point."

We got out of the car and walked a little ways down the footpath. It was not hard to guess, even from a distance, which was the plot that we were looking for—one of the headstones was still much whiter than its neighbors. Cheryl must have felt me slowing down as we got closer. She adjusted her own pace to match mine and took my arm.

"It's chilly when the wind blows, though, isn't it?" she said.

"October for you, I guess."

"October."

We stopped in front of the plot. Old stone outlined its borders, and the three graves filled it up completely—there would not have been room for a fourth. As we stood there neither of us read the inscriptions aloud, but I had the feeling that we were reading them silently at the same time and in the same order. "Stanley Riordan, Beloved Husband and Father." "Marjorie Riordan, Adored Wife and Mother." "Stanley Riordan."

"You would think they could have put something on it," said Cheryl. "'Cherished Son,' or a quote, or even just 'Sothum.'"

"I bet he didn't want anything. He probably insisted on it."

"That does sound like him."

Cheryl withdrew her arm from mine and folded her hands in front of her, and we stood in front of the grave quietly for a minute or two, about the length of a prayer.

"I'm sure I've already told you the story about the soap company a hundred times," I said.

"Tell me."

"One Friday night, late—this would be our sophomore year still—my phone rings, and it's Sothum. He tells me that my 'firefighting services' are required, and that he'll be picking me up in ten minutes, and that I should bring a change of clothes and a toothbrush. Ten minutes later I'm waiting on the front steps of my dorm as instructed, and Sothum pulls up with Buddy already in the front seat..."

"This was still in the blue Lincoln, right? I want to visualize the whole scene correctly."

"That's right, this was in Bertha. She gave out that summer. Incredible that she lasted even that long—she was a hand-me-down from Big Stan. Anyway. I get in and off we go. Sothum tells me we're headed to New Jersey to resolve a situation with his soap business, and when I tell him I wasn't aware that he had a soap business, he starts to tell me the story.

"But you know how he was at telling stories. One tangent leads to another, and twenty minutes later I still don't know anything about his soap business. I do know all about how he stole chemicals from his high school's chemistry lab and painted an enemy's desk with a thin coat of nitro-glycerin, and about the time that he got paid by the entire football team to help them find a way to cheat on a history exam."

"He told me that story once," said Cheryl. "They didn't end up cheating at all."

"Right, he told them that the trick was to be able to write all the material small enough that it would fit on a piece of paper the size of a postage stamp, which they could then smuggle into the exam for reference. For two weeks he had them meet every day after school and practice writing all the material smaller and smaller, and he helped them come up with mnemonic devices to reduce the amount of text that they had to write in the first place. Then the day before the exam, when all of them could write everything small enough to fit on a postage stamp, Sothum told them to throw the paper away—because by now they had copied everything down so many times, and developed so many mnemonic devices, that they knew it."

"And they passed, as I recall?"

"To a man. I don't think they wrecked the curve in the class or anything, but they got to keep playing football, which was what they had been after in the first place."

"And Sothum got paid," Cheryl said.

"Indeed he did. He started a tutoring business after that. Apparently he was quite the young entrepreneur. He actually started a number of businesses, but none of the others were as successful as Abluo Soap. He had created the formula himself during his senior year—he stole the original supplies from the chemistry lab—and he started selling soap door to door to the housewives of New Jersey on nights and weekends.

"He would always make a big deal of the name, saying things like 'Abluo, which, as you have probably already realized, is from the Latin.' He printed up his own boxes and everything, with 'Abluo' up at the top in block letters, and below it his slogan: 'The soap for those who know soap.'"

"And he moved units?"

"Like hotcakes. Those housewives went nuts for Abluo soap. Pretty soon he had to hire some younger kids to help him sell, manufacture, deliver. It was a regular little business running out of his garage. When he went off to college he got one of the other kids, a kid named Vinny, to run the day-to-day for him. And I guess for a year and a half Vinny had done a great job. Then without warning he up and vanished, taking a good chunk of money with him.

"After Vinny split, Sothum's mother had started getting angry phone calls from customers with outstanding orders. She passed the complaints on to Sothum, and he recruited Buddy and me to drive down and help him fulfill orders, issue refunds, and basically shut the operation down in an orderly fashion. Which, after an epic breakfast from Marjorie the next morning, is exactly what we did."

"He didn't want to want to keep it going? Maybe with a new Vinny?"

"I guess he'd had his fill of the soap business. Some of his customers were really upset when we told them. A couple of them said it was the best soap that they had ever found. One woman almost cried! Sothum gave her the formula so that she could make Abluo herself. I don't remember exactly what it was, but I remember thinking it was pretty simple to make. And cheap."

"What made you think of that story now?"

"I don't know. I guess because years later, after Big Stan died, Sothum told me that at the funeral an old friend of his father's had come up to him and said 'I just want you to know how proud your old man was of you. He told all the guys about that soap business that you started. He talked about it all the time.' Sothum didn't come out and say so, but I got the feeling that his father hadn't really been in the habit of telling him that he was proud. I guess I was wondering what Big Stan would think now, if he knew about everything that had happened since. Would he have been proud? Would he even have understood?"

We let the conversation hang in the air for a few minutes, as if I had actually just delivered a eulogy at Sothum's grave side, and then Cheryl asked me if I wanted to walk around a bit. She took my arm again as we started out and I thought how easy it would have been, if anyone had been watching us, to tell that we were an old couple recently reconciled. The familiarity combined with the novel joy in each other's presence—the newlywed pains we took with each other instant to instant, pointing out rocks on the path or low-hanging branches—it would have been unmistakable. Not to mention the encouragement that Cheryl had offered me while I told her the Abluo soap story for what must have been the third time in our marriage. At least.

It was pleasant, being an old new married couple walking around the cemetery. To begin with there was the tremendous luck of our still being on this side of the grass—the unavoidable arrogance of the living—but there was something other than that, too. I felt connected—through the bond that held me to Cheryl and her to me—to the men and women who had gone before, those who were now below and nourishing this unusually green New Jersey grass. They too had paired off, grown old together, and died. And though I was in no hurry to reach the end of that story ourselves, there was something to the idea that we were walking in their paired footsteps. It wasn't comforting exactly—we were in a graveyard after all—but it added something to the fact of our lives at that moment. Another dimension of significance.

The feeling also reminded me why I had chosen as I had. Why I had chosen the money. More accurately, perhaps: that in fact I had not chosen the money at all—not exactly. I had chosen my wife. Or as one of my professors in college had summed up a scene in *Paradise Lost*: Adam didn't choose the apple, he chose Eve. I chose the money for the "higher cardinalities" of human freedom upon which, lifting us up like a wave, it could deposit us together. That "together" was the key.

And in fact it was a bit overwhelming, this freedom at which we had arrived. Before all this had happened our future, if I were to imagine it in such terms, had seemed like a railroad track. For the most part, month by month, semester by semester, everything was straight and unswerving as could be. Of course at other times there were switches to choose between, spurs to take or not to take, scenic routes to enjoy or skip if we were in a hurry. Things weren't entirely set, there were options—but the options were clear. There was a map, and the borders of that map were well defined: our careers, our responsibilities, our means. Now when I looked out at our future I saw something vast and pathless—nothing you could possibly have mapped. An open sea, flashing and glinting and changing at every second. It was exciting, yes—oh, it was more than that. It was thrilling. It called to you like a new ocean to an explorer. But it was a bit frightening as well. Railroad tracks I could handle. I could navigate them. This was beyond that—worlds beyond that. Maybe, I worried, it would even prove to be too far beyond what I was familiar with—too much for me to handle. It was disorienting if you looked at it too long. You couldn't possibly take in every flash and glint. You had to blur your vision a little just to accept what you were seeing.

"Don't you ever regret it just a little bit?" asked Cheryl, as if she had heard my thoughts. "Don't you ever wonder what was in the envelope?"

"Not really," I said, and though Cheryl did not reply I could tell that she thought me a noble liar—and a bad one.

Actually I was more or less telling the truth. Yes, in the odd moment I still wondered whether it had been the blueprints to the Godphone, or the formula for the Specul8 engine, or a secret so profound that it had not even been hinted at in Sothum's apology—a secret life below the secret life. But what I had realized back in Eldred—what had helped me make peace with my decision—was that Sothum was not really offering me the choice between the money and the contents of the envelope. Not exactly. He was offering me the choice between the money and *knowing* the contents of the envelope. That had been his point at the end of his apology. He had been trying to show me something—something about who I was, and who I wasn't. And on this rare occasion Sothum and my wife had been in agreement. I wasn't a philosopher. That was his message for me. A warning: don't attempt what you have just seen at home. You are not a trained stunt man. You are not a philosopher.

Sothum, you see—if offered the same choice—would have gone for the envelope. Every time. That was his character. He would have been compelled to—he simply would have needed to know what was in that envelope. Whereas I—while I would certainly have liked to have known—did not need to know. I could live without it. Proof: in the end, I chose the ten million dollars, and I was still alive. Sothum had never intended for me to choose the envelope. He had known from the beginning that I wouldn't do it. The ten million dollars was there to soften the blow—to make up for the disappointment that he knew I would feel upon being forced to make this realization. Because—unlike Cheryl in this respect—he understood what the difference between lover of wisdom and lover of philosophy meant to me. He could predict how difficult it would be for me to accept. He knew all this beyond a doubt.

In fact his apparent level of certainty had inspired an attractive idea in me the other day. I remembered the end of his apology—the sure phrasing with which he had signed off. "You'll do fine. I know it." Those were his exact words. "I know it." Unlike most of us, Sothum didn't just bandy the word "know" around. I believe that in this case he used it because he meant it—because he really had known what I would choose. And I started to wonder how exactly he could have known this so surely. Was he just a human version of the genie he had built to resolve Newcomb's paradox, able to see deeply into my character and thereby to classify me as the kind of man who would eventually choose, 99 times out of 100, the money? Or was something else going on here?

During those long days and nights out in Eldred, after Cheryl had left, I had plenty of time for reading. Often I had re-read the materials on the laptop, over and over again. But at one point, both for variety and to please Mildred, I had read through Buddy's notebooks—all of them. I had skimmed through quickly, reluctant to pay enough attention that I might notice the kind of connections to real events that Sothum had, and after I had finished I did not remember much of what I had read—only the general feeling of surreality, of significance that went just wide of the mind. What I did remember the other day, however, as I had been pondering Sothum and his preternatural sureness, was that among all the notebooks stacked up along the walls of the trophy room there had been a single missing page. Only one. It had quite clearly been ripped out, just as the page that Sothum had packed up in the box for me to find had been ripped out of the notebook he had sent to Buddy's mother.

And it occurred to me: what if Sothum, in his wide reading and interpretation of Buddy's notebooks, had come across something that he had remembered later, as he was figuring out exactly how to construct the riddle he intended to leave me? What if something had rung a bell, an image or a situation, and he had realized that Buddy had already predicted the outcome? That Buddy had already predicted in one of his bizarre prose poems that I would choose the money? It would have been just like Sothum after all—just like him to track that page down, rip it out, and seal it in the envelope. A final ironic joke for no one but himself to get: sealing up in the envelope that I wasn't going to pick the very prediction that I wouldn't pick it. I liked this option a great deal. It appealed to me. So I had decided that I would go with it—that this is what I was going to believe. And if I was wrong? Well luckily I would never have to find that out. And now I was tired of speculating. I had other things to worry about—things like a long-promised honeymoon, and the question of whether or not I was going to publish Sothum's work on Featherstone.

"We had better go," said Cheryl, glancing at her watch, "or we'll miss our flight. And don't forget we have to call Buddy's mother from the airport. No faces—you promised."

"Did I really? That was foolish."

"Sounds just like you."

"Doesn't it just? Seriously, are you sure this won't break Mildred's heart?"

"Maybe it will. Maybe it won't. She'll have the house, even if Buddy goes—and maybe it will be a good thing for her to get out of that house every once in a while. Maybe she'll go play bingo at the Monticello Fire Department's fund-raiser one night and win 30 dollars and meet a man with a name so tragic that he'll want to become the future Mr. Mildred Rosebush. Anyway, it's not our choice to make."

"That's true. And maybe that's a good thing for us. Because we have so many choices to make already."

"Rome or Florence? Munich or Berlin? Paris or Paris?"

"Right," I said, picking up the pace. "Off we go then, into uncharted cardinalities of human freedom."

"That's catchy," said Cheryl. "You should see if you can sell that slogan to a travel agency."

"Or the lottery."

As we walked back to the car the wind began to pick up, and a cloud blew across the sun. I thought unaccountably of Sothum's face that night as he drove us down to New Jersey, his eyes blue and intense and jovial in the rear-view mirror, the right side of his face gone dark as we would pass momentarily out of range of headlights and streetlights, and then suddenly a blinding white.